PENGUIN BOOKS

GUYS LIKE US

Tom Lorenz received the Sue Kaufman prize from the
American Academy of Arts and Letters for *Guys Like
Us*. He teaches writing at the University of Kansas.

GUYS LIKE US

Tom Lorenz

PENGUIN BOOKS

PENGUIN BOOKS
Published by the Penguin Group
Viking Penguin, a division of Penguin Books USA Inc.,
40 West 23rd Street, New York, New York 10010, U.S.A.
Penguin Books Ltd, 27 Wrights Lane, London W8 5TZ, England
Penguin Books Australia Ltd, Ringwood, Victoria, Australia
Penguin Books Canada Ltd, 2801 John Street,
Markham, Ontario, Canada L3R 1B4
Penguin Books (N.Z.) Ltd, 182–190 Wairau Road,
Auckland 10, New Zealand

Penguin Books Ltd, Registered Offices:
Harmondsworth, Middlesex, England

First published in the United States of America by Viking Penguin,
a division of Penguin Books USA Inc. 1980
Published in Penguin Books 1990

1   3   5   7   9   10   8   6   4   2

LIBRARY OF CONGRESS CATALOGING IN PUBLICATION DATA
Lorenz, Tom.
Guys like us/Tom Lorenz.
p.   cm.
ISBN 0 14 01.3154 X
I. Title.
PS3562.O753G8   1990
813'.54—dc20   89–28526

Printed in the United States of America

To Warren and Virginia,
with gratitude and love

GUYS LIKE US

II

On his thirtieth birthday Buddy Barnes received a reindeer sweater and a ten-dollar bill from his mom, as well as the following gifts from the Sticks: two Big Mac certificates, a package of ribbed prophylactics, three pairs of toe socks, a bottle of Wild Turkey, a free pass to the motorboat show, a Richard Nixon fright mask, a humidor of White Owl cigars, a new aluminum stick, a United States savings bond, a lid of Colombian, and a plastic nose.

From Jo he received a heavy brass alarm clock, which she fired into his abdomen from a distance of ten feet after he had butted open the bedroom door with his new aluminum softball stick at three o'clock in the morning. She had been aiming for his nuts. The blow had doubled him over, and as he staggered back he asked himself: what's the story here? Then he sprang at her.

Jo had been thinking along the same lines. She had been wondering what the story was for a long time, but particularly since the day he had lost his job with the Chicago Park District for leaping out of a lawn mower into a tree.

"You what?"

"I was cut, given my notice." He had flounced down in his barber chair and popped open a can of Old Style. Jo stared at him, her face framed by her new curly hair. "I was fired," Buddy explained.

"Come off it." Jo laughed.

"I'm serious."

"Nobody gets fired anymore. What did you do, burn down the gym?"

Buddy told her about the tree.

She had been spraying her plants with water from a clear plastic bottle and she paused, the bottle pointed at him like a canister of mace. "Let me get this right: you jumped out of a lawn mower into a tree?"

Buddy nodded, rubbing his cheek with the sweating can.

"Why?"

He shrugged. He was going to explain that he'd been thinking about doing this ever since he saw the tree with its low and inviting limb, perfect for leaping into. He wanted to say that ever since he was a kid he had always wanted to leap out of something into it. All his favorite cowboys had leaped into trees at one time or another; Zorro, too. The tree was familiar to him, warm and friendly. Fat birds nested in it; happy squirrels crouched on its branches. As a kid he had climbed around in it like a monkey, carved stuff in it, necked under it with built Italian girls. He and Herm had belted shots into it in the glory days of the old school. Just that day he had pointed at it with a shoestring potato in the cab of Herman's beer truck while they ate their meatball sandwiches, and Herman had smiled broadly under his green beanie and said, "We put our share in that mother, didn't we." Then there had been the bet with Ferd and the two young chicks in the salmon-pink halters, slurping on their malteds and giggling at him from a park bench while he rode back and forth on the mower cutting grass into haphazard patterns and getting closer and closer to the tree, his shirt off, his pecs bronzing in the early May sun, feeling

good, more than a little high from the weed Ferd cultivated
in a remote corner of the defective-equipment crypt in the
gymnasium cellar. And before he knew it, without exactly
having planned on it, he made a beeline for the tree and
stood up on the mower and leaped, catching the limb and
dangling with one hand, laughing his head off and waving
to the girls while the mower veered across the field in the
direction of the swimming pool. He would have liked to add
that, unlike a lot of things, leaping into the tree had been
as much fun as he imagined it would be, easily worth any
number of custodial jobs. However, he'd had many beers
and words eluded him.

"Big deal," he finally said. "So I got fired. So what. It was
a two-bit gig anyway. I was tired of it."

"You were tired of it." Jo had applied her wrist to her
forehead as though she were taking her temperature. The
pain in her chest had started again; it felt like something
clawed was loose in there, fastened to her heart. She felt like
she was being eaten from the inside out.

"Sure. I was tired of cutting grass and spearing trash and
sweeping up shit. I was tired of the dyke and her yak." He
grinned, seeing again the hulking shape of the Major standing hands on hips at the lip of the empty pool, staring down
at the smoking mower which had crossed the field, passed
uncannily through a narrow gate, and plunged into the deep
end. There had followed a series of small explosions. "What
am I anyway, a goddamn janitor?"

"I don't know." She was appraising him curiously, as
though she had known him once a long time ago. "What are
you, Buddy? Give me a hint."

This wasn't the first job from which he'd been uncondi-
tionally released—there had been the job in the recreation
center, the Mutual of Omaha gig, the number in the pro-
motional department of her father's firm making up jingles
for the paper products they manufactured ("Wipe your ass
with a touch of class")—but it was the first one he'd lost

for leaping into trees. Jo regarded this as a bad omen. She'd been waiting nine years for him to find his true calling so she could do something with her life besides wait on tables and ring up groceries and sell Silly Putty and Evel Knievel dolls. She was an adult now, almost thirty years old—she was almost thirty years old!—and she was tired of waiting for something real to happen. Time, he had said, I need time. She had given him time. She had manned switchboards, pried quarters from under gooey plates. She had brought home bacon and waited. She had supported him for nine years; now she figured it was her turn. She had a life too, she had dreams, she could finish school, get a real job, be proud of herself. Who knew what she could do? Soon, though, it had to be soon. She couldn't stand this waiting anymore. Time obsessed her; she ticked like a bomb. More and more often at work she would find herself staring uncomprehendingly at the bins of masks, the barrels of brightly colored balls. She was beginning to feel hemmed in by slime. She had developed this pain. She was dizzy, losing weight. One afternoon she found herself gnawing on a hunk of Silly Putty, and she had rushed into the employees' bathroom in the department store and, doubled over the sink, spat blood.

She could not bring herself to tell her father that Buddy had been fired for leaping into a tree. She told him he'd been laid off, mentioning this at the birthday party she had thrown for Buddy while the three of them—Jo and her father and mother—were sitting in the dinette around a candelabrum Jo had gotten as a wedding present, sipping Lancers and staring at Jo's wedding china while the fowl simmered on a back burner and they waited for Buddy to show up.

"Laid off?" Mr. Reed said. "I never heard of anybody working for the city getting laid off." He scratched his ear with a dirty fingernail. "That's a new one on me. You sure he wasn't fired again?"

"He was laid off," Jo said carefully. No way she could

tell the truth to a man who had worked every day of his life
for forty years, who had stridden into the mill at sixteen
and manned its most vicious machinery and at a time, too,
he would point out, when safety was what happened when
a guy got tackled in his end zone—a man who had worked
his way up step by brutal step, getting his left foot squashed
and his back and shoulders permanently racked along the
way, who even now, as production manager, kept his fingernails dirty and ate his lunch out of a metal box, and who
would not hesitate to go back into the mill and take over
again when some jerkoff fell asleep on the line. No way she
could own up to Pop.

"Where is Buddy anyway?" her mother said. She had
picked up a plate and was literally holding it up to her face
to see if she could see her horselike reflection, just like in
the commercial. Jo had spent about an hour washing the
china just to cover herself against this possibility. She had
spent a lot of time on this meal. She had come home from
work and gone directly into the kitchen and started fooling
with sauces. She had had pots on every burner, timers ticking—they had put people on *Beat the Clock* for performing
less complicated feats. Buddy had come out in a baseball
suit and started putting his fingers into everything. Eight
o'clock, she had told him, knocking his hand away. At the
latest. It was now fifteen minutes to nine.

"Any minute now," she kept saying.

"You sure he isn't in the toilet combing his hair?" Mr.
Reed said out of the side of his mouth. "The guy spends
more time in the toilet than anybody I ever saw." He himself had never spent more than ten minutes in the toilet in
his entire life. He had about twenty hairs left, which he arranged with three broad slashes of his comb. He shaved on
the go, by battery. Even his shits were brief, the turds he
squeezed out hard and lean, just like himself.

Jo rubbed her temples. "He must've been held up at his
game."

"Game?" her mother said, breathing on a knife and polishing it with her napkin.

"He had a softball game tonight."

"I didn't know he still played."

"I'd check the toilet if I were you." Mr. Reed yawned. He found it virtually impossible to stay awake after nine.

"Hey, what about some more wine?" Jo said brightly. She picked up the Lancers. "Mom? Dad?" They simultaneously covered their glasses with their hands. Jo filled hers to the brim and took it with her to the kitchen and put it away in three big gulps. She leaned over the fowl, its sauces simmering to oblivion, and felt the jagged thing attached to her heart gripping tighter and tighter. She had known this was going to happen the second she saw him come out in his new uniform, parading around in the shiny yellow jersey and the sleek blue pants with a broad yellow stripe running down each leg, the stiff yellow cap cocked back on his head. The word "Stickmen" fanned across the front of his shirt in blue letters; on the back, above the big blue nine, it said "Bledsoe's Meats." There was an address and phone number on there, too. The whole suit gave off a strong metallic smell. Buddy had taken it out of the box and spent an hour fooling with it, adjusting the narrow yellow socks, getting everything just right.

"Huh?" he had said, posing in the doorway. "Huh?"

She thought he looked ridiculous, a great big thirty-year-old man walking around in a shiny yellow baseball suit with a meat sign on his back. She thought he looked like a clown.

"Don't tell me you got a game tonight?"

"Certainly I got a game tonight. What do you think I got my suit on for?" He reached over and stuck a finger in some sauce. "I'm ready, Jo. It's my year." He was tasting his finger. "Not spicy enough."

Jo pushed him away. "You know what day this is?"

"Certainly. Besides being the season opener it's my birthday, which, by the way, you haven't exactly made a big deal about." He looked up at the ceiling, squinting philosophically. "I'm thirty, Jo. The big three-oh. Some say you're through then. I've heard the talk. I won't pretend I haven't. They say you lose that crucial step, no longer get a decent jump on the pellet. Some are of the opinion that thirty is the day to hang it up." He shook his head, simultaneously reaching into his pants to adjust his genitals. "Tonight I prove that this is so much humbug."

"Forget the humbug and remember what night it is."

Buddy regarded her blankly.

"Jesus Christ, Buddy, they're coming over tonight."

"Who?"

Jo rolled her eyes. "My parents." She struck the range with a wood stirring spoon that looked like a small oar. "What do you think I've been messing around in here for?"

"I thought you were making me a birthday dinner. I thought these were my birthday sauces." He shrugged. "I beg your pardon. My mistake."

"Don't give me that act. We talked about this. You knew the story." The story had been to cajole them over for a pleasant evening, some fowl, some birthday cheer, and then he and Mr. Reed could talk business before Mr. Reed fell asleep. The story ultimately had been for Mr. Reed to offer Buddy another chance. Jo was not kidding herself about the odds on this. After his last experience with Buddy—who had repeatedly shown up for work garbed in an Olympic beer-swilling T-shirt and a pair of surfer jams, and whom he had once caught in a parking lot sharing a reefer with a carload of jerkoffs from the line—the hard-working industrialist was more likely to offer a position in his plant to George McGovern or the Son of Sam. It had been an act of high diplomacy just to get him to agree to come over . . . and here Buddy comes out in his softball suit acting like he didn't know the story. "You knew about this, Buddy. You made a promise."

"So, what are you telling me? You want me to cancel out,

let the guys down? It's the season opener, for Christ sake."
He stuck his finger in the sauce again. "Besides, you're
getting your nose out of joint pointlessly. We got the early
tilt. I'll be back in plenty of time."

"When?"

"Eight, eight-thirty. Maybe earlier if we put the slaughter
rule on them."

"Eight o'clock, Buddy. Not a minute later."

"Don't worry about it. I'll even leave my suit on. Your
old lady always had a thing for guys in uniform."

Jo wagged the oar at him. "I'm warning you: don't screw
up. And get your fingers out of there, you just had them
down your pants, for God sake."

◎◎◎◎

At nine-thirty Jo put the food on the table and they woke
up Mr. Reed, who'd been sleeping on the sofa, and silently
ate the fowl. They did not have cake. When they were done
they went out into the living room and Mr. Reed stretched
out on the sofa again, while Jo gulped down Lancers and
Mrs. Reed sipped coffee and stared fixedly at the wavy lines
on the ancient black and white Motorola with the coconut
monkey perched on top of it. She did not want to let her
eyes roam for fear of what they would see. One time when
she'd let her eyes roam, they had focused on a photograph
of Buddy and her daughter standing hand in hand, naked,
in some woods. This had not been a side or keester view, but
full frontal nudity. Another time she'd looked over and seen
the dark face of a gorilla staring back at her from a crack
in the closet door. In her daughter's apartment she'd seen
upside-down flags and stickers with sayings that gave comfort and aid to the nation's enemies; she'd seen rubber lizards
and bats stuffed inside crystal balls and all sorts of junk
she wouldn't have had in the cellar displayed in places where
everyone could see. She'd seen prurient literature. Once—
she would never forget it—she had reached down and picked

up a comic book with a picture of Mickey Mouse on the cover and, turning to a page at random, had come upon a full spread of Mickey and Minnie and Donald Duck and a host of others performing acts she considered too lewd even for consenting adults in the privacy of a bedroom, much less for beloved Disney characters. She had seen cigarette papers and suspicious-looking paraphernalia. She was no dummy. She knew what the cigarette papers were for. She knew a hookah when she saw one. All this she had seen, but never, in all the times she'd come there, had she ever seen a crucifix, a Virgin, or something else that blessed a dwelling.

The dwelling itself reminded her of a dungeon. It was stuck in a remote wing on the top floor of an old apartment building that was covered by some type of clingy mold and always looked, even in bright sunshine, gray and dingy. Had she herself looked for months she could not have come up with a more cheerless building. Though it was four floors to get to Jo's, Mrs. Reed always took the stairs. There was an elevator, but she refused to take it. It was a big cage that had a huge iron latch in front and made loud thumping noises when it moved. It moved slowly, painfully. It always seemed to be coming down just as she had started up the stairs, like it was trying to trick her into getting on, but she refused to set foot in it. Once, when she was hurrying to get past it, the elevator had descended, thumping and groaning, and she had looked over at it and had a distinct vision of a man hanging inside it, strangled by his tie.

The actual apartment was just what you'd expect in a building like this. It had high ceilings and a few small, oddly shaped rooms—including the living room which was deformed by a curved, turretlike window—and bare wood floors that squeaked when you walked over them. There never seemed to be enough light. Through the rough white walls seeped an incessant murmur of voices from adjoining apartments that Mrs. Reed tried hard not to listen to. There were four locks on the door. Jo had done the best she could with it through the creative use of throw rugs and knick-knacks and innumerable plants, which she hung in imaginative formations in baskets affixed to the ceiling, but what could you do when the man of the house papered the living room walls with posters of Bears and Bulls and Cubs, the bedroom with White Sox and Blackhawks, and had stuck a miniature basketball hoop above the closet door? What could you do when the breadwinner couldn't even bring enough home so they could buy some decent furnishings? The stuff they had now she wouldn't keep in the garage. It looked like the type of furniture people took to the river and dumped at night. This furniture had lumps and bumps and springs that jabbed. Arms were frayed; stuffing sprouted from split cushions. You could beat these items for hours with a stick, and still the dust would fly. The newest furnishing in the place was the pastel-blue vinyl barber's chair with adjustable foot and head rests, so that Buddy could get comfortable after a hard night of playing ball. The chair she herself was sitting in was a thronelike business made from some cheap velvety material that gave off an ineradicable air of must. It had long stiff arms and a high stiff back, so that when she sat in it her feet barely touched the floor. She had a nervous habit of wedging her hands behind and under the cushions of chairs, and under the cushion of this chair she had discovered at various times a banana peel, a twenty-dollar bill, an athletic supporter, and a set of rubber fangs. "There they are!" Buddy had said, and rushed over and snatched them out of her hand and popped them in his mouth without even rinsing them off first under the faucet. "I been looking all over for these babies," he had mumbled through the jutting blood-red rubber choppers. "Don't mention it," Mrs. Reed had said.

He called the place their little love nest. Mrs. Reed called it something else. Sometimes when she thought about her daughter working hard in the department store all day and coming home to those high dark ceilings and squeaking floors and murmuring walls and Salvation Army furnishings with fangs under the cushions, not to mention the four locks on the front door and the man hanging in the elevator, she would burst into tears at the dinner table and Mr. Reed would put down his knife and say, "What do you want me to do? Look, take my word for it, pretty soon she'll come to her senses and ditch that idiot and be sitting right there at the table again. It's just a matter of time. Quit worrying about her and pass the spuds."

She had tried to be charitable. She had tried to meet him more than halfway. Still, when she got there, she would find him stretched out in the barber chair, sucking on a Pabst Blue Ribbon and wearing a pair of dark glasses with hypnotic whirling eyeballs taped to the lenses, and she would think: for this I bore and raised a baby girl? Some people got married in a church, with an organ and flowers and parents and a man there to take pictures which you could put in a book and look at every once in a while. These two got married in the woods, and the only picture they had she was mortified just to think about, much less look at. She had sent her daughter away to college to get an education, and the girl had returned with nothing to show for it but a man who wore a rubber arrow through his head, who filled up the place with Blue Demons and Boilermakers and Fighting Irish, who introduced her sunshine to smut and treason and Zig Zag papers, and who, instead of coming home tired from a hard day of winning bread, went out at night wearing a shiny yellow uniform with a meat sign on his back. "Give it time," Mr. Reed would say, and roll over and go back to sleep, and she would think: time? What's nine years, a fly-by-night romance?

She had tried her best to keep out of it. If a certain person wanted to talk, fine, she had words to say, she was the mother around here. She hadn't lived fifty-three years through depression and recession, hot and cold wars, and the age of the Beatles and remained totally stupid. Until such time, though, she would keep her words to herself, locking her mouth shut tight with her teeth if necessary. No one could accuse her of being Mrs. Buttinski, not with Jo or any of her children. She had always given them a free rein. Roy Jr., the oldest, worked side by side at the mill with his pop and had three of his own. Randy, the youngest, wore his nation's uniform and flew jumbo jets in the Strategic Air Command. Jo—who for all-around looks and brains and personality had been the pearl of the trio—had gone off into the woods and married a man who wore the uniform of Bledsoe's Meats and who had not once in the last nine years made enough money to file with Uncle Sam. You figure it out.

Lately she'd been hoping—Jesus forgive her—that something would happen to him or he would just disappear. He had gone away once, to Alaska, and she had thought: free at last. She had told Jo not to worry, the Church had liberalized its thinking on certain matters, she had checked into it, marriages made in woods could be dissolved—and three months later he had showed up again in that Sherman tank he drove around in, with his hair down to here and accompanied by a freak dog who immediately chewed everything in the apartment to a pulp; the first night he was back he had gotten drunk and practically burned the place down by turning on the wrong burner and setting a package of Fig Newtons on fire. He hadn't budged since. It was becoming more and more evident he would not just disappear but sit there forever in the barber chair, swilling down Pabst Blue Ribbons and reading *War of the Worlds*. It was becoming perfectly clear that it was time for a mother to speak out. She cleared her throat preparatory to launching into the speech she had said to herself a couple of hundred times. "Jo . . ."

"More coffee?"

She shook her head, started over. "Jo, you know I've always believed in letting all you kids have a free—" She paused. Her fingers, rooting under the cushion again, had brushed against something. It was warm and smooth, with the disconcerting texture of human skin. Shifting her weight, she lifted the cushion and withdrew the object, holding it up to her face. It looked like a human scalp. She immediately flung it to the floor.

"What in the name of God is that?"

Jo went over and picked it up. "This? It's just Buddy's skinhead wig. See, it fits over your head and makes you look like you're completely bald." She placed the thing on the coffee table. "He's been looking all over for it. What were you saying?"

"Never mind," Mrs. Reed said, and went to wash her hands.

oooo

After they had left, and after Jo had hacked up the new birthday shirts she had gotten him with a kitchen knife and put her fist through all three layers of his cake, she finished off the Lancers and went to bed. She lay like a corpse, her body rigid, her eyes wide open and staring at the poster of Doctor J Buddy had taped to the ceiling. She waited for him, waited to hear the clacking of his spikes in the corridor, the fumbling of his keys in the locks—it would take him at least five minutes to get them open—waited to hear the crash of something heavy being knocked over as he lurched through the hallway and into the kitchen to get a beer. She waited, her teeth set directly on top of each other, to hear the popping open of the beer can as he lurched back through the hallway into the living room and switched on the television and flung himself in the barber chair—she could hear its sigh—and settled back to watch the *Late Late Show*, possibly wearing the skinhead wig she had throttled and fired against the door in her rage. And as she waited, listening to the melodramatic ticking of the heavy brass alarm clock on the bedside table with a porcupine in her chest, she wondered again what she was going to do.

Jo had a friend, Murphy, who worked in a travel agency in the shopping center where Jo worked and who, every night for over a year, had dreamed of murdering Cliff, her husband. She told this to Jo one afternoon while Jo was in there, looking at the colorful travel brochures that were plastered all over the walls. Jo had developed the habit of wandering into the agency every afternoon on her breaks to look at the travel brochures, and in this way she and Murphy, a torturously slim woman with a gigantic bushy hairdo, had become friends. Jo had been leaning into a poster of Tahiti the time Murphy started telling her how, for as long as she could remember, she had lain awake at night thinking of ways to kill Cliff, who slept beside her making noises like a tractor stuck in heavy mud. She told Jo she had imagined shooting him and poisoning him, setting him on fire, she had thought about drugging his beer and then smothering him with a pillow while he was out of it. She said that the very shape of his head made her want to scream. She asked Jo if she thought she was a sick person, and Jo didn't know what to say.

Jo had a friend, Sara Lee, who disappeared one day. They had shared an apartment in college, during which Sara Lee had spent most of her time asleep in her room. When she wasn't sleeping she drank malt liquor and made sarcastic remarks, many of which she directed at herself. She often referred to her chest as "two bumps on a log." Like Jo she didn't have many dates, and they went to a lot of movies together and came home and drank malt liquor and watched television while Sara Lee made sarcastic remarks at the screen. At parties they sat side by side for hours on the floor, smiling brightly. About the same time Jo met Buddy, Sara Lee met Bernard, a graduate student in biology engaged in insect research. Sara Lee joked that Bernard got his inspiration for his work when he saw the two mosquito bites on her chest. She and Bernard got married about the same time Jo and Buddy got married, and Sara Lee moved with Bernard to a downstate university where Bernard was continuing his insect research. They kept in touch, and when Bernard came to Chicago to attend a symposium or to deliver a paper on his insect research, which was receiving attention in the scientific community, Sara Lee and Jo would get together. Buddy would excuse himself and get out of the house, and the two of them would sit around talking and drinking malt liquor. When Jo would ask Sara Lee about the nature of Bernard's insect research, Sara Lee would make a face and say, "It has something to do with bug genes." She no longer made any jokes about her chest, and after two or three malt liquors she would switch to gin.

One day Jo heard that Sara Lee had disappeared. Then, a few months later while Buddy was out and Jo was lying in bed listening to the alarm clock and waiting for something to happen, Sara Lee telephoned her from San Francisco where she was working for a realtor that specialized in apartment complexes for the twenty-five-to-thirty singles crowd. She told Jo that she had been losing her mind, and that one day, while Bernard was away delivering a paper on his insect research, she had broken into his laboratory and gassed his bugs with Raid. Then she had gotten on a plane for San Francisco. She liked San Fran. She had a free apartment in one of the complexes, she leased an expensive Italian-made sports car, she had had some cosmetic surgery, she didn't know what to do with the money she was making; she and someone she kept calling Stew had just returned from the mountains where they shared a bungalow with another couple from the complex. "Not bad," she said, "for a girl named after a coffee cake."

Jo had found herself thinking a lot about Sara Lee lately, especially when Buddy was out and she was lying in bed alone at night being gnawed. She pictured Sara Lee tooling up and down the hills of San Fran in the Italian sports car,

Stew beside her, the wind in her hair. She thought about Murphy too, picturing her and Cliff lying there, Cliff making tractor noises and Murphy staring at his head and thinking about running him over with the Cordoba. After she had thought about these things for a while she would shake her head and turn and face the wall and think: not me. She was dissatisfied certainly, changes were going to have to be made, but it was nothing that couldn't be worked out. She could not imagine them not working it out. They were two mature adults, they'd been together nine years, how could they not work these things out? She couldn't picture it. She couldn't picture leaving him. Where would she go? She didn't even have a decent suitcase; she would have to get out that enormous bag with its hide peeled off and pack her stuff in it and tie it shut with one of Buddy's old belts and then, once she was ready, then what? She couldn't go home. When she tried to picture herself back home, in her old room, sitting at the dinner table with her father and mother, a feeling of extreme nausea would sweep over her and she would grit her teeth and pull the sheet up over her head. No, she couldn't go home. She would have to go off somewhere alone, and when she thought about that, of being alone, without Buddy, she would get this cold damp feeling like she was lying in a pit or at the bottom of a well. She didn't like this feeling at all. She didn't like to think about it.

She lay in bed a long time waiting for him, her brain spinning, the pain getting worse and worse, and eventually, as often happened when she waited for him alone at night, she got the distinct impression that she was fading away and that unless she got up and did something, she would disappear altogether. Bolting out of bed, she put on a pair of jeans and one of Buddy's old letter jackets and rushed out into the night.

She got into her Pinto and started driving. She had had a lot to drink, and she occupied herself entirely with keeping on the road. Stopped at lights, she composed her face in a determined expression so that anybody looking at her would see that she was about some business and had a definite place to go. Once, she glanced in the rear-view mirror and saw a police car behind her, and she pulled over to the side, her heart thumping, until it went past. She drove some more, passing through commercial zones, the dark shops stuffed with merchandise, mannequins jailed behind iron lattices. She passed the mental hospital, one of the largest in the country, she'd been told, which looked exactly like the university she'd attended except that it was completely enclosed by a high, sharply spired fence. She hurried by. She was doing quite well. Soon she came to a large residential district with block after block of small triangular houses set side by side on tiny patches of grass, and she remembered that this was where she grew up. At nearly every big intersection there was a tavern and a church. Soon she was out of the city altogether and driving down a two-lane highway that cut through woods. The black road began rushing up at her faster and faster. Behind and above her she heard a sudden roar, and glancing up, she saw a jet disappear below the trees, and she realized where she was going.

The woods fell away, and she came to the outskirts of the airport and pulled over alongside the fence at the side of the road. About a hundred yards away, two silhouettes were pawing each other in the back seat of an old Chrysler. Jo kept her eyes on the sky where, even at this hour, one of the big ones would take off about every ten minutes with a concussive roar, the long silver belly soaring directly over her head. In the distance others circled waiting to come in— three, four, sometimes she could see five at once, arrayed in great wheeling patterns, red lights blinking. In the middle of all this wind and whine the terminal gleamed like a vast shopping center.

When Jo drove around late at night she often found herself coming to the airport. She was attracted to the size of things here, the noise, the sense of stupendous motion. She

liked it even better than looking at the travel brochures in
Murphy's office. Sometimes she pulled over along the fence
and watched from a distance, her mouth open and her face
transfixed like a kid at a magic show, and sometimes she
drove right in, parked, and entered the terminal and walked
back and forth observing the crowds of people, wondering
where everyone was going. Wherever it was it was somewhere. People here were on the move. They had places to
visit, business to attend to. She would watch them for a
while, noting the stickers on suitcases, and she would become conscious of her empty hands. She was surrounded by
people who were about to take off. They would sip drinks
at 25,000 feet, leaf through important papers at 500 miles
per hour. She herself was at ground level, going nowhere.
Here she was, almost thirty years old, and never had been
out of the Midwest, never even been in the sky. This dissatisfied her no end. It made her wonder about all the other
things she was missing. Sometimes when she thought about
this she would begin to feel like she was living in a different century, and a voice would say to her, the world is moving fast, hop aboard, girl, get your ass in gear, and she
would begin walking very fast from one end of the terminal
to the other, bumping into people, her dissatisfaction growing bigger and bigger until she would finally have to rush
out and get in her car and drive home, where Buddy would
be leaning back in the barber chair with a pair of headphones jammed over his baseball cap, sucking on a joint and
listening to the Grateful Dead.

⊙⊙⊙⊙

This time when Jo got back from the airport Buddy had still
not returned. It was about quarter to two—Buddy was
standing on top of the bar in the Hot Corner doing the bump
with a pair of young girls. He was feeling fine. He asked the
girls, who were sucking fancy pink drinks through flexible
straws, how they were feeling, and they too were feeling

fine. And the Sticks? Not bad at all, thanks. The whole team was there—Harv, Red, Sammy, Doc, Stretch, Froggy, the Bull, even Whitey, who stood off to one side with his arms folded across his chest, his right hand absently flashing a series of signs. Del stood behind the bar in his white sponge hat speaking into a megaphone. Having stomped ass, they were living it up. They bumped bellies, gave each other monkey burns. They danced unusual dances, the alligator, the funky chicken—some guys were throwing in moves that had not yet been categorized. Strange hoots and yodels issued from their mouths. The Bull roared. Every so often Buddy called for his trumpet and blared out some riffs, impressing the girls with his lung and lip work. These were young girls with long tan legs, asses like pairs of clinchers wedged into tight blue shorts. Inside their yellow halters their boobs were round and snug as Hostess cupcakes. Buddy's hands roamed, taking liberties. The jukebox played "I'm a Man."

Earlier, much earlier, they had opened the new season by emasculating the Ball Busters, a bunch of college guys with big reps—Buddy went four for five and registered his usual quota of sensational snags. And then they had piled into vehicles and motored to the Corner where, after a certain amount of preliminary brew-swilling and monkey-burning and goosing, they had hoisted the birthday boy onto the bar and handed him a duffel bag stuffed with gifts. While the Sticks crowded around with their fishbowls and lopsided grins, Buddy had reached into the bag and removed the swag item by item, holding up the rubbers, the toe socks, the White Owls, the plastic schnoz . . . what could you say about guys like these? These were good eggs, guys you could count on. If you were down in the dumps, slumping, they'd pick you up. Their digs were your digs. He'd known these individuals a long time; they'd gone to school together, played ball, horsed around. He'd stood up at their weddings, was Uncle Buddy to their kids. He'd bailed them out of slammers, driven them across state lines, moved them out in the dead of night when landlords were beating at their doors. He'd clothed them and fed them and visited them when they were sick, slipping them cigarettes and Blue Ribbons until the fever broke. A few he'd buried. When called upon he'd been eyes, ears, nose, and throat for them, as well as the prevailing cooler head, and from them he expected, and got, the same in return. For guys like these he gave one hundred and ten. They took the field together in the Stick gold and blue.

"Shut your lamps," somebody yelled.

Buddy closed his eyes, and the next thing he knew somebody was prodding him in the nuts with a long cylindrical tube wrapped in tinfoil. Buddy grabbed it and tore it open —a brand new aluminum stick! He hefted it, snapping his wrists. He swallowed with difficulty; was there something in his eyes?

"You think you can still use that thing?" Red needled.

"Me?" Buddy said. "You questioning my ability to make solid contact?"

"Can you slug?" the Bull inquired.

"I'm no goon but I'll get my share."

"I don't think he can get it around," Sammy observed.

Buddy said, "Stand back." He waggled his new stick a few times then went into his stance, leaning back with the barrel resting on his shoulder, relaxed but ready. Doc produced a clincher, lobbed in the big yellow ball. Buddy made solid contact, driving it hard against the back wall and catching it on the rebound and nonchalanting it down to Doc. Sticks went wild.

Harv leaped up on the bar. He was a hirsute guy, about six-four, almost as tall as Buddy. He had graying temples, Popeye forearms, and the largest pair of ears Buddy had ever seen on a human being. He was a butcher for the A&P and played right field. His shiny new uniform was soiled in front from when he'd dived into second, stretching a gapper.

At thirty-seven he was dean of the Sticks. "Listen up a minute. I've been a Stickman for fifteen years. I'm not a Chi-Guy or an Amalgamonster. I'm no Dwarf. I play with the Sticks. Here's another thing: I been around. I played on every goddamn field in the city of Chicago. I played on fields where they had to stop the game to let the traffic through. I played on fields where there isn't a field anymore, just a bunch of cement with a chicken joint on it. I played in boneyards with balls that fell apart."

He paused, took off his cap and looked inside it as though he had a speech in there. "This is what I'm getting at. Here's what I mean. This is the best goddamn team I ever played on. We been close before, but this year we take the city. Unless my head is completely up my ass, these Sticks go all the way."

Stickmen waved dukes, pounded callused palms on top of the bar.

"Who's going to take us?" Harv asked. "The Dwarves?" He drew out the name, sissifying it.

"Fuck, no!"

"The Chi-Guys?"

"Are you shitting me?"

"The Monsters?"

"We beat their ass!"

Somebody said, "The cheer."

Harv got down on one knee and, grabbing Del's megaphone, led the cheer: hubba, hubba, hubba, HO! Stiff new yellow caps were tossed aloft, clinchers danced like yellow balloons. The floor was a thunder of bats. Stretch threw forearm shivers into the bowling machine. The Bull roared. Harv leaped down and began to pace, all worked up. Del produced a fake headline, holding it up like a banner: "STICKS TAKE TOWN!"

Buddy hadn't meant to stay. He had meant to go to the Corner for a quick one after the game and then put in two maybe three hours of hard time with Jo's folks until Roy fell asleep and Mrs. Pain-in-the-Ass made a full inspection of the place, getting it over with so that he wouldn't have to see them again until Christmas when he and Roy got into their annual holiday argument about the meaning of life beside the Nativity scene. That had been the plan. However, what with getting the presents and playing the trumpet and dancing on the bar with the girls, who were up there in the high nines on anybody's scale, he had happened to lose track of time. And who could blame him after the night he'd had? Through? If he was through, who went four for five out there tonight, stroking shots that kicked chalk down each line? Who climbed the fence to take that shot away from their clean-up hitter, a guy the size of a wood-burning stove? Who dove, tumbled, came up showing ball? Who fired strikes to all bases? He windmilled his arm, feeling no pain. Hang it up? He begged to differ: Buddy Barnes was just now reaching his peak.

Jo, he supposed, would not see it that way. He supposed he would get the full treatment when he got back—the lecture, the threats, the gripping of hair, and the trembling lower lip. Or maybe just that look of hers that seemed capable of projecting his vertebrae against the opposite wall. He'd been getting a lot of those looks lately, particularly since he'd lost his job for leaping into a tree—a sublime act which she had not even tried to understand.

"You what?" she had said, looking at him with her face surrounded by her Martian hair and holding the water bottle on him like a ray gun.

The Major had not understood it either. Her name was DeWolfe, and she was the most repulsive female Buddy had ever seen, a big crag-faced woman who smoked a pipe and wore baggy trousers and a sport jacket with her collar flared across the lapels like a big-game hunter. She tried to run the park the same way she ran the army, with a lot of straight lines and shouting and lingo. "Police the locker room," she would say. The schedules she posted were on military time.

The fact that she had once commanded squads of dykes cut no mustard with Buddy and Ferd, a twiglike guy with a severe skin problem, who spent most of his time hiding in the basement and poking on the reefer he cultivated in the defective equipment room. The Major would say, "Swab the gym," and Ferd would go down into the basement to get the buckets and come up about fifteen minutes later with a big grin plastered across his face, his eyes squinted down to the width of nickels. At first Buddy had looked at him and thought: what's the story? Then, after he'd been there a couple of weeks, Ferd had elbowed him in the side and they'd gone down into the basement to a large cluttered room behind the boiler, where Ferd kept his plants in cardboard boxes on some tables in a corner, a pair of high-powered grow lights trained on them and his watering can on the floor.

"Huh?" Ferd had said, proud as Eli Whitney.

"Not bad," Buddy said, sampling some of the product, "but what if they bust this stuff?"

"No problem. I been here almost two years and nobody comes down here but me."

Buddy could believe that. Besides being jammed with torn wrestling mats and cracked backboards and an assortment of whistles and medicine balls, the room was occupied by a family of rats which Buddy spotted nosing around in a corner. Mice, Buddy could handle; rats were an entirely different thing. Blanching, he began edging back.

"Them? No problem." Perching on a stack of bases, Ferd took several rapid pokes on his reefer. "We're all partners down here." He exhaled, coughing violently. "We even get high together."

Buddy and Ferd got high just about every morning and stayed that way just about all day. Buddy had been high the day he bet Ferd he could leap into the tree, and Ferd had taken one look at it and reached into his pocket and said, "A double sawksi says you won't." Later, after he had eaten the meatball sandwich in the cab of Herman's beer truck, after they had gotten out the hard ball and gloves and tossed a few—Herman squatting down behind the plate and giving his usual solid target with his old floppy Campanella— Buddy had gotten on the lawn mower and started riding around, cutting the grass into haphazard patterns. In a while he stopped and removed his shirt, not just because it was unusually warm for May but also to honk off the Major who, he knew, would be watching from her office in the field house. The Major hated it when Buddy took off his shirt. She told him that societies without shirts had never produced a damn thing. "Take Africa," she had pointed out. Buddy suspected that she disapproved for other reasons. He suspected that taking his shirt off had an effect even on her. He could understand why. Unlike a lot of the guys, who had started flabbing out a few years ago, Buddy remained in fine form. He still had the build of a twenty-year-old, long and angular, hipless. He still did his sit-ups and jumping jacks. He ran in place. Fine sandy hairs curled in the hollow between his pecs. Like Duke Parnell, the flame-throwing protagonist of several short stories he had written during that time when he believed his true calling was to be a writer, Buddy had a face like the guy in the Old Spice ad—strong jawed, ruggedly appealing. His teeth were big and white, the size of Chiclets. His hair tumbled forward in a natural mop of curls, cresting above his sensitive brow. His blue eyes twinkled. He was six foot five.

In a short time Buddy grew bored cutting grass into haphazard patterns. Needing a quick pickup, he paused and crouched down by the side of the mower to take a few hits on the jay Ferd had slipped him, and glancing back, he noticed two girls watching him from a park bench about fifty yards away. He had seen them before. They usually came by in the afternoon and watched him while he monkeyed around with some humdrum task, and sometimes he would take off his shirt—occasionally even in snappier weather—

and display his physique to them. They were sweethearts, about sixteen, with long legs and fawn-colored hair, and when they saw him glance over, they giggled and hunkered down behind their malteds. Ferd was watching from a clump of bushes by the tennis courts where he'd been hiding most of the afternoon with his trash spear, waiting on his bet. The Major was watching between the blinds. The tree stood at the edge of the field, the limb jutting out like a long friendly arm. Buddy climbed back on the mower and, yahooing loudly, veered directly at it. At the last moment he drew his feet onto the seat, reared up in a half crouch, and leaped. He made it easy. Dangling like an ape, he watched the mower continue along without him, watched it move across the field in the direction of the swimming pool and pass uncannily through the narrow gate. An instant later he heard the explosions.

From Ferd he collected his twenty. From the Major he received his dishonorable discharge and a tongue-lashing which he advised her to can. From Jo he got the long silence and the X-ray glare.

"What are you, Buddy?" she had said. "Give me a hint."

He was no custodian, that was certain, nor a jingle guy for Captain Industry. He had talent, brains, had compiled a 3.0 G.P.A. without even trying; it was there in black and white, anyone could check. On aptitude tests he had consistently scored in the high percentiles right across the board; counselors couldn't get over it. He could play the trumpet—guitar, too. He had the soul of an artist, the hands of a fly-chaser. If forced to pin a label on himself he supposed it would have to be: Renaissance Guy. People were naturally drawn to him, attracted, he supposed, by that certain something. All in all, he was a highly qualified individual. Just the other day when he stopped in to see his old mom, who seemed to be getting thinner and paler every time he stopped in to see her, with her nose jutting out of her bony face and her pants hanging loose, after she had given him the reindeer

sweater and brought out the cake with the thirty candles she
had meticulously inserted with her arthritic fingers, after
they had eaten some—Buddy's an enormous piece, hers a
bird's portion—and talked awhile in the stonelike presence
of the old man who sat on the porch and snarled in his camel-
colored easy chair, and after Buddy had made his old mom
laugh with some elementary legerdemain and a few rudi-
mentary hand shadows, she had reached for the dishrag and
wiped his mouth and told him what she'd always said:
"Buddy, you can be whatever you want to be." Buddy
nodded. His mom was right. He just hadn't figured out what
it was yet. Like Lonesomeboy Jones, his persona in a score
of ballads he had written in his Mississippi Delta blues stage,
his true calling still eluded him. But unlike Lonesomeboy,
an aging Negro far far from home, Buddy was a white guy
with plenty of time.

∞∞∞∞

He got back in the wee of the morning, toting his bat and
the bag of presents, fumbled open the four locks which confounded and infuriated him for a good five minutes, and
tiptoed in. The next instant he was on the floor, cursing, with
a small end table and several potted plants on top of him,
his toe socks and White Owls and Tricky Dick fright mask
and schnoz scattered all over the place. He threw off the
plants, got up, and snapped on the light to see what it was
he had stepped on, and discovered his skinhead wig which
she'd been purposely hiding from him and which, in an act
of guerrilla warfare, she had placed right in front of the
door for him to trip over and maim himself.

Jamming the rubber scalp into his back pocket, he aimed
for the kitchen to get a beer but was arrested in the dinette
by remnants of a party: a candelabrum, an empty bottle of
Lancers lying on its side, a cake defaced by several fist
prints. He also found some colorful new shirts hacked to
pieces and a card with "Happy Birthday, asshole" scrawled

across the envelope. Buddy stood there a moment, swaying, assessing what lay before him. He surveyed his cake. It had been a three-layer job with swirled white icing embedded with green and red and yellow flowers. He speared a flower on the end of his finger and tasted it. He asked himself why someone would want to punch out a birthday cake. Distressed, he whirled and directed himself toward the bedroom meaning to get the story behind this senseless pastry destruction.

He tried the door but it was locked. Buddy was in no mood for locks. He didn't mind saying he had had it up to here with locks. He got his new aluminum stick and butted it open. She was ready, nailing him in the solar plexus with a heavy brass alarm clock which took the wind out of his sails. They confronted each other on opposite sides of the bed, Buddy doubled over, Jo with narrowed eyes and taloned hands. He lunged, missed, tumbled. She clouted him a ringing blow to the ear. He caught her leg and pulled her down.

They wrestled on the floor, and after a while Buddy got a little worked up and fished it out and slipped it to her in the manner they'd grown accustomed to, he holding her down with a forearm across her throat, she pummeling and heeling him and wishing she had a sharp metal object to rake across his eyes. Pretty soon their shouts of rage and pleasure had people pounding on the walls again.

2

The Laundromat was full of guys. They were sitting in flimsy schoolkids' desks with foldover tops, gazing vacantly, sleeping in their palms. Some were up against the wall. These were oddly dressed guys, decked out in sweat suits, pajamas, Texaco shirts, hockey jerseys, and heavy woolen suit pants. They flipped through soggy magazines, played cards; every so often a machine would buzz and one of them would have to get up and rearrange his load, opening the lid and peering in carefully like there might be a small angry animal hiding inside. In one corner a heavily muscled dude in a brown pocket-T was in a lot of trouble with the fitted sheets; on the other side two homosexuals in black mesh undershirts were arguing about bleach. It was about a hundred and twenty degrees in there. The machines went round and round.

Buddy was leaning up against the soap machine, showing a guy named Morrison the funny marks on his stomach. "Check this out." He lifted up his shirt.

Morrison took off his Polaroids and squinted. "What is it?" Right in the middle of Buddy's stomach was a dull red circular welt containing a series of knoblike imprints and what seemed to be the faint outline of a word at the bottom. It looked to Morrison like some type of brand.

"You know what this is?" Buddy said. "An alarm clock. I come home last night and wham, she nails me with this heavy brass number the minute I come through the door. I took it point-blank. Hurt?"

Morrison whistled through the gap in his front teeth. "How come?"

Buddy lowered his shirt. "How do I know? Don't ask."

He went over to the tables and dumped out his load and began sorting it into lights and darks. He hogged up a whole table. He was in no mood to share. Every now and then he would reach under his shirt and feel the clock marks on his stomach, simultaneously breathing curses, so that the guys sorting their own loads at adjoining tables would glance over at him with cagey eyes. She had lain in wait with a hard brass object, that's what he couldn't get over. What if he had taken it upside the skull or in the jewels? Had she thought about that? Had she considered that it was only his superb muscle tone that had prevented internal injury? Sure, they had their disagreements just like everybody else —where did it say it was all gravy?—but this introduction of deadly weapons was an entirely new development.

He felt he was going to have to speak to her about this matter of lying in wait. He was also going to have to speak to her about these goddamn lists she kept leaving for him every morning. Today, for instance, he had gotten up with his head feeling like an anvil and found himself barricaded in by a huge pile of dirty wash with a list of laundry do's and don't's propped on top of it. He had kicked his way through and gone into the kitchen and discovered twenty-five dollars and a grocery list taped to his Wheaties. It was a long list filled with little irritating items like Windex and Brillo pads which, he immediately deduced, were harbingers of lists to come. Ever since he had lost his job for leaping into a tree, she had him slaving away like a washerwoman; she had him running errands, painting stuff, a guy of his caliber she had on his hands and knees scouring the bathroom bowl. They were going to have to reach an understanding. He felt he was going to have to put his foot down—on her neck, if necessary.

He had discovered the marks on his stomach that morning while taking his usual leisurely hour-long toilette. He had also discovered hives, which had appeared overnight on his hands and the insides of his arms in ugly red patches. He had picked them up when the plants fell on top of him after he had tripped over the skinhead booby trap she had set by the door. Buddy was allergic to certain varieties of plants and tried to keep his contact with them to a minimum. This had become a lot harder ever since Jo had turned the apartment into a scaled-down version of the Borneo jungle. The goddamn things were everywhere. It seemed like every place he wanted to lean his arms or rest his feet there was a plant, and every time he turned around he was cracking his head against a new one hammocked from the ceiling. The windows were so thick with them he could hardly see out. There was a rubber tree in the dinette, ferns in the kitchen; he undressed each night observed by Wandering Jews. During his toilettes he had to share the facilities with several bushy growths of the variety that thrived in dank, humid atmospheres, a grow light shining in his eyes. He ate his morning Wheaties surrounded by cacti.

He supposed he had only himself to blame for the plants. He had given her the first one, a hardy little fern which he'd surprised her with one day for no reason but to make her smile, little realizing that from this one modest growth a teeming rain forest would bush. He couldn't see the sense of it. A pet he could understand. He could handle a bird or a cat or some kind of rodent that hung around in a cage, although in his opinion even these creatures couldn't hold a candle to a good old hound. Buddy had had a dog once. He had bought it from a grease monkey somewhere in Minnesota. At the time he'd been returning from Alaska, where he had gone to find his true calling, but he had not found it there. After a few months it had become evident to him that that vast land had little to offer besides large groups of hairy men, poisonous plants, and gigantic biting insects. He was on his way back to the toddling town all hairy and itchy and smelling like an elk, when he pulled into a gas station and spotted a young dog standing alertly between the pumps with a rag in its mouth, like it was waiting for a signal to wipe his windshield. Buddy was immediately impressed with the dog's ingenuity as well as its appearance; he had never before seen a dog with the body of a German shepherd and the face of a Scottie.

"How much?" he had asked the grease monkey, gesturing at the beast.

"Ain't for sale."

Buddy reached into his pocket and pulled out the wad he had amassed fighting forest fires. Though depleted by massive gambling losses, it still amounted to almost fifteen hundred dollars, by far the most money he had ever had. He peeled off three tens and a twenty and stuffed them into the grease monkey's shirt pocket, above which he wore his name: Bart. He then opened the passenger door and whistled, and the dog, without hesitation, clambered in.

Mutant was a big frisky guy who rarely barked. He sat up, rolled over on his back. He gave of himself unstintingly and crapped outside. Within a week, however, he had chewed everything in the apartment to a pulp. He and Jo had a series of tremendous arguments about the animal. One night Jo issued an ultimatum: either the dog or me. Buddy thought it over. The next morning, heavy-hearted, he drove to Herman's and persuaded him to adopt Mutant, throwing in a bottle of Wild Turkey in the bargain—which included visiting privileges.

It was about that time that Jo started going crazy with

the plants. Instead of man's best friend they had philoden-
drons. Buddy couldn't understand it. What could you do
with a plant? You couldn't wrestle with one or put your wrist
in its mouth. A plant couldn't guard your place from murderous intruders. It couldn't do anything but take up space.
He had heard somewhere they were supposed to produce
oxygen, but he didn't believe this for a minute. He was sure
it was the reverse: they breathed. They were sucking up his
air, splotching up his arms, crowding him out. It seemed like
every time they had an argument Jo would bring home another plant. Pretty soon the place was infested with them.
She spent a ridiculous amount of time fooling with them; it
occurred to Buddy that she talked more to growths than she
did to him. He felt he finally had to put his foot down when
she hung a bunch of plants right in front of the hoop he had
fastened above the closet door, setting up a defense he could
penetrate only by standing inside the closet and leaning forward for underhand lob shots. This seemed like an ideal way
for him to make a complete monkey out of himself, and he
had gotten a kitchen knife and hacked them down.

She had made a big deal out of it, of course, lugging the
plants over and setting them down in front of him like so
many beheaded innocents and giving him the X-ray glare,
the same glare she had first given him the night he had set
the Figs on fire and which she had most recently given him
the day he had lost his job for leaping into the tree.

"What's the big deal here?" Buddy had said. "They were
in my way. I got my rights. Look, if I've told you once I've
told you a thousand times: leave my hoop alone."

But his finding a true calling—now there *was* a big deal.
She acted like it was nothing, like it was the easiest thing in
the world to figure out. His true calling! He had tried to be
patient, pointing out such factors as the slumping economy,
recession, government interference in the free-enterprise system. He had reminded her of the difficulty of finding meaningful work in a mechanized society. He wasn't talking about

writing jingles or delivering pizzas or tending bar or selling Ferd's weed to adolescent hipsters. He wasn't talking about fooling with huge metal coils at the copper mill. He wasn't talking trash. He was talking about his true calling, which wasn't easy to find in this age of affirmative action, double-digit inflation, and the superabundant work force.

She didn't understand. She would give him the glare, her face puckered like she was tonguing a headache lozenge, and tell him that after nine years she had reached her own conclusions about what his true calling was: namely, to sit all day in his barber chair with a pair of headphones clapped over his head, hogging down Old Styles and reading *Twenty Thousand Leagues Under the Sea*.

"And don't give me that shit about your arm either," she would add. At times like this Buddy was prone to remind her that he'd been cut down in the flower of his youth by a cruel and mysterious elbow pain and was haunted by the fear that his true calling would forever be denied him. He'd call her attention to this and to the fact that he'd had it all: namely, speed, the hook, and deadeye control.

Jo, however, was tired of hearing about it. "Quit pointing at your arm," she would say. "It doesn't have anything to do with anything anymore."

"It's still my fucking arm, isn't it?" Buddy would say. "It isn't your arm."

"What I'd like to know," Jo would say, pruning off dead jade leaves, "is if your arm hurts you so much, how come you can still go out and run around with those clowns every night of the week?"

This was the place where Buddy would jam on his cap and go down to the Corner and have eight or nine beers and talk ball with Stretch and Bull and Harv and Red and play the machines and try to get his mind off why he continued to stay with a woman who wouldn't let up on him for a minute.

She could not appreciate his position. She refused to entertain his point of view. She called him a bum. A guy like him, a bum! As though he'd been passed out on the floor all these years or zombied out on weed like that idiot Ferd. As though he hadn't had his face lashed by auto-antenna-wielding youths in the rec center parking lot after he had tried to teach them a few simple pick and rolls, the ungrateful turds. As though he hadn't delivered pizzas, tended bar, written jingles, hawked insurance, speared trash with a stick. As though he hadn't sweated his nads off in the copper mill and awakened each morning with claws hanging on the ends of his arms. As though he hadn't ventured all the way to goddamn Alaska.

"Maybe," he had pointed out to her, "just maybe I could find my true calling if you'd give me the least tiny bit of support. Begrudge me a measly pat on the back once in a while. You may not know it," he had added, "but I'm an extremely sensitive guy. I've got an artistic temperament. I've got certain creative needs."

"God," she had said, gripping her head.

∞∞

No faith. No support. When he came home that time with the gigantic typewriter balanced on his back, she had looked at him as though he had just grown a hump. "What's that?"

"A typewriter, what do you think it is." He stood there, panting and red from the exertion of lugging the thing up the stairs.

"Where did you get it?"

"I found it in the park. Make way, will you? This mother is heavy."

He went in and put his machine on the kitchen table and sat down in front of it and immediately began pecking at the rusty keys. Jo observed him. After a minute she came over and asked him what he thought he was doing.

"Writing."

"I see. What are you writing?"

"I'm not sure yet. I'm one of those writers who has to write a while to discover what it is I'm writing."

"Oh," Jo said. "One of those writers." She went away, blinking. Buddy continued to peck in a blizzard of creativity. He was convinced that finding the typewriter had been a sign. He'd been shagging flies in the park and had gone after a long belt of the Bull's and had nearly stumbled over what seemed like a boulder buried in tall grass. He got down on his hands and knees and parted the grass and discovered a big black square metal case plastered with travel decals. He crouched down and touched it. He might have been an ape-man poking at the monolith. He pried open the top, and inside was this gigantic typewriter with round black keys running steeply up the carriage and a blank piece of paper locked inside the rollers.

He brought the thing home and sat down in front of it and didn't get up for about a week. Jo couldn't believe it. She would come home from the department store and find him sitting there, wearing only his jockeys and a pair of glasses with a piece of tape holding one temple together, the floor directly beneath him covered with crumpled balls of paper.

He started with sketches, just to get the hang of it. Then he wrote a couple of Duke Parnell stories. He was building up, of course, to a book, one filled with life and death and blood and sex—and plenty of laughs, too. He planned to draw on his own experiences. He had experienced a great deal. He had traveled, for instance, and known women. He knew what it was like to be down and out without a nickel in his pocket. He knew the thrill of victory and the agony of defeat as only an athlete can know it, knew too what it was like to be cut down in the flower of his youth.

Convinced he had found his true calling at last, Buddy didn't mess around. He wrote a story a day. Some were Westerns, set in the town of Tumbleweed Junction and starring a lawman named Tex Wilson who had only one eye—

but it was an exceptionally keen eye. Some were science fiction tales that had to do, in one way or another, with the end of the world. One was set on a grim planet covered by a radioactive haze and inhabited only by funguslike growths endowed with the capacity to communicate with each other and remember. At the very end of the story this devastated planet turned out to be earth. Most of the others were Duke Parnell stories. In one, called "Achilles Elbow," Duke was cut down in the flower of his youth.

His longest was a combination of sports and science fiction. It was called "The Year the Cubs Won the Pennant," and starred Billy Zapski, an alien who came down to earth in the guise of a switch-hitting rookie center fielder, a position the Cubs had been trying unsuccessfully to fill for years. Everyone knew there was something mysterious about Billy —his phosphorescent spikes, his enormous cap, his oddly shaped, seven-fingered glove—but he was such a great player that nobody bothered with these trivialities. Annihilating eleven individual records, Billy led the Cubs to the pennant in a cakewalk. The story ended unhappily, however. Just before the start of the World Series, as the mayor was drawing back his arm to throw out the first ball, a spaceship appeared, hovering over the center field scoreboard, and Billy vanished in a beam of light, returning to his native planet where he was a second-grader. Utterly demoralized, the Cubs lost the series in four straight games.

It took Buddy almost a week to write this story, which he considered his masterpiece, and like all his stories this one had a moral: everything's relative.

After a month Buddy had accumulated a corpus of fifteen stories. He had not showed them to anyone. He had especially not showed them to Jo. Typically, she had regarded his writing as yet another albeit bizarre way to avoid going out and getting a real job. She had suggested he put the typewriter to good use by typing up some résumés. This statement was so ignorant that he had not bothered to reply.

He would let his fellow professionals judge his work. His stories would speak for themselves.

One morning he loaded his stories into the box his winter boots had come in, toted them to the post office, and mailed them to a prestigious literary agency, whose name he had gotten out of a book. After considerable thought he had decided to include all his stories, not only because he couldn't decide which ones to leave out—they were all good—but because he wanted the agency to get a load of his versatility and the breadth of his vision. He did include a letter stating that the agency was under no obligation to take all the stories, just the ones they liked the best. He went home and waited, knocking off a silly little thing about a parrot who became chief adviser to the president of the United States, just to keep his hand warm. After a couple of weeks he found his stories on the landing outside the door, stuffed inside a ragged tan envelope with its ends burst open, the whole package looking like it had been tossed through the window by someone in a hurry. He swooped it up and carried it furtively into the bedroom and tore it open. The first thing he saw was a terse and humiliating note scribbled in pencil across the title page of "The Year the Cubs Won the Pennant." The note had said: "Give me a break."

As soon as Jo got home that night he dumped the stories in her lap.

"What do you want me to do with these?"

"Read them."

"How many?"

"All of them."

She picked out the funguslike-growth story and started to read. Buddy leaned over her, his jaw jutting, his hands balled into fists. She read the first paragraph, then paused and said, "This planet isn't actually earth, is it?"

He snatched the story away from her and riffled through the stack until he came to a Tex Wilson tale; he shoved it in her face.

She started to read. "Well, do something, will you? I can't read with you standing over me like that."

Buddy went into the bedroom and lay down, a warm wash-cloth draped across his forehead, and occupied himself by mentally crashing the office of the agency, barging past squads of snotty receptionists and smashing down the door of the wimp who had scribbled that shit all over his master-piece. He had the toad by the throat when he heard a peal of shrieking laughter, and he sprang out of bed and bounded into the living room and found Jo on the floor, kicking her heels and laughing hysterically.

"Something funny?" Buddy said.

"I'm sorry," she sobbed. She was holding up the Tex Wilson story, pointing at the place where Tex's gun said "Blam."

∘∘∘∘

No consideration. Zero trust. The day he brought the large guitar home she had looked at him as though he were hope-less.

"Now what?"

"It's a beaut, isn't it?" Buddy flourished the instrument which was unusually large and bloated-looking, as though it had been soaking at the bottom of a lagoon for many years. It had a yellowish-green cast and a threadbare shoulder sling. "I won it from this old shine in a poker game." He struck a sour chord. "Get me the Pledge, will you? I want to dust this baby off."

He curled up on the floor with it and stayed there for over a month, tuning and polishing it, plunking on it interminably. The fact that he had no idea how to play had not fazed him in the least. He planned to get the hang of it by ear. "I'm musically inclined," he pointed out to Jo. "It's just some-thing I was born with, I guess." He did in fact know how to play the trumpet and was good enough to have blown with a few very bad jazz bands in his college days, never lasting long with any of them primarily because he felt that practice damaged his creative spontaneity. He still had the trumpet but blew it only at parties, on top of the bar at the Corner, and in the bleachers at Wrigley Field, where he used it to encourage rallies.

Jo had never cared for his trumpet; she liked this large guitar even less. Every time she came home from the department store, her feet killing her and her head frazzled by brats who razed her toy displays, she would find him curled up on the floor next to the stereo she was still paying for, listening to scratchy recordings of Negro music and plunking on the guitar in a manner that mimicked the peculiar and monotonous style of Mississippi Delta blues. Occasionally he sang in a garbled voice, slurring the words.

"What are you listening to this type of music for?" she would ask him. "You're not black."

Buddy would pause, lowering the large urine-colored guitar. "What's the matter with you? Don't you know anything? The blues isn't just for Negroes. It's for anybody who's ever been down in the dumps, broke, fucked over, and shat on. It's a state of mind." He lifted the guitar, rapidly strummed a few times, and sang in a garbled voice: "I'm a hog for you, baby; I can't get enough of your love . . ."

She had never tried to appreciate his music. She had never listened to any of his songs, including his Lonesomeboy Jones ballads which he felt were particularly meaningful. She had not even attended his audition in that hole in the wall on Sheridan Road, which had been halted prematurely when a bunch of Sticks who came to give him support got into it with hecklers from the kitchen crew. Buddy leaped off the stage and joined the disagreement, which lasted for most of his allotted twenty minutes and had taken the manager, the bartender, and a platoon of cops to break up.

Depressing? Sure it was depressing, particularly since the large guitar had been ruined in the fight when Buddy smashed it over the bartender's shaved noggin. He had moped home with his caved-in ax cradled in his arms and a gash on his nose, and Jo's only reaction had been to hand him the telephone. Emitting a low guttural sound, Buddy had seized the receiver and dialed the Major's number, wondering whatever happened to the sweetheart of his college days who, wearing a rose and a pioneer dress, had married him at sunrise in the woods which were out of bounds on the university golf course, who used to put down saucers of milk for six different strays, who went with him to see Long John Baldry, Atomic Rooster, George Benson (before he went commercial), and John Mayall and the Bluesbreakers, who—scented with sandalwood incense and wearing only a string of Indian beads—used to sit on his lap and suck on his fingers, and who had soaked his foot in Epsom salts when, as a rookie Stick, he had sprained his ankle on a close play at the plate.

oooo

They had first met in the men's room of the administration building in the aftermath of a demonstration in which some students had occupied certain key offices, setting fire to trash cans and dumping on important desks. Buddy had gone in there to take a leak and found her coughing and gasping into a brown paper towel. The corridors were thick with gas.

He had fished a rag out of his pocket, run some cold water over it, and handed it to her. She blew her nose in it and handed it back. Buddy studied her. She was a slim girl with a heart-shaped face and frizzy brown hair that came down to the middle of her back. She had an overbite and a long narrow nose that turned up at the end in a small bulb, as though someone had stuck a piece of putty on it and left it there. Buddy liked this nose a lot; it seemed to have a sense of humor.

"You okay?"

She nodded, sniffling. She had her purse slung over her shoulder, and she gripped it tightly, her eyes fastened on the door. "This is the men's room, isn't it?" she said. "I better get out of here."

"What's your hurry? There's just a bunch of gas out there." He cracked open a window. "Relax a minute. Get some air. Have a look around while you're at it." He gave her a brief tour of the men's room. "Nothing much. You got your stalls, your mirror, your towel machine. I don't know how it is in your place, but these goddamn things are always stuck and you wind up wiping your hands on your pants. Over there you got your urinals." He led her over to inspect the urinals, which were filled with gum, cigarette butts, small amounts of piss. "Bad news," he said, taking a whiff. "See those mothball cakes? I know a guy who ate one once on a bet. You feeling any better? C'mon, I'll buy you a drink."

He took her to his place, poured her several glasses of wine, and then jumped on her. She elbowed him in the kidney. It was like that for a whole month. He would show her a good time, take her to parties where drugged people of all races mingled hiply or to an Antonioni film, then they'd go back to his place, smoke a joint, he'd jump on her and she'd come down hard on his instep. He couldn't believe it. Even before the age of sexual liberation and the greening of America, it had never taken him more than three nights to score. He had techniques, lines. Hard-to-get knockouts had melted under his charm, and here was this skinny girl with frizzy hair and a funny nose who kept coming down hard on his instep.

"What's the story?" he asked her one night after she had dinked him expertly in his painfully tender nuts. "This is the age of Aquarius."

"I don't care what age it is," Jo had said. "Keep your hands to yourself."

Buddy pondered the situation for a whole week. One night he threw a pebble at her window at three in the morning. She came to the door in a bathrobe and yawned. "What's up?"

"Okay," he said, tugging on a sideburn. "Let's get married."

Jo studied him closely. "You stoned?"

"No."

"Drunk?"

"No, I am not drunk." He threw his arms in the air. "What do you want me to do, get on my knees?"

"Not really," Jo said, unsashing her robe. "I got a better idea."

The following Saturday Jo put on her pioneer dress and Buddy got out his hairy brown sport coat, and they went out to the golf course with a few close friends they had managed to get out of bed. A hip cleric wearing Bermuda shorts, a sunburst T-shirt, and a collar he whipped out of his pocket and stuck on for the occasion pronounced them husband and wife. The ceremony was legit, even if it was briefly interrupted by a man in an alligator shirt who came hacking through the underbrush with a nine iron in search of his Spalding Dot.

After the honeymoon, which they'd spent at the Wisconsin Dells riding the roller coasters high as kites and looking at themselves in funny mirrors, they moved into Buddy's love nest—a dusty two-room flat above a Laundromat, furnished with a mattress, a legless maroon sofa, and a couple of lawn chairs. Like Gandhi, Buddy was not a materialist. Jo didn't mind. She put curtains in the windows, hung erotic prints on the walls, cashed in some savings bonds, and bought furniture at the Salvation Army store. Together they rode in his rust-chewed Oldsmobile, a urine-colored car with split vinyl upholstery, year-round snow tires, and a passenger door held shut by a piece of rope. What did they care? It got them to Goose Lake, didn't it? Together they made the scene, checked out what was happening. They caught the Mahavishnu Orchestra, Hound Dog Taylor, Canned Heat, CSN&Y. They went to a Raoul Walsh retrospective and a Bulls-Lakers playoff game. Together they saw *2001* seven times and watched Nixon resign on the old Motorola, the picture flip-flopping and shrunk to about half its original size.

While he searched for his true calling, Jo worked, manning switchboards, ringing up groceries, serving seven different kinds of hotcakes, and prying quarters from under gooey plates. For a while she even wore a jungle girl suit and served voodoo punch in the Bali Hi Lounge until Buddy found out about it and made her quit. She had done it for him, she explained, understanding in the good old days that a true calling took time to find.

In the evenings she went to his games, sitting right up front where Buddy could see her and wearing one of his old windbreakers that came down to the tops of her knees. In the good old nights they made love, acts that had little in common with the grim grapplings they now performed. Jo then was easy. She had her tricks. One night she would play the nymphet, putting her hair in pigtails and sticking a Tootsie Pop in her mouth; the next night she'd give him the tease, showing him a little of this and a little of that while he lay back on the bed and watched, his wang swelling to formidable proportions. Horny in the morning, he'd fish it out before she went to work and she'd put her legs up on his shoulders, her tight wet center making a Hun of him. She'd go down, driving him nuts with teeth and tongue and swirling hair. He'd eat her completely, leaving her covered with little purple marks like clusters of berries on a long white vine. After, he'd pull one of his gags, do his Victor Mature impression or rooster his fingers against the wall, and she'd laugh her laugh, which was moist and vulnerable, like she was coming down with a cold. There wasn't a sound he liked any better. Each night she'd curl up against him and fall asleep, and he'd wrap himself around her and stroke her like a tide.

Those, however, were the good old days. In these strange new days Buddy couldn't get a yuk out of her to save his life. He would sneak up on her wearing one of his funny schnozzes, and she would just look at him with a tremendous weariness in her eyes. He'd hide behind the rubber plant and surprise her as she came through the kitchen, establishing position and drawing the offensive foul, and she would mutter something into his chest and walk around him, shaking her head. She would come home from work and walk right past him without even a glance, leaving him standing there like an idiot in his antler cap. Just the other day he was walking around in his giant rubber feet, and she had glared at him with her mouth shut tight around her teeth, like she had a tremendous squawk locked up inside. Beneath her strange new curls her nose jutted sharply, like a stinger. The curls themselves surrounded her face in a fierce brown bubble. Buddy didn't like this hairdo at all. He hadn't liked it when she first showed up with it, and he still didn't like it. It reminded him of something a chick from another planet might show up with.

"What's that?" he had said.

"You mean my hair? What do you think?"

Buddy told her. "You look like an alien."

They had quarreled about it. Buddy found this new hair unpleasant to look at and unpleasant to touch. It was the hairdo of a woman who, provoked, might take you apart with a series of blows to the Adam's apple, genitals, and other, lesser-known vulnerable spots.

"Why don't you get rid of that hairdo," Buddy suggested from time to time. "It looked a lot better the old way."

"Listen," Jo said. "You better get used to it, because this is the way it's staying."

"Okay," Buddy said, "but in my opinion you still look like the Chick from Mars."

"Don't call me that."

"Don't call you what?"

"Chick. I hate that." She said it again, turning her mouth inside out.

"Christ," Buddy had said.

He didn't understand any of it. Wasn't he the same easygoing guy he'd always been? His sense of humor, his hair, his lopsided grin—he hadn't lost any of those, had he? He hadn't gone fat and crabby like a lot of guys, nor did he regularly give her the knuckle sandwich. He still brought her little surprises, hot Sams and corn dogs from the corner snack man, baubles and beads he had lifted from Woolworth's, he even brought her plants. And didn't he still have that certain something? Better believe it. But now, all of a sudden, he was a clown, an idiot, an immature child. An inept and selfish guy in the sack, he ignored the clitoris. He was a bum, walking around with an alarm clock on his stomach.

What really hurt was the fact that she no longer came to his games. Out in left, surrounded by his fans—the old guys, the young turks, the chicks who would wave to him and call out his name—Buddy would search the crowded bleachers in vain. He retaliated by monkeying around, picking up women at the zoo, the International House of Pancakes, the mummy room of the Natural History Museum, but every time he did it he felt so lousy he'd mope around for days, banging his fists together and peeking at her with guilty eyes. In these strange new days Jo never even noticed.

OOOO

Buddy was still going through the wash—he kept losing track of Jo's complicated sorting system and would have to start over again—when he spotted a small dark guy wearing a white shirt and a glossy black hat dart into the dry cleaner's next door. Buddy thrust out his head and looked at the man for a minute, his hands gripping down hard on the edge of the table. The man was going through his pockets looking for his ticket while the proprietress, a toothy woman with her hair swathed in colorful rags like a fortune-teller, observed him from behind the counter, resting comfortably on her chest. The man was extremely thin; his shirt hung like a flag on a windless day. He could not find his ticket. He began arguing with the woman, pointing at a garment hanging from the rack inside a plastic bag. Finally the woman went over and put her foot on the pedal, activating a bright merry-go-round of clothing, and the skinny guy leaned sideways on the counter and glanced idly back into the Laundromat. Buddy, who'd been watching the entire exchange with his whole body angled forward like a big wary hare, suddenly jumped back behind the pop machine, flattening himself against the wall.

The skinny guy's name was Noselli, and Buddy owed him some money. He owed him from the Super Bowl when he had taken Denver and the spread. He had made a generous wager on the game, figuring Denver was a cinch to beat the spread, but then they had gone out and played like bozos and he had gone down the tubes. He remembered how Noselli, who'd been covering Dallas all over town, had grinned at him when he placed the wager. This grin had not sat well with Buddy, and he had doubled his bet right there. Not only did Buddy owe him on the Bowl, he felt it was possible that he owed the skinny bookman on several other wagers. He couldn't remember, but he felt that he did. He'd been avoiding him now for several months.

Buddy knew Noselli from around. He remembered when he first set eyes on this meatball a couple of years ago. He had been hanging around in the Corner drinking Old Styles and talking ball, and then this skinny guy in a black leather jacket and a glossy black hat had come in and started scuffing balls around the pool table. Buddy had observed him for a moment, licking suds off his lips. The guy was jabbing at the balls, wielding the cue in an obviously sham manner. He was torturing the table. Grinning, Buddy had picked up his beer and gone over and asked him if he'd care to shoot a game.

Buddy was well aware of the clown's gambit. They each

hustled the other once, and then, with a bill on the table, Billy had chalked up and run fifty straight. He plucked the bill off the table and dropped it in his pocket, and Noselli, without once changing expression, had put his stick carefully back up on the wall and pushed his hat back off his forehead and walked out the door.

There had been subsequent, less pleasant encounters. Buddy remembered very well the time he had sat in on a poker game with Noselli and some of his meatball friends, and he had not gotten a card to save his life. Every time Noselli dealt—he was up big—he would snap out Buddy's card and toss it down and look over what he had and say, "Jack shit." He said it every time. Finally, Buddy had looked over at him and said: "What's this Jack shit noise?" He was burning. He was sure Noselli was slipping himself cards, but what could he do with a table full of meatballs in the room? Noselli had shrugged and worked his toothpick and said, "Play it, then." Buddy had, losing just over one hundred dollars, and after he was cleaned out he had gone home and locked himself in the bathroom and beaten up the shower curtain.

They still ran into each other from time to time—in the bleachers at Wrigley Field, at Buddy's games, sometimes at the track—and sometimes Buddy wired in a little side action on his games and sometimes he played the Noseman's football cards. He did not fare well on the cards, and then he would have to avoid the guy for a while, jumping behind Coke machines. Once—Buddy would never forget it—he was cornered by Noselli in a racetrack urinal and, producing a small black book in which he kept his outstanding accounts, Noselli had showed Buddy how much he was down and then inquired whether Buddy ever had a bad game from time to time.

"What are you talking about?" Buddy had said. He knew very well what the meatball was talking about, but he wanted to hear it out loud with his own ears.

Noselli made himself clear. "I'm not talking about a clown act. Just drop one from time to time. Lose one in the lights."

"Let me get this straight," Buddy had said. "You're asking a guy like me to drop one? You're asking me—a Stickman, a left fielder—to lose one in the lights?" He had the punk by the lapels of his leather jacket. "Chew on this. I'm a Stick. I go all out. I catch everything. I take the extra base." He reached into his pocket and counted out a couple of bills—he'd been up big at the track that day—and stuffed them into one of Noselli's innumerable jacket pockets. "Here's your cash. We're straight. Get out of my face." He threw Noselli out of the toilet. There were a couple of other guys over at the urinals, holding themselves and listening over their shoulders, and Buddy told them to zip up and get out of there. He was burning. When the room was cleared, he had gone over and ripped the towel machine off the wall.

Buddy was still hiding behind the pop machine when Noselli came through the door, holding the plastic bag with his black leather jacket inside. He held it daintily, as though it were a holy vestment. He wandered over to the pop machine and rooted out some change. He glanced with disgust at the selections. They were out of everything except Mountain Dew, and Noselli hated Mountain Dew. Frowning, he slipped in his coins anyway, and then he glanced briefly at Buddy, who had turned his back and had his face pressed up against a bulletin board.

Noselli said, "Looking for hot tips, Barnes?"

Buddy spun around. "Nose, baby." He was all smiles. "Howzit going?"

"Same as always. Some days are good, some days not so good."

"I hear you."

"Of course it's always good to run into an old friend you haven't seen in a long time."

"It hasn't been that long." Buddy stroked his jaw. "Couple of months, maybe."

"More like four." He was staring at Buddy beneath the brim of his hat, which had slid down to his eyebrows. He was working a toothpick from one side of his mouth to the other. "The way I remember it, I haven't seen you since the Bowl."

"Naw," Buddy said. "I've seen you since then."

Noselli said nothing.

Buddy ran his hands under his shirt and began stroking the clock on his stomach. "Seems to me I saw you in the Palace that one day. It was two, three months ago, remember?"

Noselli said, "No way."

"Sure," Buddy said. "I came in, we had a drink, and then we settled up on the Bowl. It was sometime in February, as I recall."

Noselli put down the plastic bag and, reaching into his back pocket, produced the black book. "Barnes. Down half a bill. Took Denver and the spread." He laughed dryly at the idea of such an idiotic wager. "You're also down on a couple of Bear games."

Buddy narrowed his eyes. "No way, Nose. I'm clear on those."

Noselli pushed his hat back off his forehead. "I got your markers in the car. Don't make me get them."

Buddy shrugged. "Maybe so. I could've sworn I settled with you, but never mind. My mistake. No sweat." He was thumping his stomach like a tom-tom. "Hey, you know I'm good for it anyway, right?"

Noselli just looked at him.

"Guys like us, we go back a long way. We understand each other. Hey, haven't I always been good on any business we've done?"

"Sure," Noselli said, "after I have to hunt you up. The last time, I had to hunt you up in the toilet, remember?"

Buddy laughed. "I was running a little short at the time."

"That's the trouble with you, Barnes. You're always running short." Noselli picked up the plastic bag and slung it over his shoulder; the weight of the jacket caught him off balance and he staggered back a step or two. "I'll be expecting you this week, Barnes. Don't make me have to hunt you up again."

"For sure, Nose."

"By the way, what happened to your stomach?"

"This? I ran into the fence over at Clarendon."

"Yeah? I thought maybe your old lady hit you with a clock or something." He laughed dryly, then spun around and walked out, sagging under his jacket.

As soon as he had left, Buddy turned on the pop machine and jarred it with several powerful elbow smashes. He gave it the boot. The big talk, the hat, the leather jacket—everything about the punk got under his hide. Here was a guy who did his business in a bowling alley: who did he think he was kidding? Still burning, Buddy scooped up his wash and crammed it haphazardly into five machines, sprinkling in detergent and ramming down the lids. He fired in his coins with cruel, open-handed thrusts, and went out, pushing past a fat guy in a fuzzy yellow robe who was blocking the door. They exchanged words. He moved down the street, walking into a wind that blew swirling grit and clouds of bus exhaust directly into his face. In the distance tall buildings loomed in a smoggy mirage. Across the street two guys in pea-green leisure suits, their sports cars locked at the bumper, threatened each other with fists and tough talk.

In a thoroughly lowdown mood, Buddy walked a couple of blocks with his hands jammed deep into the pockets of a pair of baggy, paint-splattered pants. Then he ducked into the Corner. Some Sticks were sitting at the bar—Red, Stretch, Froggy, the Bull—still in uniform, as though they had never left, their long-visored caps pushed back on their heads. The Bull had a nasty gash on his arm from chasing a pop foul into the fence. Del was feeding the tarantula.

Crawford was there showing people his new plastic hand, his real hand having been recently ground to a pulp in heavy industrial machinery. He showed it to Buddy.

"Check it out."

"Nice," Buddy said without enthusiasm. "Looks real natural."

"I'm still getting used to it." Behind his safety goggles he had small pear-colored eyes that didn't catch much. "It's a hard thing to get used to. It isn't like a real hand."

"I'm hip." Buddy brushed past Crawford and took a stool off to one end of the bar. Whipping out some of the grocery money, he bought a shot of Wild Turkey which he downed all at once, cowpoke fashion. He shuddered and bought another, leaning forward with his elbows balanced on the counter and sucking on his teeth and wishing to Christ he had a game tonight.

The Sticks were drinking Pabst Blue Ribbons and talking ball. As usual Red was doing most of the talking, juggling his hands and fidgeting like a hyper Howdy Doody. He was a substitute teacher and a pesky singles hitter. Hunkered down beside him was the Bull, his huge ass engulfing the stool, his huge arms, equally adept at digging six-foot holes and launching goon shots into parking lots, lying like shovels across the bar. Now that Herman had left the team for good, he was out of position at third and knew it. Next came Stretch, erect as a fence post, staring at his lobster hands and wondering when the layoff at the copper mill was going to end. Froggy and Crawford sat side by side, the former examining Crawf's prosthesis with his veiny, magnified eyes. He was a certified public accountant and kept the team's books. Then came Buddy, three stools over, wishing to Jesus he could climb a fence tonight, sprint for the corner, dive and tumble and come up showing ball.

Suddenly he lifted his shirt, inviting the Sticks to get a load of his stomach and the marks thereon. "Look at this bullshit, will you? It's my birthday, and she hits me with this clock, a big heavy mother. On my birthday! Sore? Let me tell you."

"What for?" the Bull inquired.

"How do I know? So I was a little late. What was I supposed to do? Say, 'All right, fellas, hurry up and give me my stuff, I got to be running along'? I'm thirty years old, for Christ sake."

"I know where you're coming from," Red offered. "Didn't that chick spray me with some kind of jazz in P.J.'s parking lot last week? I was just talking to her, and all of a sudden she's got this can in my face. My fucking nose turned red, let me tell you. I couldn't see for two days."

"Some of these chicks are armed to the teeth," Bull observed. "They got knifes, pistols, hat pins. They know the kung fu. You don't know what a chick is going to pull on you anymore."

"Didn't that chick blow a whistle on me outside of Walgreen's that time?" Red said.

Froggy removed his glasses and spoke with a naked face. "The way I see it, you got to establish guidelines right from the start. Draw up rules. Get it down on paper. That way when somebody gets out of line you got it down right there in black and white. It's in the books."

"I'll tell you this," Bull said. "If my old lady doesn't get the ants out of her pants, she's going to get it good. First I come home and there's a load of bricks in the yard. I ask her, 'What do you think the bricks are for?' 'We need another room,' she tells me. 'Is that so?' I say. I got them out of there in a hurry, let me tell you. Then I catch her reading one of those how-to-do-it books in bed one night. It's put out by one of those outfits where they put wires on your dick and hook you up to a machine, you know the kind I mean. I ask her, 'What's with the book?' She starts whipping through it, reading stuff at me. She's got stuff underlined!

'What's the matter with you?' I say. 'I know how to do it. I haven't heard no complaints.' I got that thing away from her fast, believe me."

Buddy slid over. "We're talking life here. We're talking men and women and certain ways of doing things. This stuff goes back a long way. It isn't new." He was stabbing his finger into the bar. "We're talking, what—fifty thousand years of recorded history? This stuff came way before Christ. We're talking basics now. You can't change something like this overnight. You don't change the rules in the middle of the game. No way, Jose."

"Where we make our mistake," Red said, "is letting them get together to bullshit all the time. One says this, another says that, pretty soon you're dealing with a whole committee. Bad news." He shook his head. "In my opinion nothing good can come from all this yak."

"I still say it's a matter of ground rules. If you have it all down in the books you don't run into this type of thing."

"Our forefathers, guys who came over on boats—you think they'd put up with this kind of noise? We're talking fundamentals here. You can trace this back to the caves if you want to."

"I'm not through. Now she starts in on me about the team. 'What do you have to practice for?' she asks me. 'Isn't it enough you play every goddamn night of the week?' I say, 'Woman, how do you expect to win the city if you don't practice?' She thinks it's easy to hit the seats. Get this: she's ironing wrinkles in my uniform. She's fucking with my hat. The other night she says to me, matter-of-fact, 'I might not be home when you get home.' 'Oh yeah,' I says. 'Oh yeah.' "

"I know what you're saying. My first wife left me on account of the team. One night she says to me, 'Me or the team.' I mean, Jesus, she puts it to me like that, what can you say?"

"Tell me this: she ever lay in wait for you? *Look* at this sucker. Do you think this hurt or what? I'm talking about a big fucking brass number she nails me with—wham—the minute I walk through the door. Let me say, gentlemen, that I am honked."

Stretch, who had been silently shredding paper napkins, suddenly smashed his long claws on the bar. "Let's do something."

"Like what?" Red said.

"Let's go to the track," Del said. He had put on his white sponge hat and was reading the racing form. "I got some hot ones . . ."

"You and your hot ones," Buddy said. The last time he had gone to the track with Del he had lost a lot of money, most of it under very weird circumstances. One of his horses had fallen over backwards in the gate. Another had been disqualified when the jockey had gotten into a whipping match with another jockey down the backstretch. Nobody could remember anything like it. Buddy had stuffed his tickets into his mouth and eaten them. "I'm staying away from there," he said. "They got nothing but Mexicans riding anymore. You never know what those beaners are going to do."

"Listen to this horseshit," Del said.

"I'm talking facts."

"Well what do you want to do?" Bull said.

Buddy cracked a smile. "How about some cards?"

"Listen to the guy," Red said. "He's got more cards up his ass than Carter has liver pills."

"All right, how about some pool? I'll give you an even shot and play lefty."

"Don't do me any favors."

"Jesus Christ," Stretch said, snapping his neck. "Let's do something."

"I wish to Christ we had a game tonight," Buddy said. "Hey, Frog, how come we don't have a game tonight?"

Frog swallowed. "Bye."

"Bye? What do we have a bye for? The season just started."

Red said, "Let's go out to the field and hit a few."

"Too early," Froggy said. "The high school broads'll still be out there."

"Maybe not," Bull said. "Buddy, lift up your shirt there and see what time it is."

"Get bent."

"Check out the mouth on this boy. The guy won't even give me the time of day."

"I'm warning you, Bull, I'm in no mood to be trifled with. I'll knock you out."

Moving with surprising agility for a three hundred pounder, the Bull pounced on Buddy and got him in a bear hug and began lifting him off the stool. Buddy put his feet against the bar and, applying sudden pressure, catapulted backwards, the two of them reeling into the bowling machine. They went down in a heap and wrestled around on the floor.

◍◍◍◍

Many hours later—it was dark, all the blinking signs were on—Buddy bopped down the street with a little yellow plant drooping out of the palm of his hand. It came in a small square pot and had a narrow stem growing up out of a patch of dirt and ending in several tongue-shaped yellow leaves. The leaves were speckled with brown and green spots. Buddy had seen it in a plant shop on his way back from the Corner and had immediately been attracted to it. It was sitting on a table by the window, surrounded and dwarfed by a bunch of big green bushy angry-looking plants, the kind that looked like they would give you the hives just by coming near them. Buddy had looked at the little yellow plant for a minute, his nose pressed up against the window, and then he had ducked into the shop and snatched it off the table, plunked a few bills on the counter, and walked out with it in the palm of his hand.

Driving home, Buddy looked at the little yellow plant from time to time. He felt there was something exotic about it. He felt that it might be rare. There was a balmy hint of the trade winds in its generous yellow leaves. He felt as though he had a little tiny desert island right there on the front seat of the Olds with him. He couldn't wait to get home and show it to Jo.

Jo was watering the jungle when he got back, spraying plants with mist from a clear plastic bottle. When she sprayed, the water made a faint hissing sound. She was wearing a red terry cloth robe, considerably more faded than the one he remembered. Her hair was a tangle, her eyes were dark; she had about her the haggard air of an Italian movie actress. As soon as he came in she put down the bottle and said, "We have to talk."

"In a minute. I want to show you something first." He had the little yellow plant behind his back. "Close your eyes."

Jo pinched the bridge of her nose. She knew he had a stupid present for her. The last time she had closed her eyes he had stuck a roach clip that looked like a real roach about two inches from her face. She no longer found these gewgaws charming. She was no longer amused by his surprises. She was tired of surprises. She understood that the enchantment had gone out of their lives. "I don't want to close my eyes," she said. "I want to talk."

"Just close your eyes a minute, will you?" Buddy said. "I want to show you this."

Jo closed her eyes.

"Okay, you can look."

Jo opened her eyes. There was a big yellow tongue about two inches from her face. The tongue was wagging at her. She made a face at it and jerked back.

"Well," Buddy said. "What do you think of this little guy?"

Jo took the plant and looked at it for a minute. She sized it up from various angles, inspecting the drooping leaves, the thin brittle stem. She stuck her finger in the pot and felt sand.

"I think it's tropical," Buddy was saying. "I think it might be rare."

Jo was touching the tip of a leaf. It wagged several times, synchronizing itself with the pain in her heart, then dropped off and fluttered to the floor. Jo wondered if she were going to go to pieces. She did not want to cry.

Buddy said, "I might be wrong but I think it's exotic."

"It's dead," Jo said.

Buddy looked at her. "What do you mean?"

"They sold you a dead plant," Jo said. She was chewing her lips. "I'm sorry."

"What are you talking about, dead." Buddy snatched the plant away from her and, grabbing the water bottle, began spraying it vigorously. "It probably just needs a little water, is all. You got to be careful with these exotic plants. They're tricky." He continued to spray it, and as he did so, several more of the tongue-shaped leaves came off and fluttered to the floor. Finally only one remained. Buddy held it to the light and saw a network of brown veins. Disgusted, he tore the leaf off and crumpled it in his fingers. It left a sticky paste in his hand.

"So I bought a dead plant," Buddy said. "So what. Big deal. How was I supposed to know it was dead. What am I anyway, a goddamn gardener?"

"You don't have to shout," Jo said. She was trying to keep from going to pieces. She was trying to keep the riot in her head under control.

"Well, what do you expect?" Buddy said. He was hunched over in the barber chair like a big buzzard. He could feel it, there was a rage circling in, waiting to land on him. "I bring you a plant and you get pissed off at me. What in hell do you expect?"

"I'm not angry," Jo said. "It was a nice thought. Thank you."

Buddy said, "You've been giving me that look ever since I walked in the door."

"What look? I'm not giving you a look. All I want to do is talk."

Buddy abruptly got to his feet and came over to her. He put his arms around her. It was like embracing a scarecrow. "I don't want to talk. Why do we have to talk? There's too much talk." He nodded, remembering what Froggy said, or had it been Red? "That's where we make our mistake." He began moving his hands up and down her sides. It was like stroking a coat rack. "Let's lie down on the bed for a minute."

"We can't."

"Why not?"

"I'll show you why not. Come over here." She led him to the bedroom, pushed open the door. Buddy peered inside. Clothes were strewn everywhere—blouses, pullovers, jeans, unmentionables—draped over the bureau, over lamps, on towels spread across the bed. Much of it was tinted red. "I had to go and get it myself. You weren't there, Buddy. You left me with five unbalanced loads."

Buddy slapped himself in the face. "I forgot."

"Did I tell you not to wash anything with the robe? Didn't I say that? Now it's all ruined." She held up a red brassiere, flung it down. "Ruined."

Buddy picked it up and held it to his chest. "Why can't you wear this? Just because it's a little red—"

"You don't know what you're talking about. By the way, where's my money?"

"What money?"

"The grocery money. I gave you a list and I come home

and there's not a goddamn thing to eat. C'mon," she wiggled her fingers, "fork it over."

Buddy reached into his pocket and pulled out what was in it: a handful of golf tees, a matchbook cover with a telephone number on it, some fuzz, two crumpled bills, and change. The grocery list was also in there. Buddy stared stupidly at these objects, as though some magic had been worked in his pants while he was wearing them.

"What's that junk in your hand?"

Buddy handed it to her.

"Where's the rest of the money?"

"That's it."

"No." Jo laughed.

"So I bought a few drinks. Can't a guy buy a few drinks for his friends?"

Jo flapped the bills at him. "You're paying me back. Every nickel."

"Don't worry about it."

"From now on I'm keeping track."

"Take a break."

Jo's eyes were wide. "I can't go on like this, Buddy. I'm losing my mind."

"Young love has its ups and downs, doesn't it."

"Talk to me, Buddy. Make sense."

"Talk? I been talking all day. I'm telling myself forget about it. I'm saying forget that she lay in wait with a hard brass object on my birthday. I say forget about the cake. I come home in a good mood, I bring you a plant, and I get nothing but grief. Over what? Twenty dollars and some red underwear. Look." He lifted up his shirt, displaying his branded belly. "What about this?"

"I'm sorry," Jo said. "I'm sorry about the clock. I'm sorry about the plant." She had her face in her hands, holding tight to her expression. "All I want to do is talk. I thought that if we could talk some of these things out—"

"Why bother?" He brushed past her, grabbed his cap, and headed for the back door.

Jo watched him go down the hall, knocking plants out of his path. "I have to talk to you!"

"I don't wanna." He stopped at the refrigerator, grabbed a beer, and went out the back, zigzagging down the steps and cocooning himself in the Oldsmobile.

He sat there awhile, hunkered over the wheel, slugging on the beer and staring at the peak of his hood like he was sighting down a rifle barrel. Suddenly a pair of balled-up red socks dropped down in the middle of the hood like a hand grenade, followed by several more. They were his. The sky began to rain socks and shorts and pocket-T's. Buddy sprang out of the car and, glancing up, saw Jo emptying his underwear drawer down into the alley on top of him.

"Hey," Buddy shouted. "Quit that."

Having emptied it, Jo dropped the drawer itself on him; Buddy dove for cover.

He zigzagged back up the stairs two at a time, but she was ready, confronting him on the landing with his very own stick which she jabbed in his face repeatedly, keeping him at bay.

"Are you insane?"

"I'm warning you: keep back."

Buddy commenced a series of feints which ended when Jo bopped him squarely in the nose with the knob of the bat. The blow brought tears to his eyes. He saw stars. Having immobilized him, Jo drove him back down the stairs with pokes to the chest until he finally lost his balance and tumbled backward down the last three or four, landing flat on his ass in the alley.

He lay there for several moments, seriously injured, while she emptied his stuff on top of him. She emptied his shirts, his trousers (including his brand-new checked double-knits), his shoes. A plastic bag containing his toiletries exploded like a mortar round right beside him. His shiny gold softball uniform came down preceded by his spikes. His library thudded down in a big cardboard box—Westerns, comic books, sports mags, *The War of the Worlds*—all of it in a sprawling heap. Bedroom windows were filled with curious cold-creamed faces. A man in purple pajamas watched impassively from his porch. His Nerf set—ball and hoop—floated down. She threw out everything, including his hairy brown sport coat and his skinhead wig.

Buddy thought: she's pushed me too far.

It took her about twenty minutes to empty the place of his belongings. The last thing to go was his trumpet. Buddy, thinking the siege was over, sat up and removed a pair of his shorts from the railing. They were threadbare Jockeys, with a Swiss cheese of holes around the waist and the elastic nearly gone. He looked up, glimpsing a patch of muddy sky between the buildings, and observed a shiny gold object appear in this space attached to the end of Jo's upraised arm. She propelled it down on him. He ducked and it smashed into the railing just above him, caroming into the middle of the alley. Buddy dragged himself over to it and picked it up. The horn was in bad shape, dented and bent, useless now for rallies.

3

It was a little after midnight when the urine-colored Olds with the piece of cardboard stuck in a back-seat window and the passenger door tied shut with rope pulled in front of Herman's house, making a formidable, tanklike rumble. Buddy was behind the wheel, his things heaped all around him, a bandana obscuring the middle of his face. His nose was killing him. It had begun to swell. He was convinced it had now swelled to remarkable proportions, and he pictured it as one of those cartoon noses caught in a slammed door—red and pulsating. His chest and ribs ached from being poked with the bat. His ass hurt from falling down the stairs. He wondered if he'd been injured internally.

He eased himself out of the car and walked to the rear of the house, a one-story, barrackslike structure, and stuck his head into an open bedroom window. "Herman."

Herman withdrew his head from under the pillow and looked around. Sam, his wife, slept beside him with plugs in her ears.

"Over here."

Herman blinked at him. "What's up?"

"Let me in, will you?"

"What time is it?"

"How do I know? Get your ass out of bed, will you, and open the door."

"Around front."

Buddy went to the front door and Herman let him in. He was a bulky guy with a huge head that had squashed his neck back down into his shoulders. His face was lugubrious, wreathed with jowls. Thin, straw-colored hair was gathered in a small stack on the top of his head. He was wearing a faded blue robe with "Champ" stitched above the pocket and stood looking at Buddy with his sad hound's eyes.

"What's the matter with your face?"

"I'm killed, Herman. She assassinated me."

"You're all fucked up."

"We had it out, Herm. She got me with a cheap shot. She nailed me in the beak with my own stick—do you believe it?"

"What for?"

"You wouldn't believe it even if I told you." He was standing in the middle of the living room, gently tweaking his nose. "How is this son of a bitch? I'm afraid to look. What do you think, is it busted?"

Herman studied Buddy's nose from various angles. "Nah. It's just swollen. I think it's gonna go purple on you, though."

"It better not be broken, that's all I can say. If she broke my nose I'll kill her." He collapsed into an easy chair that seemed to swallow him up and closed his eyes. "You got anything to drink?"

Herman scratched his jaw. "Yeah. The thing is, we got to keep it down a little bit. The kid, you know."

"Certainly."

Herman tiptoed into the kitchen. While he was out there Buddy heard him talking to Sam. "It's just Buddy," he heard him say. "Go back to sleep."

He returned with a couple of Blue Ribbons. Buddy popped his open and took several enormous swallows, his Adam's apple bobbing, and began telling Herman what had happened. Herman listened attentively with his hands on his knees, his topheavy body tilted forward at an extreme angle as though at any moment he might fall over onto the floor. Every so often he would raise an enormous hand, the knuckles like thick rope, and remind Buddy to keep it down.

"So there it is," Buddy said, finishing up with the part where she threw the trumpet at him.

Herman was shaking his head. "She really did all that, huh?"

"And more. And for what? Over twenty dollars and some red underwear." The phrase had stuck in Buddy's mind; it had an appealingly ironic ring to it. "Nine years and she throws it away over twenty measly dollars and some red underwear. Pretty ironic, huh?"

"It's ironic, all right," Herman said.

"It's fucking uncivilized is what it is. Hillbillies pull that kind of stuff." He made a small ironic noise in his nose. "Well, that's it. I got my stuff in the car. I packed up and left her. I tried, Herm. I put up with it as long as I could, but a guy like me can only take so much horseshit."

Herman waved his hand nonchalantly. "You're all worked up now, certainly. Perfectly understandable. But give it a few days and this thing will blow over."

Buddy launched himself forward. "Blow over! We're talking about assault, Herm. Mental and physical cruelty. Possible disfiguration. There were witnesses." He was stabbing his finger into the arm rest. "Don't tell me about blowing over. This is serious, Herm. She called me stuff. Everybody heard."

"I know, I know," Herman said. He had picked up his

son's rubber hammer and was using it as a kind of gavel, tapping it into his palm. "All I'm saying is, we all have our arguments. Sam and me—we've had it out. You remember some of the battles we had."

"She ever take a stick to you?"

Herman shrugged.

"She ever throw your trumpet out in the alley?"

"No, but—"

"Look, we're talking about two different things. You're talking about disagreements between rational adults. I'm talking about guerrilla war. Did I tell you about the clock?"

"Yeah," Herman said. "You showed me the clock." He was sitting with his head drawn between his shoulders, turtle-style, thinking: why can't people try to get along? "So, what are you gonna do?"

"Don't know for sure. I was thinking about getting my own place. Nothing fancy, just a couple of rooms, a little shelter, you know what I mean. I don't need much. A bed, a place to set my hoop up." He glanced up at the irregularly plastered ceiling. "It's a whole new ball game, Herm. I'm out on my own. I figure I might need a few days to get myself organized. I got to think things out, figure out my strategy." He peeled the label off his Blue Ribbon and plastered it across the back of his hand. "I was thinking that maybe I could crash here for a few days. Just until I get myself straightened out."

Herman wrung his hands, remembering the last time Buddy had stayed. The couple of days had turned into three weeks of him coming in loaded at two in the morning and turning on some crime-stopper show. Sometimes he would hiss in the bedroom door, inviting Herman to join him for a nightcap. Herman had missed several days of work in this way. On the days he made it he would be severely hung over, exhausted, cranky in the cab of his beer truck while Buddy sprawled on the couch until noon, his big feet propped up on the arm rest, his dog gnawing on one of

Herman's shoes. One night he had blown the dials off the stove while trying to heat up a pot pie. Another night he'd brought a bimbo home, scandalizing Mitchell, who was five. Sam said, "He's got to go."

Buddy made amends by repairing things around the house. He was a handy guy. He could paper a wall. He could hammer and screw and glue. He glued a chair together. He screwed the dials back on the stove. He fixed a leak in the ceiling, heaping a big mound of plaster over it which hung there like a blob waiting to drop down on someone. He cut the grass, Mutant romping beside him, trampling things. He entertained Mitchell when the kid got back from kindergarten. They got along fine. They were pals. They played ball. Mitchell rode on Buddy's shoulders like a tiny sultan. Buddy hid. One afternoon Buddy took him to the park, got into a pick-up hoop game, and forgot about him. Mitchell wandered off, and the police had had to retrieve him. That night the blob dropped down on Herman when he came out of the shower. He sat in the chair picking plaster out of his hair and the chair fell apart, Herman falling backward and thudding on the floor. Mutant took advantage of the commotion to clamber onto the table and slobber down everyone's supper. Sam screamed in the bedroom. "Look," Herman said, "we're partners, but you got to go."

"I figure just a day or two," Buddy was saying. "Just until I get my game plan down."

Herman hung his head. "I don't know, Bud. It isn't me. You know it isn't me."

Buddy sighed. He wasn't sure but he seemed to recall that the last time he had crashed at Herm's it had caused certain small inconveniences. He seemed to remember a problem about his hour-long toilettes. "Sure. Look, don't worry about it. I can always stay at the Y."

"If it was up to me you could crash here all year. You could have my fucking bed."

Buddy put his bottle down smartly on the table and got

to his feet. "Hey, I understand the situation. Forget about it. I don't want to cause any trouble."

Herman, who had avoided looking at Buddy, now peeked over at him. He was thinking. When Herman thought, his thoughts were almost visible, moving across his forehead like the headlines in Times Square. "Where you going?"

"Out in the car."

"You gonna sleep in the car?"

Buddy shrugged.

Herman wrung his hands again. He was working his jaws rapidly, as though they were connected to his brain. "That's bullshit, sleeping in the car. C'mon, sit your ass in the chair there. Crash here tonight. The only thing is, we gotta keep it down a little, you know?"

Buddy paused in the doorway. "You sure?"

"Yeah, I'm sure."

Buddy came back over, biffed Herman on the shoulder. "Hey, how about another beer? You want another brewski?"

Herman moved his shoulders. "I guess."

"Don't get up," Buddy said. "Allow me."

ΟΟΟΟ

They stayed up awhile, drinking Blue Ribbons and talking ball. Buddy mentioned that the Sticks were off to a fine start. We're making the plays, he pointed out, hitting in clutch situations. Herman asked what kind of a start Buddy was personally off to. "Good," Buddy said. "I'm making solid contact, spraying to all fields." "And the arm?" Herman asked. "It's holding up," Buddy said, checking his fingers. "So far I'm firing strikes."

Herman wondered how the Bull was doing at third. Until he gave it up, third had been his. He owned it. The guardian of the hot corner, he'd swat down shots like a bear and charge all dribblers; he'd take a guy's best shot in the chest and throw him out laughing. When he came to the dish his big black stick was feared throughout the city. He'd given it up, though, and now he wondered how the Bull was doing.

Buddy tilted his beer, swallowed. He looked around. "Between you and me, Herm," he said, "not so hot. He's getting handcuffed, throwing the pill away. Just between the two of us, we need you back to make a run for all the marbles. We miss your hands, your stabilizing influence in the infield. We could use your big black stick."

Herman tilted his beer, swallowed. "I miss it," he admitted. "If it was up to me I'd be out there."

Herman got up to take a leak and Buddy went out to the Olds to get the bottle of Wild Turkey he had stashed in the glove compartment. While he was out there he sneaked around to the garage where they kept Mutant and brought him back into the house. They were glad to see each other. Mutant stood up and put his paws on Buddy's chest, licking him from chin to forehead. He gnawed affectionately on Buddy's wrist. When Herman returned, wobbling through the hallway, the two of them were wrestling around on the floor.

"What's the fucking dog doing loose?"

"I let him in." He had Mutant in a headlock. "It's okay, isn't it?"

"I guess," Herman said. "Just so long's he keeps it down."

Buddy went out into the kitchen and began banging cabinets, returning momentarily with a pair of Yosemite Sam glasses. He picked up the bottle of Wild Turkey and filled his glass halfway up. Herman stared uncertainly with glowing eyes.

"Look out for that shit," he said, finally observing the Turkey.

"C'mon, Herm. Just a short one."

"No way. I can't handle that stuff anymore."

Buddy toasted him. "The Glicker. Herm the Germ." He drank and grimaced, feeling the hooch go from his stomach directly to his brain. His gums went numb.

They talked old times. They'd been a pair—Buddy and

Herm. Herm a big strong dude, even in grammar school, Buddy always long and loose. They'd taken the field together in the old gold and blue. Herman crouched behind the dish in the tools of ignorance, Buddy toed the slab. Herman flashed the signs. He made a solid target. Buddy hit the glove with mustard, low and away. He broke off the hook. Herman talked it up. He put down his big clattering leg and blocked the plate—nobody got home. Buddy put his leg in the guy's face and came straight over the top—nobody touched him.

Cagers too, a pair even there. Corner men. Buddy used finesse. He hit from the wings and the top of the key. He had the touch. He went one on one, faking right and taking the baseline. Herman set picks. He charged, sure, but he picked it up at the other end playing the good D. A hatchet guy, he mauled stars, upset their timing. He went up and got the ball. He went to the floor too. There were no jumps when Herm got his hands on it.

"You were one rough monkey," Buddy remembered.

"You had it all," Herm said. "Number one, number two, and control."

"Nah," Buddy demurred. "I lacked consistency."

"Don't tell me." Herman took umbrage. "I know what I'm talking about. Half these stiffs in the league now couldn't throw with you."

"The arm, Herm."

"Yeah. The fucking arm."

Buddy poured himself another drink. "C'mon, Herm. Just a short one."

"Sure," Herman said. "Why not?"

They talked the old crowd—Bull and Sammy, Doc and Red. They talked Pud and Spike and Sparrow. These were wild individuals. They'd raised the roof, taken their chances. They never gave a shit. Two of them were in the ground and Spike you couldn't sneak up on, having left several toes and most of his mind in Asia. Others too had fallen on the thorns of life—Crawford, for instance, with his plastic hand. The rest were hanging tough, plugging away, driving forklifts and beer trucks, selling shoes and cheap hammers and other crap. They were putting up aluminum siding, digging graves, working the meat squad at the A&P. Several had never been gainfully employed. Some were cops. They had kids that were reaching a certain age, wising off. Their wives were spreading out, beginning to look like floats in the Rose Bowl parade. They themselves were no Romeos. They'd lost hair, gone fat, wore caricatures on their faces. Some sported tits. They looked at the world through dull sheep's eyes.

"You're lucky," Herman philosophized. He was breathing heavily through his open mouth. "Compared to the rest of us, you got a relatively shitless life."

"Lucky? Shitless? What about this?" Buddy pointed clumsily at his nose, jabbing it inadvertently and wincing with pain.

"That," Herman said, flapping his hand. "That's nothing. It'll be purple for a while, and then it'll be okay again." He drank, baring his teeth. "What's a nose?"

"It isn't just the nose, Herm. It's more than that." He put his hands over his ears to stop the roaring. "I'm in a whole new ball game now. I got to get lined up, get some irons in the fire. Let's face it, Herm, I got to get a job."

Herman shifted his weight and squeezed out a mute one. The room had begun to recede on him like a tide, the ship hanging on the opposite wall was sailing away. Sprawled at his feet, Mutant was doing a job on one of his shower clogs. "You're in good shape. A guy like you can do anything. You got that sheepskin, don't you?"

"Not on me."

"Yeah, but you still got it, and nobody can take it away from you. You're in the books. Somebody rips it off, you just go down and get another one."

"Yeah, but I'll tell you straight, Herm, it isn't doing me a whole lot of good. It's just sitting there. I got to find a way to get some action with it. I'm talking something good, now. No more bartending. None of that factory shit."

"I'm hip."

"I gotta sit down and think, check stuff out."

"So?"

"So it might take time."

"So take your time. You got time." He flicked his hand, shooing something. "What's time?"

"So where am I gonna stay?"

"Here! Right fucking here!" He lifted his glass and poured what was left in it over his chin. "You always got a place to stay as long as the Glicker's around."

"I don't want to cause any trouble, Herm."

"Trouble? What trouble? Who says there's trouble?"

"I don't want to start any arguments."

"There's no argument about it. I say you stay here, you stay here." He lifted the bottle and poured, splashing Turkey liberally over the coffee table. He began quarreling loudly with someone. *"Argument? There isn't going to be any argument."*

"You sure?"

"Sure I'm sure. I'm the Glicker, right?"

"No doubt about it."

"We're partners, aren't we?"

"Better believe it."

They shook.

"Hey." Buddy got up, swaying slightly. "Where's that stick of yours? You still got that big fucking black stick?"

"Wait here."

Herman got up and charged through the hallway. He disappeared into a closet and began shoving things around, making a tremendous racket. Buddy could hear him talking to Sam. "I'm looking for something," he heard Herman shout. Something heavy fell and Mutant barked huskily. "You're dreaming," Herman shouted. "There isn't any dog."

After a minute he emerged, dragging a huge black bat behind him. He looked like the Java man hunting something.

"There it is." Buddy laughed. "Lemme see that thing." Herman tossed it over to him. "Jesus Christ," Buddy said, wielding it, "this thing must weigh fifty pounds."

"C'mon, you banjo hitter, give it here." Herman took the bat away from him and assumed his stance, crouching severely, peeking at the pitcher over his left shoulder. "Stand back."

Buddy stood back.

Herman's eyes widened, following the pitch. At the last instant he uncoiled, whistling the air with his murderous cut.

"Pow!" Buddy said. "Ka-blam!"

"Definitely," Herman said. "Better believe it."

Herman took three more cuts. On the fourth he let go of the bat. It whistled across the living room and smashed directly into the center of a large mirror hanging above the sofa. The mirror hung poised an instant, then split into two big pieces and disappeared from the wall.

◊◊◊◊

They woke up clutching their heads.

"Jesus Christ."

"My head!"

Buddy was sitting on the sofa picking small bits of glass out of his hair. His tongue felt like it had been plied with vulcanized rubber. Herman was doubled over in the easy chair, trying to pry open his eyes, two tiny red specks in his puffy face.

"What time is it?"

Buddy checked his watch. Spiro's hands were together at twelve. "Noon."

Herman groaned. Whiskey and beer stains had dried in the shapes of continents on his blue champ robe. There were Blue Ribbons on the floor, the table, the windowsills.

"Call in sick."

Herman waved his hand, dismissing the suggestion. He got up and began to pace, gripping his head. Suddenly, he stopped and looked over at the big bare spot on the wall. "Where's the mirror?"

"Back here. You nailed it with your stick, remember?"

"No shit?"

Buddy reached back and produced the huge black bat. "You were taking your cuts, Herm. You were swinging good. You got to remember to hang on to your stick, however."

Herman stepped over Mutant, who was gnawing on his other clog, and peeked behind the sofa. He immediately drew back, as though a corpse were back there. "Holy shit." He covered his face. "What did Sam say?"

"To be honest, she wasn't real happy about it, Herm. As I recall, she categorized us both as swine."

Herman began pacing about the room again, banging his fists together like a mechanical monkey. "I'm dead," he was saying. "I'm completely fucked."

"Relax," Buddy said. "Here's my plan. We'll go out this afternoon and pick up a new one, have it up there before she gets back. Maybe throw in a pair of earrings in the deal. She'll forget about the whole thing, believe me. I know how to handle this type of situation."

Herman was grimacing. "You know what those things cost?"

"Charge the mother."

Herman sat down in the easy chair and applied a head-lock to himself. Buddy went into the kitchen and got the last beer. He popped it open, suds foaming onto his chin and T-shirt, took a swig, and offered it to Herman.

"C'mon, Herm. Hair of the dog."

oooo

They were still sitting there when Sam returned from the bakery at four. She was a stocky, freckled woman, wearing a white bakery suit stained here and there with various jellies. She had Mitchell with her—a husky chip off Herman's block—shielding the youngster from his old man, who was still in his robe, holding a tall boy from the cold pack Buddy had gone out and gotten. A Foghorn Leghorn cartoon was playing on the television.

Sam turned to Mitchell and said, "Go to your room." Mitchell moped off while Sam assessed the situation, taking in Buddy, the dog, the cartoon, the beers, before zeroing in on the baseball bat lying in the middle of the floor. Then she went over and seized the can from Herman, who continued to hold his hand up, the fingers clutching air. After a second he lowered it to his knee. Buddy began straightening the sofa cushions.

"Don't start on me," Herman warned. "I don't want to hear anything about it."

Sam extended her hand, the fingers spread, and began ticking off Herman's transgressions. "You missed work. You broke the mirror. The dog is loose. You started drinking again. You're drinking now . . ."

Herman made a hacking sound in the back of his throat and stared at the television.

Sam was looking down at the small bald spot on the top of Herman's head. "I'll tell you one thing: you better not start pulling your old shit again. You know how it was the last time. We agreed."

"I know it."

"What's the matter with you? You know you can't drink."

"I said I didn't want to hear about it, didn't I? Get away from me."

Sam jerked her head toward Buddy. "What's that asshole still doing here?"

Herman rubbed his eyes. "For Christ sake, the guy's sitting right there in front of you."

"So what. I don't care what he thinks. He's an asshole and I want him out of here. I told you I wanted him out of here, didn't I?"

"Be reasonable." Herman winced. "The child." He gestured at Mitchell who had sneaked out and was listening from the edge of the room.

"I don't care if he hears it," Sam said. "You act like swine and he might as well know it."

"Swine?" Herman said softly. "Are you calling me a swine, Sam?"

"I'm married to a boar." She went behind the sofa and, picking up a shard of glass, showed Herman its jagged edge. "See? It breaks. When you hit a mirror with a baseball bat, it breaks."

"Aw look, Sam," Buddy said. "He didn't mean anything. He was just taking his cuts and his stick got away from him."

"Oh. Well. That's different. I understand now. I guess when you're swinging a baseball bat in the living room those things will happen from time to time."

"Sure. I've done it myself."

"I'll bet you have, shit-for-brains."

Herman was shaking his head. "No, I won't have this. There's a child present."

"Makes no difference," Sam said. "The kid's here, the kid's not here: the guy is still a dick."

"Wait a minute now. You're talking about my partner here. Your partner comes to you for help, what are you supposed to do, throw him out in the cold?" Herman thumped his chest. "Not me. Not the Glicker."

Sam wasn't buying it. "Wise up. Every time he shows up here he either destroys, explodes, or loses something. The last time he was here he lost the kid. He brings us dogs," she added, scowling at Mutant.

Buddy jumped up. "I think I'll take him out to the garage now. C'mon, Mute." He picked the dog up by his forelegs and began dragging him across the room.

Sam said, "While you're out there, keep going and don't come back."

Herman was holding the top of his head to keep it from

flying off. "No sir. I won't have it. I will not have this kind of talk."

"Get this," Sam said. "I want him out of here. Immediately."

Herman rose. "You get this: he's my friend and he goes when I tell him to go."

Buddy said, "I'm going."

Herman said, "You keep out of this."

Sam picked up Herman's huge black bat with both hands. "He's going if I have to drive him out myself."

"That's all," Buddy said, eyeballing the bat. He let go of Mutant and started edging toward the door. "I'm gone."

"Stay right where you are," Herman said. "Freeze. Woman, put down my stick before I take it away from you."

"Try it, you big fool."

"I'm warning you, Sam."

"I'll knock you on your ass."

They squared off. Herman feinted ponderously and made his move. Sam clipped him on the leg and he went down howling. Buddy fled. He jumped into the Olds and started it up, while inside the house came terrible howls and heavy crashings. Neighbors involved with various aspects of their lawns stopped what they were doing and listened. Buddy revved the engine. In a minute Herman reeled out of the house backward in his bathrobe, his arms extended to ward off the blows from Sam's relentless attack. He turned and sprinted for the car, ducking just as Sam whistled the black bat at his head.

oooo

They drove around the West Side awhile, Buddy keeping his yap shut and both hands on the wheel, his battered pal over by the door staring woodenly at the bumps and bruises on his forearms. He had the look of a man who was methodically assembling the ingredients of a high explosive inside his head. Buddy had the visor of his cap pulled low to keep the sun out of his eyes. Traffic was heavy, and Buddy fidgeted his leg when they were stalled in a line. He felt a lot better when they were moving. Every so often Herman tenderly flexed a knee.

"You okay?"

"Okay? What are you talking about okay? I was beaten to death with a baseball bat. How could I be okay?"

"I mean, are you all right? She didn't get you in the coconut, did she?"

"No," Herman said, probing his pate. "She didn't."

Buddy paused. "Where do you want to go?"

"Just drive around."

Buddy drove around some more. He drove slowly and avoided holes, not wanting to dislodge his exhaust system which was affixed to the car with tape and twine.

"She nailed me," Herman said from time to time. "She used my own stick against me."

"You'll be okay."

"We fight. We have our disagreements, who doesn't. But she never took a bat to me before."

"Just be thankful there wasn't a firearm lying around somewhere." Buddy stuck his head out the window and yelled at a guy who had cut him off: "Fish head!"

"She beat me in front of the kid," Herman mumbled.

"Mitch's okay. Don't worry about him. He's seen worse on *Kojak*."

"He saw his pop beaten."

"Kids forget."

"Not me! No way. I'll be fucked before I forget this." He looked at Buddy. "What was that she called me?"

Buddy thought a minute. "A boar."

"I'm no boar. I work hard and she beats me to a pulp. You saw it. And for what? A mirror. A lousy piece of glass." Herman burned, his hands throttling the black bat wedged between his legs. Abruptly he shouted, "Stop the car!"

Buddy slammed on the brakes and Herman sprang out.

He walked directly over to a trash can sitting by the curb and lifting the bat high over his head, began to demolish it. He gave it nine or ten savage whacks, knocking it over and smashing it flat, and then continued beating it, the clanging blows summoning people out to their porches. They watched as Herman beat the trash can from various approaches and angles. When he was finally finished with it, it looked like it had been crushed by a bus. A small trail of garbage bled from its open mouth.

∞∞∞∞

The Sticks were already taking their practice cuts when Buddy and Herman screeched into the lot, churning gravel. Guys were spread across the outfield in loose formations, stretching limbs and making hot dog stabs as one Stick after another rushed in to take ten. The sun was oozing down behind the center field fence, where old men in gray raincoats clustered under a tree drinking cheap wine out of paper bags. The bleachers were filling. In the distance tall buildings loomed in a smoggy mirage.

Buddy had eeled into his suit in a Texaco station but Herman approached the field in his blue champ robe, his bat tucked under his arm like a blunderbuss.

"Herm the Germ!"

"The Glicker!"

There were biffs and gooses all around.

"You retire already?" Whitey said, appraising Herman's garb.

"Hell, no. I come to play."

"You wanna play?" Sammy said.

"Hell, yes."

"You think you still can, old dude?" Red needled.

"Watch me, punk."

"What I want to know," Bull said, "is can you still slug?"

"What's this?" Herman displayed his bat. "My dick?"

"Wait a minute." Buddy took charge. "The guy can't go

out there in his bathrobe for Christ sake. Who's got an extra suit?"

The Sticks took stock and came up with a suit for Herman. It did not become his odd body. The shirt was long in the sleeves and tight in the shoulders, the pants came down over his feet. He rolled them up and wore them pirate-style. He didn't give a shit. His cap perched on his huge head like a small yellow bird.

"Shoes," Buddy called out. "Who's got some shoes?"

Nobody could come up with an extra pair.

"I'll play in my feet," Herman said. "I don't give a shit."

They took the field against a bunch of wise-guy dagos in flashy red suits. This was softball Chicago-style, the big yellow clincher and ten guys out there with nothing but their hands. They knew about the other game but would have no truck with it. They sneered at guys who played softball with gloves and the midget sphere. Anyone who was a player could take it barehanded, hide on hide.

It was clear tonight they were up against a hot dog squad. The dagos wore their caps backward and opened their shirts to bare hirsute chests. They yelled stuff. It was no contest. The Sticks were sticking. They were sharp in the field. Red and Sammy turned two. Doc was keeping them high and tight, and it was nothing but melons for Buddy in left. He was feeling loose, getting a good jump on the pill, firing strikes to all bases. The ball hung yellow in the clear black sky. The moon was full, the crowd rowdy, and a row of chicks in salmon-pink halters had their eye on him. He hit one in the gap and took second standing. He went the other way and kicked chalk. Stretch gooned one out, the Bull too. Herman began finding the range. The first one was a high pop to left. The second was off the fence. The third was out, a tremendous goon shot over the scoreboard and into the back of a pickup truck parked in a vacant field. Herman went around laughing, and in the dugout it was fives and tens all around.

Routed, the dagos clammed up. They tried to pull stuff on the bases, but Herm was at third and the Bull behind the plate, so they went after the slighter Sammy at second, a squat, boulderlike guy coming in high and spiking him in the shin. Herman charged over and chested the asshole into center field. In the last inning he played the shortest third anyone had ever seen, practically even with the pitcher, and challenged any greaseball to hit one past him. The first guy wheeled and hit a shot that Herman took in the gut. He moved in a little closer. The second guy went for his face—Herman knocked it down and threw him out easy. The third guy got under his and lifted a lazy one to Buddy, who went fancy and took it behind his back. The crowd went crazy—nobody could remember anything like it. Buddy sauntered in and, planting a kiss on the ball, tossed it to the girls in the salmon-pink halters.

OOOO

After, at the Corner, it was homecoming night for Herm. The whole team was there—Harv, the Bull, Red, Sammy, Stretch, even Farber, the odd one, who stood behind the bar with his shirt off examining his bodybuilder's torso in the smoky mirror. Some skinny punks wearing shiny lids and black leather jackets tried to weasel in, but the Sticks ran them out. It was Herman's gig, the return of the Glicker.

Buddy and Herm drank peppermint schnapps. Buddy's nose had turned the color of raspberry jam, but he didn't mind the ribbing his teammates dished out. He was feeling fine. There was nothing like a big win under the lights to get the ammonia out of his blood. He reached over and poked Herman on the shoulder. "Wake up."

"I'm awake." Herman was keeling far off to one side, like a sailor in a high wind.

"How you doing, big man?"

"Fine. Never better."

"You were looking good out there tonight. You were slugging."

"I hit that one, didn't I?"

"You caught it all."

"Ka-blam."

"We beat their ass, didn't we? Put it to them."

"Bunch of wise guys. Big talk."

"They tried some bullshit."

"Smart-ass jerks."

"You nailed that one guy, though. He never knew what nailed him."

"Shithead."

They drank.

Buddy leaned back, his hands cupped behind his neck. "I'm feeling okay, Herm. I'm having a fine time. And yourself?"

Herman cupped his hands around his mouth and hooted.

"I'll tell you, Herm. You know what I was just thinking? Why don't we give those bags a call? What the hay."

"Now?"

"Sure. Why not? Invite them down here, have a drink, bury the hatchet. What's your opinion?"

Herman put his chin on his fist and thought it over. "I don't know. You think they'd come?"

"Certainly. Why wouldn't they? They don't like this hassling all the time any more than we do."

Herman was rubbing at some imaginary fuzz on the tip of his nose. "I don't know. You think it's a good idea?"

"Sure it is. Believe me. I know what I'm talking about." He gave Herman a little shove. "Go ahead. Get Sam on the horn there."

Herman procured some coins from Del and went over to the phone. Zeroing in on the slots, he dropped them in and stood for a moment with the receiver in his hand, trying to remember his phone number. Finally it came to him. He dialed clumsily and waited, an impish smile flattening his face. He waited a long time.

" 'Lo, Sam? This is the Glicker."

Almost immediately he snatched the receiver from his head as though it had bit him. He turned and gave Buddy a stricken look. "She hung up."

"You're kidding."

"I told her it was the Glicker and she fucking hung up."

"Look out." Buddy brushed Herman aside, dropped in his coins, and dialed. He counted fourteen rings before she finally answered. "Jo? Buddy. Look, let's cut out this bull-shit—" There was a sharp click, then the dial tone.

"What happened?"

"She hung up."

They looked off in opposite directions, then simultaneously began smashing their fists into the wall.

"Goddamn!"

"Do you believe it?"

"I've had all I can take."

"I told her it was the Glicker, didn't I?"

"I'm way past my limit. I mean, what kind of noise is that?"

"I says, 'Sam, this is the Glicker.' The Glicker! And she cuts me off. I mean, how rude can you get?"

"Let's get outta here."

They stormed out the door and around the corner to the Olds, making loud strangling noises. The car rocked from the force of their slammings.

"That's about all of that," Buddy said.

"The Glicker!"

Buddy started the car, which made a formidable, tank-like rumble.

Herman said, "Let's go."

Buddy said, "Where?"

They looked at each other.

4 Danny Noselli was sitting in the cocktail lounge of the Pin Palace waiting for the guy with the headphones to show up. The guy had said he could get his hands on thirty pair, topnotch merchandise. "I'm talking quality stuff, run you forty, fifty bills apiece," the guy had said. His name was Threefeathers and he billed himself as an Indian. He had a long jaw and thick dark eyebrows that met at the bridge of his bulbous nose. He didn't look like an Indian. He wasn't red. He looked to Noselli like just another hill-billy.

"How many?"

"Thirty—maybe more. You interested?"

"Maybe." A toothpick ran back and forth between Noselli's small even teeth.

Glancing around, Threefeathers had reached into a paper bag and produced a set. He slid the box across the table and Noselli picked it up and opened it, withdrawing the phones. They were heavy in his hand. He shrugged. He didn't know beans about headphones. He removed his hat, a glossy black job with a gray band and a narrow upturned brim running all the way around, and put the headphones on. The long black cord spiraled down, bobbing. Feeling asinine, Noselli took them off and put them back in the box.

"I'll give you two bills for thirty."

The Indian screwed up his face. "C'mon, man. These are top quality phones. Like I said, you can unload these babies for half a bill apiece."

"Two bills. Take it or leave it."

Threefeathers lit a Lucky and thought it over. "Okay. Half up front and half on delivery. I can get them to you day after tomorrow."

Noselli reached into his pocket and pulled out his roll. He peeled off a ten and two twenties. "I'll front you fifty. And make it tomorrow. Three o'clock. I'll be right here."

It was now quarter to four and Threefeathers still hadn't showed. The toothpick danced between Noselli's teeth. He had decided to subtract a dollar for every minute the red man kept him waiting. You had to teach these Indians. If you gave them half a chance they'd keep you waiting all year, diddle around, walk all over you. Noselli found this to be true of most people. They would diddle if you let them get away with it. His motto was: nobody diddles the kid.

He finished his drink and snapped his fingers at the waitress who, evidently missing the signal, strolled right past him.

"Hey."

She turned around and came back to his table, walking very slowly, as though her feet hurt. She had a large bony face and hair that was several shades of red.

Noselli tapped his drink.

"Well, what is it?"

"V.O. and water."

"Anything else?"

"Yeah," Noselli said. "Bring me some nuts."

He sighed. It was a jungle, there was no doubt about it. Let up for a minute and people would diddle with you all day. If it wasn't an Indian, it was a woman. You couldn't relax for a second. People wised off, were late for appointments; ask them for nuts and they look at you like you got two heads. This nasty waitress, for example. She had just blown her tip.

Noselli pushed his hat back off his forehead, a gesture he repeated about two hundred times a day. The hat was slightly large for his head and kept slipping down around his ears, and every few minutes he would have to push it back again. Besides the hat, Noselli was wearing a faded white shirt with a tab collar and a pair of shiny black pants with a single gray stripe running down each leg. They looked like tuxedo pants and, in fact, were—one of about a dozen pair he still had from a batch of hot tuxedos he'd been unable to get rid of. He felt the pants were a classy touch. He wore them all the time even though he couldn't come up with a pair that fit him right. The ones he had on today were too big for him and bunched around his ankles, so that every few minutes he would have to hitch them up by the waist. He still had the tuxedo shirts too, but the frilly fronts struck him as faggoty, and he refused to wear them. He stuck with regular white business shirts, most of which had a tendency to blouse around his middle and creep down his wrists. The truth was, he was a little guy and had trouble finding clothes that fit him right. He would try on a shirt in the store and it would look okay, but the minute he took it home and tried it on the goddamn thing would start to blouse on him. He couldn't figure it out. It seemed like everything he put on looked rumpled, cheap. It bothered him. Even his black leather jacket, which he considered his cloak of authority and wore constantly, no matter the weather, came down to the middle of his legs.

His face didn't fit him either. He had a dark, hollow-cheeked, sensitive face, like a saint's face on a holy card. People had a tendency to diddle with a face like his. They would mess around with him, take liberties, and he'd have to straighten them out. He was used to it. By now he expected it. He'd been straightening people out all his life, having learned at an early age that the only justice was the swift variety he meted out himself. When he was a kid other kids had wised off, called him "Nose," punched him, pushed him down stairs—he'd come back later with a metal pipe and mess up their bikes. He poisoned dogs, blew up model trains, set clubhouses on fire. It was all part of life. People diddle, what else could you do?

He'd even had to straighten out his own mother who'd nursed him at her breast and raised him all alone, his father having been crushed by heavy industrial machinery when Noselli was still in his brother's diapers, which were too large for him and chafed his bottom. She was a huge woman with a voice that could bring ships out of the fog. She listened to opera and sang baritone. Danny was her baby. He'd hummed at an early age and she had bought him a piano and made him sit and monkey at it two hours a day. She held him up, displaying him to relatives. "Look," she would say, squeezing his cheeks, "did you ever see such a face? Another Vivaldi, with a face like that. A Paganini!" Noselli, however, didn't want to play the piano. He wanted to watch *The Untouchables*. One afternoon while she was out shopping, he went into the piano with a pair of garden shears and rendered it unplayable. She bought him a horn. One afternoon on his way back from a lesson, the horn was run over by a laundry truck. She bought him a violin. He swapped it for a zip gun which he kept in the case and which he used against individuals who had diddled with him. Mama Noselli despaired. She worried over his poor grades and his record of arrests for juvenile offenses. She wondered what he was going to do with his life. He told her without hesitation: join the Mafia.

This was true. From the time he was sixteen, Noselli looked for a family contact, a mobster relative who could take him under his wing. It was with great bitterness that he realized all the Nosellis were upstanding citizens. His brothers were teachers, lawyers. His uncle was a judge, his sister a nun. There wasn't an illegitimate businessman among them. As always, he would have to make it on his own. He hung out, never squealing, engaging in petty criminality in the hope that some underworld talent scout would discover him.

Eventually an auto thief introduced him to Mr. K, who operated a series of illegal enterprises from his tavern on the Near North Side. Mr. K let the eager young hoodlum run numbers and parlay cards among the Mexicans and hillbillies who peopled the area. Noselli was grateful for the chance, although he considered it beneath his dignity to work for a Polack. Recently, he'd set up his own base of operations in the Pin Palace and begun doing some free-lance fencing and loan sharking, not out of disloyalty to his boss but to impress him by his ingenuity and business acumen into giving him a bigger share of the action. He'd gotten hold of the tuxedos in this way. Now he was waiting for this Indian to show up with the headphones. The Indian was late, wasting his time. He was bad news. Noselli hitched his pants and pushed his hat back onto his head. He sipped his drink and then, grimacing, spat it back into the glass. It wasn't V.O. and water. There was some kind of Seven-Up shit in it. Noselli couldn't stand Seven-Up.

◐◐◐◐

While Noselli continued to wait on the Indian, Buddy and Herman pulled up in front of the Pin Palace with a fierce grinding of metal inside Buddy's brake shoes.

"You sure he's in there?" Herman said.

"Sure I'm sure. The guy's always in there. I'll be right back."

He got out and pushed past a bunch of minipunks who were blocking the door and went inside. Herman hunkered down in the seat and started cracking his knuckles. He was on edge. He was always on edge when running short on cash, and he couldn't be running any shorter than he was now. He worked one hand and then the other, recalling the argument he had had that morning with a pair of small, balding employees in the savings and loan association where he did his banking. Intending to tap his savings, he had waited in line at a window and presented his passbook to a young woman wearing the largest pair of eyeglasses he had ever seen. The woman took it and went over and called someone up on the phone. Right away this pissed Herman off. He took it as an insult, implying that he was either too stupid to manage his money or a crook. He waited, cracking his knuckles and listening to people impatiently shuffling their feet behind him.

The woman came back and slid his little green book under the window. "I'm sorry, but this account was closed this morning."

Herman stared at her. "You're nuts."

"If you'd care to open a new—"

"I want my money," Herman said. He had his hands on top of the window as though he meant to vault over the side. "Who's in charge of this joint?"

She got him the manager and also his assistant, both of whom tried to explain the legitimacy of the transaction. Buddy, who had parked the Olds directly in front of the bank with the motor running like a getaway car, glimpsed the scene through two large potted plants in the window. He saw two small, balding men explaining something to Herman, and then he observed Herman threatening them with what appeared to be a nameplate. As far as he could tell no cash was changing hands. Seconds later Herman was charging through the sunshine, his ill-fitting baseball suit a yellow glare.

"The bakery," he shouted, banging shut the door.

Buddy drove to the bakery, which was crowded with housewives holding tickets and eyeballing long johns and fancy cakes displayed in glass cabinets. Herman barged through and confronted Sam near the eclairs.

"You've gone too far, bitch."

"Hah," Sam said. "Beat you to it, didn't I?"

"I want my dough."

"Dry up."

Herman put one hand on the counter and vaulted over the top, scattering containers of sugar cookies. Sam took sanctuary in the bathroom. Herman tested the door with his fists and shoulder while a woman ran out into the street and started screaming for the police. Buddy, who had been shoveling cinnamon twists into a paper sack, raced to the bathroom and flung himself on Herman's back, getting him in a full nelson, the paper sack between his teeth.

"You're breaking my fucking neck!"

"The police, you lunatic."

He wrestled Herman out of there and pushed him in the car and they sped away, Buddy taking evasive action. When they got to six corners he pulled into a parking lot and shut off the engine and ducked down in the seat. He was sweating, out of breath. He felt he was too old to be ducking down in car seats. In the next car a couple of miniature dogs with painted nails and red ribbons around their necks were yapping their heads off at Herman, who was leaning forward and gripping the dash as though he meant to catapult himself through the windshield. When he was sure the coast was clear, Buddy reached across and shook him.

"You okay?"

"Leave off." He shrugged off Buddy's hand.

"You went ape-shit in there, Herm. You lost it for a minute."

"She wiped me out."

"Forget about it. You'll get it back. She's just afraid you'll go hog-wild and spend it all. She thinks you're fiscally irresponsible. These women." Buddy shook his head. "The way they act, you'd think we were ten years old."

"I made it and I want it. I drive the truck."

"Don't worry about it. Relax." He opened the sack and reached in for a pastry. "Here," he said, getting another, "have one of these tasty guys."

Herman took it and bit off one end. He chewed methodically for a minute, then glanced sourly at what was left in his hand. "I don't want a goddamn doughnut." He threw the tidbit out the window. "I'm starving. I missed my breakfast."

"I hear you. Let's get some breakfast."

"I could eat about forty eggs right now and that's no shit."

"Mr. Egg?"

"Yeah."

Buddy started the car. He then paused, tapping the wheel. "Hey, Herm, you got any money?"

Herman frisked himself and produced his wallet. He peered into its alligator depths. "Nothing," he said miserably. "I'm completely tapped out."

Buddy turned his pockets inside-out and came up with a half-eaten roll of Necco wafers and thirty-seven cents. This sum would have to last him until Froggy collected the weekly payoff from Bledsoe the meat man, who paid top dollar for the privilege of sponsoring the best. They stared straight ahead, Herman cracking his knuckles, Buddy beating on the steering wheel. The dogs yapped and yapped.

"I got it," Buddy said. "Little place on Diversey. I know a chick there who'll slip us some free cakes."

"Good deal. Then let's spin by my place and pick up my stuff."

Buddy pulled out into traffic. He drove a few blocks, his elbow out the window and his hand thumping on the roof. Then, without warning, he hit the brakes and swerved the Olds into a screeching U-turn. There was a harsh clashing of horns.

"What was that?" Herman said.

"Never mind the cakes," Buddy said. "I got a better idea."

◌◌◌◌

Noselli was sitting at his usual table in the rear of the cocktail lounge when Buddy came in. He was quarreling with a big waitress.

"I said V.O. and water," Noselli was saying.

"And what's that?"

"I don't know. There's some kind of Seven-Up shit in it." He pushed the drink at her. "Bring me a V.O. and water. And some nuts."

"Nose, baby." Buddy slid in opposite him. "Howzit going?"

"Same as always," Noselli said. He hated to be called Nose. The name did not carry appropriate respect. All his life he'd been evening up with guys who'd called him that. "I'm waiting on an Indian right now."

"You got to watch out for those guys," Buddy said. They nodded, assenting to the truth of this observation. Out front bowling balls rolled incessantly. Pins crashed.

Noselli had his black book out and was thumbing through it. "Let's see. Barnes. You're down half a bill on the Bowl and—"

"Yeah, I know about that." Buddy reached out and put his hand over the ledger. Noselli looked at it. "Actually, Nose, I came to see you about something else."

"Like what?"

"Well, I'm running a little short at the moment, see, and I was wondering if you could spot me a clam or two for a couple of weeks." He was drumming his fingers across the gouged tabletop. "You know I'm good for it."

Noselli took a toothpick out of his mouth and studied it. It had little tiny nicks in it from his little tiny teeth. "I don't think so, Barnes. You're way late on this other matter.

You're out of line. If I didn't know you better I'd say you were diddling."

"Me? Diddling? C'mon, Nose. We go back a long way. You know me better than that."

Noselli jammed the toothpick back into his mouth, working it around until it was pointed at Buddy's eye. "How much you talking about?"

"I don't know. Not much." He calculated in his head. "Four bills."

Noselli's face remained expressionless. "You got any collateral?"

"Collateral? Since when are you taking collateral? If I wanted to hear collateral I'd be down at the bank."

"Go ahead. Who's stopping you?" He made a noncommittal gesture with his hand. Buddy felt the blood pounding in his head; his temples were beating like tiny hearts. "Look, I don't care who you do business with," Noselli said. "If you do business with me you do it on my terms. You went bad on the Bowl, and now I got to have some collateral. Besides"—he moistened a finger and rubbed out a speck of soil on his wrist—"I hear you been canned for jumping into trees."

Buddy arched his brows. "You hear that?"

Noselli nodded, smiling out of one side of his mouth.

"You know, I heard it too. Ridiculous, isn't it? Utter bullshit." He tried to laugh, but it came out like a bark. "That's a good one. C'mon, Nose, you know me better than that."

Noselli shrugged. "I don't know. You always impressed me as the kind of guy who'd do something stupid like that. You took Denver and the spread, didn't you?"

"Hey." Buddy hunched his shoulders in disappointment. "What are we talking about here?"

"We're talking about collateral."

"What are you talking about? Like I said, I'm running short at the moment."

Noselli's eyes, which had been darting around like hummingbirds, settled finally on Buddy's hand. "You got that ring, don't you?"

Buddy jerked his head down to look at it. "This? My wedding ring?"

"What's it worth?"

"Christ, I don't know." He studied the ring, clenching and unclenching his hand. It was a plain old gilt job worth less than fifty dollars. Jo's was just like it. It was the only set they'd been able to afford. Since they needed the rings to go, and since the jeweler didn't have anything in stock that fit him right, Buddy had had to wear his on his pinky. He examined it, turning his wrist back and forth.

"What's the story?" Noselli said. "You want the money or not?"

Buddy slid his hands under the counter and began twisting the ring loose. It came off with reluctance. He flipped it over to Noselli who caught it and stuffed it into his pocket without looking at it. Producing his roll, he peeled four bills off the top and slid them across to Buddy inside a half-eaten bag of potato chips. "You know my terms."

Buddy grunted.

"Don't let this get away from you, Barnes." He was jotting in his little black book.

"Don't worry about it."

"Don't make me have to hunt you up."

"I'll be around."

Buddy went out, pushing past the punksters who were tossing quarters at cracks in the sidewalk and spitting several different ways, got into the Olds, and immediately began beating up the upholstery. Herman watched.

"What happened? Did you get the cash?"

Buddy was digging his fist repeatedly into the spongy material protruding from the cracks. Dust flew. "He pushed me, Herm. He went way too far. He tells me I'm diddling. Collateral, he says." His hands were strangler's hands. "Picture it, Herm. See him sitting there in that greaseball coat of his and that little wop hat. Check out the toothpick." Buddy ground his teeth. He was burning. He could not remember when he had been more infuriated, not even when the Noseman had cornered him by the urinals and tried to get him to lose one in the lights. "Imagine him sitting not two feet away from me in that meatball outfit and telling me I'm out of line. A guy like me! I'm telling you, Herm, I came this close to putting his lights out."

"Yeah," Herman said, "but did you get the money?"

"I got it. I'll tell you straight, Herm, he better stay away from me. The next time I see him I'll make him eat that fucking hat of his." He stuck his head out the window and shouted, "Kiss my ass!" through the front doors of the Palace.

"All right. Forget about it." Herman patted his belly. "Let's chow down."

Buddy would not be calmed. He itched for revenge. The score had to be settled. Let him go off and hide somewhere, he would find him. Let him hide in the sleaziest bar in town, he'd hunt him down. Not tomorrow, maybe, but someday, punk, you won't know when. He'd strike by night. No place was safe. He made a minute distance between his thumb and forefinger. "This close, Herm. I'm not kidding." He started the Olds and steered into traffic, cutting off a gleaming Cordoba, his left hand jammed deep into his pocket.

Inside the Palace Noselli fingered the ring. It looked to him like a pretty nice piece of merchandise. He put its worth at a couple of bills, maybe more—he'd have to get it checked out to be sure.

The waitress came by with his drink, putting it down smartly on the table. "I hope this suits you."

Noselli sipped it and nodded. "What about the nuts?"

The waitress looked at the ceiling. "What kind you want?" She started ticking off nuts on her fingers. "Almonds, pecans, pistachios, nigger toes . . ."

"Cashews. Bring me some cashews."

"I don't know if we got cashews."

"Check."

She went away. Noselli stirred his drink, glancing at his watch, a hot Bulova which he had to wear high up on his forearm to keep it from creeping down to the palm of his hand. The Indian was now almost two hours late. Very bad. There were times, like now, when Noselli wondered what was life if not one big diddle after another.

5

They moved in with Doc, who had a small, cluttered flat above a delicatessen, redolent of cold cuts. It had one bedroom with a cot in it. Doc slept on the cot. Buddy and Herman flipped over Doc's lumpy sofa.

"Call it," Buddy said.

"Heads."

They both looked at it. Herman made a face. "You're all right," Buddy said. "Just take those cushions off the chairs there, throw a blanket over them, and you're all set."

In the dark that night Herman sat up and poked Buddy on the shoulder. "Tomorrow we switch."

"Sure," Buddy said, rolling over. "Tomorrow."

The flat was situated across the street from a branch of a large university, and in the afternoons Buddy and Herm would sit in the window with meatball sandwiches and watch the coeds work out, whole fields of them in shorts and T-shirts, doing jumping jacks, playing softball, stretching their slim tan limbs. On occasion Buddy would produce a pair of binoculars.

"My God!"

"Where? Lemme see."

"Second base. See what I mean?"

"Oh yeah. Definitely."

"You guys," Doc would say. He was a short compact guy with rimless spectacles that emphasized the roundness of his monkish face. He had stringy red hair that had completely disappeared from the top of his head and hung in a fringe over his ears and down his collar. He spoke with a slight lisp, which gave certain people the impression they were dealing with a pussy. This was a misconception. Buddy had personally seen him cut off the air of a heavyweight catcher in Riis Park one day, scissoring his legs around the slob's throat with some fancy jujitsu work.

Doc spent most of his time reading at a desk piled high with five-pound volumes of literature. He was a student. He'd been a student as long as Buddy had known him, and Buddy had known Doc a long time. Buddy wasn't sure which degree he was now studying for, but he did know that he was in no hurry to get it. He had bilked the government for several sizable loans, none of which he had any intention of repaying. Doc was tricky like that.

Buddy found him an interesting guy. Like Buddy he was well read, and his apartment was a librarian's nightmare. There were books in shelves and books in boxes; you had to step over and around piles of them to get to the john. He had books on windowsills and stuffed in drawers. There were books in the kitchen cabinet, next to the wheat germ. Doc would get up early, mix a blender full of health drink— a puce-colored brew consisting of bananas, carrots, eggs, and a whole bunch of other ingredients he tapped in like fish food—and sit at his desk all day, sipping and reading. He read constantly. He was an authority on odd subjects— medieval superstitions, for instance, and Australian mammals. Buddy found it refreshing to talk to the guy. He was one of the few guys around Buddy considered his intellectual equal. They shared an enthusiasm for science fiction and cowboy stories.

"Louis L'Amour," Buddy would say.

"Sure. Then there's Max Brand."

"In the field of sci-fi it all started and ended with Verne."

"I'm hip," Doc agreed.

While Doc hit the books, Buddy and Herm took it easy. They considered themselves on vacation. That's what Herman told Skovich, his dispatcher. "I'm on vacation, Skovich," he had said. "I got it coming. Don't give me a hard time." He slammed down the phone.

"He gives me a hard time," he said to Buddy.

"You ought to trash that job," Buddy said.

"I been thinking about it."

"Sure." Buddy's face was as earnest as an eagle scout's. "I always said a guy like you, with your qualifications, has no business being a beer hack."

"You think so?"

"Absolutely. Gigs like that are a dime a dozen. You ought to get in a line that takes full advantage of your abilities."

Herman paused, considering his abilities. "I can do things," he admitted. "I'm a qualified guy."

"Herm." Buddy put a hand on the big man's shoulder. "If I were looking for guys, you'd be the first guy I'd hire."

"Really?"

"Absolutely."

They went to the ball game, slipping in to the executive boxes right above the Cub dugout and thrusting their upside-down faces inside to offer advice in clutch situations. Well-rounded guys, they availed themselves of the town's cultural attractions. They went to museums, observed the rise and fall of ancient civilizations and the finest flowerings of technological man. They played ticktacktoe with a computer. They were everywhere accompanied by a thousand Cub Scouts who had poured out of their buses and into the high-ceilinged halls like ants attacking a sugar cake. Annoyed, Buddy and Herman went to the aquarium and gawked at weird fish. They saw stars in the planetarium, became acquainted with nebulae and white dwarfs. They stopped in at the zoo. "Hah," Herman said, "check out the asses on those monkeys, will you?"

On sunny afternoons they went down to the beach and, lounging on the hairy tan blanket Buddy used as a seat cover in the Olds, displayed their admirable physiques to sunning sweeties. They watched them for hours, cultivating imaginary harems. They listened for cries from bikinied things in sham distress. Occasionally they would saunter to the water and wet their calves. Buddy played it cool behind slate-gray Polaroids, but Herman had to be physically restrained. At times he seemed capable of the cartoon maneuver of swiveling his head a full 360 degrees. His eyes bulged. He clutched his jewels and groaned. "For Christ sake," Buddy would say, "be cool." Herman said he couldn't help it. Once, Buddy returned from one of his leisurely strolls along the beach and found Herman, his back and shoulders already pink and blistering, leaning over a willowy blonde and inviting her to have a bite of his hot dog. Another time Herman, in a superabundance of virile energy, walked down to the water on his hands like a carnival strongman and was reprimanded by the lifeguard for clowning.

"Relax, Herm. Like I said before, you got to play it cool." They were sitting in a diner on Diversey where on certain mornings, when the Greek wasn't looking, Nan the waitress would slip them some free pancakes. Buddy had also gotten in the habit of stopping over to see Nan on certain evenings when nothing better was happening.

"Aw look," Herman said. "I was just trying to stir up some action." He nodded at Nan, a skinny girl with peach-colored hair and big nervous eyes, who was talking with the other waitress by the coffee pot. This other waitress was short and muscular, with severe dark bangs. The polka-dot outfit she had to wear did not flatter her figure. "You think maybe you could get your friend to arrange something over there?"

Buddy glanced over. "You interested in that?"

Herman shrugged. "Maybe."

Buddy picked up the menu and laughed behind it.

"Okay." Herman slammed his fist on the counter. "Never mind. Forget it."

"I'm just ribbing you, for Christ sake. Don't be so touchy. If you're interested I'll set something up. No problem." He stuck the menu in the metal slot and got up.

Herman said, "Where you going?"

"To talk to her."

"Sit down," Herman hissed. "Are you crazy?"

"I thought you said you wanted me to set something up."

"Not now," Herman said, ducking down in the booth. "Not while I'm sitting right here, for Christ sake." He was all crouched in on himself like a bullfrog. "I got my pride."

One night Buddy put on his new checked double-knits and his hairy brown sport coat, and he and Herman—a vision in plaid—went to a fancy restaurant with big torches on the door and a guy to park your car. "After you," Buddy said. As soon as they sat down he made it a point to ask the waiter for his personal recommendation in the matter of wine. "We're looking," he said, "for an amusing little bottle to go with some meat." The waiter went and got one and poured a swallow for Buddy's approval. Buddy swirled it beneath his nose, whiffing the bouquet, then downed it, smacking his lips rapidly. "This will do nicely," he said. Herman, who had been gnawing on a piece of celery, suddenly thrust out his empty water glass. "Not so fast," he said. "Pour me a slug of that, will you, chief?"

After, they leaned back, popped open their pants, and lit up cigars.

"I don't mind telling you, Herm, that I'm enjoying myself," Buddy said. "I'm having a fine time. And yourself?"

Herman belched up a little bit of his sirloin. "Couldn't be better."

"Good food, good drinks, good companionship . . ."

"Don't forget the cigars."

"Certainly not." He lipped the stogie, blew the smoke out of one side of his mouth. "We're playing some dynamite ball, too. Don't forget that."

"No way."

"It's the good life, all right."

"Can't beat it with a stick."

"You know what I was just thinking about, Herm?" He exhaled, blowing ovals of blue smoke toward the ceiling. "The bags. If they could see us now, huh?"

Herman chuckled. "It'd knock them for a loop, wouldn't it. Pissed?"

"We couldn't possibly get along without them."

"Perish the thought."

"We'd miss them something terrible."

"Yeah," Herman said. "Like the plague."

"Like a poke in the eye with a sharp stick."

"Like a hot poker up the ass."

"I think we're in trouble, Herm. If they don't take us back I just don't know what we'll do." He crooned the last part, sounding like a bloodhound.

They laughed, clutching their hearts.

The next afternoon they rode an elevator to the lookout tower on the highest floor of the tallest building in the world. From this vantage point they took in the vast panorama of the city—the gleaming skyline, sprawling factories, teeming neighborhoods, and a tidy fringe of suburbia merging with the horizon. Cars and buses crawled the narrow streets, Els barreled along their tracks. Men in suits walked to important meetings, shoppers shopped, dudes stepped lively in the latest vines. Kids romped in gushing hydrants while their mothers reeled wash off the lines. Goods were being moved by truck and rail and plane. A hundred clocks blinked the time. Buddy pressed his hands and face to the glass, gazing out with an expression of deep satisfaction. He felt like he could reach out and touch everything, just grab it all. He felt like the king of Chicago. "It's all out there," he said to Herman, nodding. "It's right there waiting for us, kid."

He glanced over and found Herman looking straight down, his eyes rolling in his stricken face. His skin had turned the color of seaweed.

"You okay?"

"Let's get outta here," Herman croaked. "I can't stand heights."

∞∞∞∞

They were squires of leisure, gents of ease. They drank Michelob and smoked twenty-cent cigars. They grew beards. Buddy's came in irregularly, a dirty blond, giving him a marooned look; Herman's sprouted a dense savage red.

"How you guys coming?" Doc asked from time to time.

"Just dandy," Buddy would say. "Couldn't be better. And yourself?"

"Not bad," Doc would say, "considering the voluminous amounts of printed matter I've got to hack through. You guys are welcome, you know. Feel free. It's just that I've got this midterm coming up. I'd appreciate it if you tried to keep it down."

"By all means."

"Hey, Herm," Doc called out. "Those cartoons. Would you turn them down a little?"

They went to the schoolyard and shot some hoops, their shirtless chests gleaming, their racket attracting the attention of coeds sitting in the window aisles. They went one on one, huffing and puffing and banging into each other. They dribbled off their own feet, turned it over. They threw up bricks that did not draw iron. Herman crashed into the standard, badly bruising his knee. Buddy reeled under a tree, gasping.

"Jesus Christ."

"No shit." Herman staggered over, his face the color of a nectarine.

"I don't know about you, Herm, but I'm in disgraceful shape."

"You? Right now I'm sitting under a tree having a heart attack."

They decided to get in shape, stopping in one afternoon at the Hellenic Institute of Physical Culture, which was located on Clark between a massage parlor and the local headquarters of a white supremacy party. Farber, the center fielder, worked out at the institute. He was in there every day. His plan was to develop the most perfect body the world had ever known and then exhibit it at various muscle conventions. "Come on down on Tuesday," he told them. "You can sign in as my guests."

"I don't know," Herman said later. He had always considered Farber a strange egg. "You think it might be a queer joint?"

"Don't be ridiculous," Buddy countered. "It's open to the general public. Chicks go in there," he added.

Herman wasn't convinced. "I don't want to work out in any queer joint."

They put down their duffel bags and signed their names in a fancy, gilt-edged book that reminded Buddy of something you'd see in a funeral parlor. The institute itself consisted of a single large, nearly square room almost completely lined with mirrors. It was matted and equipped with bicycles, treadmills, and innumerable pieces of odd apparatus fashioned from pulleys and aluminum tubing. They reminded Buddy of something a medieval inquisitor might employ to torture something out of a guy. They looked to him like racks. Powerfully muscled men were strapped into each of these devices. Other men were prone on benches, pinioned under great sagging weights. Still others were standing in front of mirrors in tight black briefs admiring their

mountainous chests, powerhouse biceps, stupendous thighs.
Flexed backs revealed numerous distinct muscle groups like
small kingdoms on a map of Europe. Men sucked air into
mighty lungs, squeezed things with hands that could rip
tennis balls asunder. There were no chicks, no talk, very
little hair. Over in a corner two men were oiling one another.

"Nope," Herman said, turning around.

"For Christ sake." Buddy grabbed him by his sweat suit.
"Don't be a jerk."

He got the attention of the closest dynamo by standing
between the guy and his reflection. "Farber?" The dynamo
pointed to the far end of the room where Farber was doing
military presses in one of the torture machines. Buddy and
Herman went over and watched him. He was working hard,
pumping an unbelievable amount of weight. His muscles
swelled one on top of another like Chinese bowls. His skin
was translucent, treed with veins. He finished his exercise
and bounded away from the machine, windmilling his arms.

"Howdy, boys. Glad you could make it." He introduced
them to his friends, Ray and Gary. Herm eyed them sus-
piciously.

"You're in ridiculously good condition, Farbs," Buddy
said. "No wonder you can slug."

"It doesn't take long," Farber said. "Go ahead. Slide down
on the seat there and work out."

Buddy sat down gingerly.

"Just grab on to the bar there and pull down."

"Easy on the poundage," Buddy reminded him. "I'm
basically a puny guy."

Farber fooled around with some gauges, then flashed the
go-ahead signal. Buddy reached up and grabbed hold of the
bar and began pulling it down. Straining with all his might
he managed to move it about half a foot. For a split second
he and the bar achieved equilibrium; then the bar started
taking over, lifting him inexorably off the bench. He gave a
loud cry and let go, the bar flying violently upward, Buddy

crashing down hard on his tailbone and tumbling to the floor.

Herman, meanwhile, was in serious trouble on one of the trickier high-powered bicycles. He had somehow lost control of it and it was pitching him forward and backward like some type of berserk carnival ride. Herm hung on, his stubby legs churning, but the faster he went the more violently the machine lurched, eventually flinging him sideways to the mat where he landed with a heavy thud.

"That's about all of that," Herman said.

"Whirlpool?" Farber said. "Sauna?"

"No thanks."

They changed in a hurry and got out of there. Back out in the street, Herman poked Buddy with an elbow. He was glancing at the massage parlor window, which was plastered with lewd suggestions and alluring silhouettes. "C'mon, Bud. What do you say?"

Buddy screwed up his face. "The day I got to pay to have my dummy rubbed," he said indignantly, "is the day I put it away for good."

Herman shrugged in disappointment. They moved on, passing in front of the Nazi headquarters where, inside, several short, terrierlike men wearing square mustaches and brown uniforms festooned with swastikas were conferring beneath a huge portrait of the Führer.

oooo

Evenings, they suited up. They played ball every night of the week, and on Wednesdays they played a doubleheader. "Huddle up," Whitey would say, and the Sticks would huddle for the Stickman cheer—"hubba hubba hubba HO!"— and break for their positions, looking sharp and confident under the lights. The fields they played on were handsomely maintained, first class all the way, a far cry from the days when they were rookie Sticks playing in prairies and odd lots with sidewalks, trees, drinking fountains, and other weird obstacles farcing up the outfields. Buddy had cracked into many a weird obstacle while chasing deep drives. Not now. He drifted back easy and flagged it down near the fence. His throws bounced true to the base. His name was blared over the public address—"Now batting, Buddy Barnes." People cheered. The Stickmen drew. They were the featured attraction, the main event. Young turks came out to see them, and knowledgeable old gents. Chicks came. They were watching the best.

The Sticks didn't disappoint them. They were jelling, putting it all together. The little guys were getting on, the goons were gooning. They were smothering powerhouse squads with line-to-line defense. They took the Strokers and the Swatters and the Chi-Guys. They blasted the Blasters, dwarfed the Dwarfs. On a drizzly Thursday before a four-figure throng they systematically dismantled the Amalga-monsters. These teams were no stiffs. Lesser outfits never made it past the fourth before the umps invoked the slaughter rule.

Buddy himself was having his greatest season. He was unconscious at the dish, a stroking machine. His bullets dissected outfields, infielders were burned by his sizzling shots. He even gooned a few. High and tight, low and away —it didn't make any difference. It didn't even matter what stick he used. He just picked one out of the rack, went up there, and swung at what he saw. He saw yellow melons, big balloons. He went with the pitch. He didn't give a shit. He ran hard, thinking at least two.

It was in the garden, though, that he put on the real show. He loved to play extra shallow and piss guys off. He loved to take them over his shoulder on the dead run, whirling away from the fence. He loved to climb the fence. Danger was his business. He dove, tumbled. He had his own fans out there. Chicks called out to him, "Hey, Buddy. Buddy, over here." He favored the sweetest ones with winks. He ran out to applause, doffing his cap.

He was on fire out there, in each and every inning of each

and every game. He played like there was no tomorrow. Most of the time he could not tell what day it was. What was the difference? Just throw out the clincher and get on with the game.

"Hey, Herm." They were sitting in the dugout enjoying another laugher. "Tell me if this isn't the berries."

"Yeah," Herman said. "Some fun."

❀❀❀❀

One evening Buddy was watched closely out in left by a woman in a powder-blue Pinto who was parked in front of a tavern across the street from the field. The woman was wearing dark glasses and a trench coat buttoned all the way up to her throat. A stained red scarf covered her hair. Every so often some Spanish men leaving the tavern would lean their heads into the window and grin at her, but the woman paid no attention to them. She stared straight ahead. She had both hands on the wheel and kept the motor running.

Jo did not know for sure what she was doing there, parked in front of the tavern. She had not intended to come to Buddy's game. All she knew was that after Jerry and Larry, Mrs. Berry's boys, brought the furniture over she had had to get out. She had been lying on the couch with a cold rag on her chest—it was over ninety, the apartment was a furnace—and the next thing she knew the Berry twins were barging in with furniture. They carried in two love seats and put them down in a corner, and Jo got up and stuck her head in the doorway, and the next thing she knew they were bringing in a big leather sofa. Jo said, "Wait a minute," and her mother, who had come up the back stairs, refusing to take the elevator, walked in and said, "Put it over there, boys," and they put the big leather sofa over in the corner next to the two love seats.

Jo recognized the furniture. It was old furniture her mother had been keeping in the basement. Her mother had been after her to come home now that she and Buddy had parted, but Jo had told her right away to get that idea out of her head, she was definitely not going back home. So evidently her mother had decided to bring the home to her instead. So far, she had brought over lacy yellow curtains for the kitchen and a flowery seat cover for the bathroom bowl. She had brought over fresh fruits and vegetables. One night she came over with a crucifix hidden in her handbag and stuck it on the wall above the mantel when Jo was out of the room. Jo had had to talk to her mother about this. She told her to quit bringing over curtains and vegetables and crucifixes. She had thought she had made herself clear on this, but now her mother was bringing her furniture. Jo didn't want it.

"What am I supposed to do with this?" she said, and Mrs. Reed said, "Sit on it."

They argued about the furniture, and then after her mother left, Jo put on the trench coat and the dark glasses and got into the Pinto and started driving. The next thing she knew she found herself at Buddy's field, an anonymous woman parked in front of a tavern with her hands on the wheel and the motor running.

Except for work, this was one of the few times Jo had been out since she had thrown Buddy's stuff into the alley. She had not felt like going out. She did not have the energy. She guessed that the act of expelling Buddy and his things from her life had taken a lot out of her, or maybe it was this disagreeable situation with her mother, she wasn't sure. All she knew was that lately she had been gripped by a tremendous weariness. Each day she would come home from work and switch on the set and lie back with a cold rag on her chest. She was drifting. The pain in her heart had been replaced by a numbness that went clear to her toes. Her plans, her dreams—they seemed to her now like fairy tales, infantile fabulations. Where do you even begin? Her plants were turning yellow. She felt that she was turning to wood.

She had been getting a lot of advice since she and Buddy had parted. Many people seemed to know exactly what she should do. Murphy wanted to give Cliff the brush and get a place with her. Sara Lee told her to get her butt out to the Coast. Even Gary, an appliance salesman in the same department store where she worked, was eager to help and told her so about fifty times a day. As for Jo—she didn't know what to think. She would come home from work and lie down with a cold rag on her chest and think: my husband and I are estranged. She found herself saying that word, estranged, quite often. She was fascinated by it. It seemed to cover the situation. Estranged. She felt estranged, all right. She certainly didn't feel like anybody she knew. She felt like some anonymous woman.

"You're going to take him back, aren't you?" her mother had said the night she brought the crucifix over, and Jo had thought a moment and then looked at her and told her the truth: "I don't know."

This answer had confirmed Mrs. Reed's worst suspicions. When she learned that Jo and the maniac had parted ways she had been so overjoyed that she had immediately gone to the church and lit lamps to thank the Lord for answering her prayers. Then she had tried to figure out a strategy to get her daughter out of that dungeon and back home where she belonged during the difficult and crucial few months that lay ahead. She wanted her daughter out of that building. She knew it was only a matter of time until the maniac came snooping around again, and she did not want her daughter to be trapped in there when that occurred. Who knew what could happen? Who knew what spell he would try to cast on her again? He might resort to drugs. No, when the maniac came snooping back, she wanted her daughter back home where she could take charge of the situation personally if she had to. He would cast no spell on *her*. She would stand in front of the house and bar the door with her very body if she had to.

Mrs. Reed had been greatly disappointed when Jo told her she wasn't coming home. After she had heard the news about Jo and Buddy, she had thought: I've got to get her out of there. But when she called Jo, the first words Jo said to her were: "I'm not coming home so don't even bring it up." These were disappointing words to Mrs. Reed. They pierced her like a crown of thorns. Here she had a beautiful clean home just waiting for her, she could stay in her old room and be surrounded by her loved ones, and she was choosing instead to remain in a building that looked like it belonged in *The Hunchback of Notre Dame*. Mrs. Reed couldn't understand it. She had thought that if there was going to be trouble it would come from her boys, but they had turned out fine; they had good jobs, had married wisely, they had given Mrs. Reed fine, healthy, clean grandchildren, and fine snapshots, while Jo, her daughter, her baby girl, had married a maniac and even now did not have enough sense to remove herself from his repugnant domain.

Mrs. Reed respected the mysteries of life. Unlike some people, she did not suffer from the sin of intellectual pride. Certain things were beyond human understanding. She decided that if she couldn't get her daughter out of that eyesore she could at least transform it into a half-decent place for a human being to live. She began to make periodic visits, always bringing something with her up the back stairs—she refused to take the elevator—that would spruce the place up. She asked Chet, Mrs. Zalinski's boy, to pick out some nice fresh fruits and vegetables at the supermart where Chet worked, and then she and Chet had brought them over. There was a little bit of trickery also involved here. In recruiting Chet Zalinski for this mission Mrs. Reed had had a little something more in mind than just fruit and vegetables. Mrs. Reed was hoping that maybe Jo and Chet could get together. Chet was single, he was about Jo's age—in fact, they had practically grown up with each other. She couldn't understand why they couldn't spend a little time together, though she didn't mean to rush things. If at some later point they got serious about each other, that was fine with Mrs.

Reed—Jo could, and had, done worse—but that could develop in its own time. For now, she just wanted them to get to know each other. Having lived nine years with a maniac, Jo certainly could afford to spend a few hours with a nice solid hardworking normal man like Chet Zalinski.

And so they had loaded the fruits and vegetables Chet had picked out himself into Mrs. Reed's car and brought them over, and Jo had not even gotten up off the couch to say hello. "We brought over some fresh fruits and vegetables," Mrs. Reed said, and Jo just lay there like a slug. "Plums," she said, holding up some plums for Jo to look at. She never budged. She looked like she'd been drugged. She looked to Mrs. Reed like one of those women in a Dracula movie, she was so pale and thin and listless. Upset and angry, Mrs. Reed had stuck her head in the refrigerator and begun making room for the produce, shoving things around and removing entirely Jo's stock of frankfurters and TV dinners. "You are what you eat," she muttered loudly, dumping a handful of frozen Mexican garbage into the trash. Chet stood at the kitchen table with a cucumber in each hand.

It was a few nights later that Mrs. Reed, operating on instinct, brought the crucifix over. She had been haunted by the image of her daughter lying there as if she were in the power of some sinister force. She had had nightmares. She'd seen a man with fangs and an unnatural scalp. She concealed the crucifix in her handbag and hung it over the mantel when Jo was out of the room. She knew Jo would squawk when she spotted it, but she felt better that she had at least brought it over. She had this vision of Jo wresting it off the wall one night and jabbing it in the maniac's face, keeping him at bay.

Jo had put up with the curtains and the flowery toilet seat, she had allowed her refrigerator to be violated, but she felt she had to draw the line over the crucifix. A large, heavy crucifix, it dominated the room with its morbid presence. It practically turned the place into a shrine.

"No way," she said, going over and wrestling it off the wall.

Mrs. Reed was looking at her. "I'm getting worried about you," she said.

"Don't. I'm fine." Jo was holding the crucifix behind her back and looking from place to place, wondering where she could put it down.

"I'm worried," Mrs. Reed said. "You look terrible, you should see yourself." Mrs. Reed was looking at the big blue veins in the backs of her hands. "You were very rude to Chet when we came by the other night with the fruits and vegetables."

"That's another thing," Jo said. "Don't bring that guy around anymore." She pointed the crucifix at her. "I know what's on your mind."

Mrs. Reed said, "What do you mean?"

"You know what I mean."

Mrs. Reed was looking at the veins throbbing in her wrist. "Chet Zalinski is a very nice man."

"I can't stand him," Jo said. "I never could." She remembered him as a small boy with gross things in his pockets—a collector of bottle caps and nails. Once he kept a praying mantis inside a mayonnaise jar. He was wearing black shoes and Bermuda shorts when he came up the other night, and Jo had been disgusted at the thick black hair on his legs. The hair on his head was like pubic hair, stiff and black and wiry, and he'd had a razor rash across his throat. He still lived at home but Jo was sure he had a woman somewhere, maybe tied up in a shed. "He gives me the creeps," she added. "I don't want him up here again—is that clear?"

"I'm getting worried," Mrs. Reed said. She could feel the blood pounding in her hands. She would not have been surprised to see it gush forth, to watch stigmata blossom in her palms. How much could a mother's heart stand? "You're going to take him back, aren't you," she said.

Jo thought a moment. "I don't know."

Finally her mother went away, leaving Jo with the crucifix. She wondered what she should do with it. She could not
get herself to throw it away. It was like the flag in that respect: you just couldn't heave it into the trash. At first she
had unthinkingly stuffed it in the bureau drawer with her red
underwear, but she quickly changed her mind: she did not
want to see the tortured Byzantine face of Jesus staring up
at her the first thing when she got dressed in the morning.
She moved it to a different drawer, the one where she kept
all the hideous earrings and glass ducks and other junk
Buddy had given her, until she could figure out exactly what
to do with it.

Now she had all this furniture on her hands, too. She
didn't know what to do about that. All she knew was that
she had to get away from it. She could smell it from across
the room. It smelled like Lysol and Lemon Pledge and
Glamorene upholstery shampoo; with a smell like that
around she might as well have been living at home. She had
to get out. She put on the trench coat and the dark glasses,
wrapped the stained scarf over her head, got into the Pinto,
and started driving. She didn't know where she was going
but just being out made her feel better. She had begun to
wonder if she would ever go out again. She was beginning to
fear that she might be turning into one of those women who
never goes out and who they find dead one day in her apartment with about fifty pails of chop suey all around and a
crucifix over her heart.

Jo found herself driving deeper and deeper into the city.
The buildings here were scarred, bunched tight together;
the streets had ragged edges. Skinny men with cans of Bud
leaned out of windows, alley kids darted between the cars.
There was a carnival going on in a church parking lot, and
glancing out, Jo could see the green tents, the Ferris wheel,
the Oldsmobile with streamers on it. She drove on. There
was no moon, no stars. Soon she saw the banked lights of a
baseball field smoking against the sky. She drove around the

field a few times, then turned onto a side street that had some small shops with Spanish writing in the windows. She parked in front of a tavern at a place that afforded her a clear view of the outfield but was not so close that she risked being seen. She definitely did not want to be seen. She kept the motor running and both hands on the wheel.

She saw him right away. He was standing out there in his gold and blue uniform with his shirt tail hanging out, spitting into his hands. The first thing she noticed about him was the hair on his face. He was trying to grow a beard again. Jo had to laugh. He should know better than to try to grow a beard. He had tried to grow a beard once before, when he went to Alaska. He'd waved his cap at her and driven off into the sunset, and three months later he came back with a freak dog and hair on his face. "What's that on your face?" Jo had asked him, and Buddy had stroked his whiskers and said, "What do you think of my beard, Jo?" and Jo had had to laugh. It wasn't a beard, it was just hair on his face. It looked like weeds growing in a vacant lot. She remembered teasing him a lot about it, and then he started chasing her around the apartment, and then he caught her and carried her into the bedroom and took her in a rough, bearded guy's kind of way, pinning her down and talking dirty Alaska talk in her ear.

She kept watching him. She watched him break for one, moving across the outfield in his graceful long-legged loping way, watched him dance across the grass and catch the ball and throw it back in one smooth true motion with his shirt tail hanging out, and she remembered how she felt when he went to Alaska. He had gone off one day, sticking his head out the window of the Olds and looking back and waving to her with his baseball cap. "Wish me luck," he had said, and he waved the cap and drove away like the Duke riding off into the sunset. She had turned her back—they had not been getting along at all—and slammed the door and danced through the empty apartment. After a few days, though, she began to miss him. She began to miss his dumb jokes, his laugh; the apartment seemed empty without a big trumpet-playing man around. She longed to come home to a funny schnozzola. She began to feel abandoned, forlorn, like his Nerf ball lying in a corner, like his Keds hanging on the wall. She missed his touch, his rough fingers tender on her neck, her wrist, her ankles. She remembered the gifts he used to bring: Reubens at midnight, hideous earrings— he had even brought her plants. She cried beside the scrawny things. Alone at night she remembered the way he used to sleep beside her with his lips parted and his hair in his eyes like a boy, and she would sit up and ask herself: what if he never comes back? and she would feel a wind as cold as a tundra blow through her bones. Sitting in the car and watching him she remembered this feeling very well; lately, she had begun to feel like Alaska all over again.

"You're going to take him back, aren't you?" her mother had said, and Jo had told her truthfully she didn't know. She supposed it was possible. She supposed she could try to live with him one more time. Before she did, though, they would have to sit down and have a real good talk. He would have to sit still and get the phones off of his head and listen to her. Certain matters would have to be ironed out. And then she thought about the times they had tried to talk it out, sitting at the table like two sober mature adults, and Jo had expressed her dissatisfaction, had pointed out the sacrifices she had made to support him while he ran around every night with a meat ad on his back and sat around all day in the barber chair reading *The Time Machine* with a pair of headphones jammed over his baseball cap and waiting for his true calling to sneak up on him and hit him over the head. She had pointed out that they were adults now: she wanted to start living like a regular person, she had dreams, she could finish school, get a real job, be proud of herself. She was not prepared to live all her life for a softball man— and pretty soon she would look over at him and find him playing with his fingers, roostering shadows against the wall, or feel him nuzzling her neck with a plastic nose, and she would think: he's missing it, he is just not getting the point.

No, there was no point trying to talk it out with him. If she was going to do it she would have to take him back the way he was. In fact, one night he had said those very words to her. "Take me the way I am," he had said, and he had put down his trumpet and gotten up out of the barber chair and walked, naked, into the kitchen for an Old Style, his giant rubber feet slapping against the tiles. There was no changing him; if she was going to do it she would have to take him back giant rubber feet and all.

She would have to take his games, too, and she remembered all the summer nights she had squandered at fields like these, sitting on a hard bench in a row of women who cupped their hands to their mouths and hollered until Jo's head hurt. They were forever shouting and screaming and whistling like large jungle birds, each with her own distinctive call. These were stout women with cotton candy hair and generous behinds. They intimidated Jo with their chests, which in hot weather jutted out of their shells like the big guns on a battleship. When it was chilly they wore men's jackets with racing patches and oil decals on the sleeves. Many brought babies to the games and passed them around —some of them could hold several babies at once in their big fleshy arms. Jo would sit off at one end and wait for the game to be over.

She would have to take the games, and she would have to take the bars after the games, too. God, not the bars. The bars were pretty much the same as the games: there was the same shouting and screaming only now it had a roof over it. Just remembering it was enough to make her clap her hands over her ears. There was a smell about those places she would never forget, a mixture of beer and piss and sweat and vomit—she would have to do her business squatting over a massed ring of toilet paper and come back to find her ginger ale glass filled with beer. She remembered being very tired; she had to get up early and go to work, she wanted to go home, but of course, Buddy was always one of the last to leave. He was always in the middle of things, laughing and joking, the star of the show. Women eyed him, she knew it, strange unattached women congregated at his side. Sometimes one would fill the jukebox with coins and saunter over to Buddy and work out right in front of him, and Jo would get up and wait for him in the car.

She would have to take the bars and the games or she would have to take the waiting. She would have to take the lying in bed and listening for him fumbling at the locks and coming in and knocking something over. She would have to take the barber chair and the beer cans and the *Late Late Show,* and just as she was falling asleep, she would have to take him climbing in next to her and pushing up against her and grabbing at her breasts with the dust of second base still all over his fingers. And she knew that someday, sooner or later, she would again find herself lying in wait with a hard brass object in her hand.

She glanced out toward the field and saw him running away from her, sprinting toward the fence in that leggy graceful way, and she put the car into gear and eased away from the curb. She just wouldn't do it. She had to give herself a chance, she had to breathe. There was the way he moved, certainly, but she refused to build a life around the fancy dance of a softball man.

She drove home and walked up the back stairs and began looking disgustedly at all the junk she was living with. She looked at the pastel-blue vinyl barber chair, the posters and upside-down flags hanging on the walls, the sofa and matching love seats from her mother's basement hogging up an entire corner. The apartment looked like some kind of bizarre warehouse. Who lived here? There was an impersonal, anonymous quality about it; she felt like she was living in an attic filled with someone else's junk. What here was ac-

tually hers? She realized she despised the place. Night after
night she had been surrounded by all this stuff, resenting it.
The pastel-blue vinyl barber chair she hated in particular.
She went over and kicked it. This made her feel good. Soon
she found herself beating on it, thumping it with her fists
and shoes and elbows, and that made her feel even better.
Suddenly she went behind it and put her shoulder to it and,
straining with all her might, began pushing it toward the
door. Suddenly, without thinking what she was going to do
with it, she had it out in the hallway and she paused, blew
hair out of her eyes, and looked at it and thought: now
what? She began pushing it down the hallway toward the
elevator, grunting with the effort, the chair making loud
squawking noises. She finally got it to the elevator and she
pushed the button and waited for the thing to come up. She
waited awhile and finally it arrived, thumping and groaning.
She worked the big iron latch, slid open the door, and pushed
the barber chair into the elevator. She took the elevator all
the way down and unloaded the barber chair in the basement, which was dark and dusty and filled with ladders and
old fans and mattress springs and old junky furniture simi-
lar to the stuff she had in her place; in fact, it looked a lot
like her place down there, except for the cast-iron lawn
dog rusting in a corner. She pushed the barber chair up
against a wall and went back up the elevator feeling like
she had just gotten rid of a dead body in the middle of the
night.

As soon as she got back she started in on the love seats.
After her fierce struggle with the barber chair she was able
to dispose of these in the basement rather easily. Her mother's big leather sofa, though, was another matter. It was on
rollers, but one of them had broken off and the sofa sagged
badly to one side; she had a hell of a time getting the thing
down the hall. At some point she grew aware that she was
being watched. All along the hall people had unlocked their
locks and cracked open their doors; faces were peering out

at her. At the apartment right next to the elevator, a buzzard-like man with a pipe and satin lounging pajamas was standing boldly in the doorway and watching her as she wrestled with the couch. She reared up and glared at him and said, "Don't just stand there. Give me a hand." The man did as he was ordered without saying a word.

She did not stop with the furniture. She was not about to stop now. Some new tremendous energy was coursing through her. She took down all the posters, the upside-down flag, the stickers. She got a big box out of the basement and loaded it with rubber lizards and crystal balls and dirty comic books and other junk. She took down the lacy yellow curtains in the kitchen, stripped the flowers from the bathroom bowl. She was ruthless: everything that wasn't hers was hunted down, nothing was spared. She hunted down Buddy's gorilla suit, pitched out the coconut monkeys. The last thing to go was the heavy Byzantine crucifix which she carried down and hung, with a certain reverence, on the basement wall.

She was completely soaked when she came back up from the basement, her hair was plastered about her face, but she still felt strong. She had never felt stronger in her whole life. The apartment had been transformed. It now had an airy, spacious quality; she felt that she could breathe. The few simple furnishings that remained—a sofa, two chairs, a table—suggested a spartan, no-nonsense mentality she felt was appropriate for the serious business of starting life. She picked up the watering can and began attending to her plants, glancing with satisfaction at the round depression in the floor where the barber chair once sat.

She was over by the rubber tree when she suddenly thought of one other thing. Grabbing a black Flair out of a drawer, she went down to the front hallway and scratched Buddy's name off the mailbox. Then she went back up, picked up the watering can, and marched through the apartment like she owned it.

6　One weekend Buddy went home to see his mom, pulling up in front of the old white house, a boxlike structure with the roof still caved in slightly from when the tree fell on it, the paint fading to gray and blistering in the sun. As he got out he could see his old man's head sticking up behind the bushes that grew around the front porch. Buddy went round back and surprised his mom while she was scrubbing the kitchen floor on her hands and knees with a Brillo pad. She lifted her head and peered up at him, looking like a turtle beached there on the linoleum.

"It's me, Buddy boy!" He removed his novelty glasses with the hypnotic whirling eyeballs glued to the lenses and planted one on her fuzzy cheek.

She made some lemonade and they went out back and drank it, sitting on rusty lawn chairs in the concrete yard and looking across at the backboard and hoop planted at the other end. They had paved the whole yard when Buddy was twelve so he could practice whenever he felt like it. She was the one who'd done it. His old man hadn't even known about the concrete until he fell down drunk in the yard one night and split open his head.

"It was a bunch of you out here," she was saying. "There was Red, Sammy, Stretch . . . who was that one who kept cutting off the net with a jackknife?"

"Spike?"

"That's the one. Spike." She nodded. "Who else?"

"Don't forget Herman."

"Herman." She laughed. "He was *always* over. Always wore that shirt with the picture of Cape Canaveral on it, remember? It had a big picture of a rocket ship on the front. Remember how he would always lean back in a chair and make those noises?"

"Yeah," Buddy said. "He was always blasting off."

They told Herman stories for a while, sitting in the sun with their memories and lemonade. They told the one about the time Buddy and Herman decided to get a paper route, and the first day a blizzard hit and they wound up stashing about five hundred *Tribs* in the basement. They jammed them into a back room where Buddy's old man kept his tools and his gin, and one night about a month later he went in there for the gin and opened the door and all the *Tribs* fell out on top of him.

"Sore?" Buddy said. "I had to hide from him for weeks." They laughed about the *Tribs* falling on the old man.

They told some stories about other money-making schemes the two of them had had, like the summer they umped the Little League and one night Herman called a kid out on a close play at the plate and his mother came out of the stands and hit him in the face with a vegetable; like the summer they washed cars and Herman hosed down Jumbo Murphy's car with the windows open, ruining his leather upholstery and leaving about a foot of water on the floor, and when Jumbo came around and saw the water he picked up the hose and turned it on Herman, drenching him, and Herman had stood there and taken his medicine like a man; like the summer they were caddies over at the country club and Herman had actually wound up in the hole from poker losses in the jock house, and Buddy split what he had made with him and they had bought identical motor bikes with the money, and the first day he had it Herman parked it in front of Walgreen's and when he came out sucking on a malted the motor bike wasn't there.

"Herman never did have much luck," Buddy's mother said.

They told stories about the rest of the gang too, about Red and Spike and Stretch and Crawford, and Buddy's mother shook her head and wondered where the time had gone.

"What a bunch," she said. "Always out here running yourselves ragged. I brought lemonade, remember?"

Buddy lifted his glass and took a sip. "It was good."

"Herman always drank three big glasses, I remember it very well. And he always said thank you. He was always polite. 'Thank you, Mrs. Barnes,' he'd say. Wearing that Cape Canaveral shirt." She smiled, pursing her mouth around her ill-fitting plate. "I used to stand by that window and watch you practice out here. I can remember when you needed two hands to heave it up there, and now look at you."

Buddy swallowed. "I'm just a big galoot, Ma."

"Even when I wasn't watching I could hear you. I always knew where you were. Thump, thump, thump . . . I could hear it all over the house." She reached down and put on the sunbonnet with the cherries on it Buddy had bought her for her birthday when he was twelve. She wore it with her head erect, as though it had been given to her by the Duke of Windsor. "Now it's quiet." A line of sweat had formed on her faint gray mustache; water beaded on her lemonade glass. "Do your mom a favor, Buddy."

"Name it, Ma."

"You know what I'd like?"

"Let's hear it."

"I'd like to see you play. Raise a racket for your old mom, Buddy. Get your ball and play awhile."

Buddy was happy to. He went and got his ball from the trunk of the car and shot some hoops in the yard, the ball thumping on the pavement, whistling cleanly through the netless rim. He threw in a few fancy moves, hooks and spin shots and behind-the-back drives, glancing back to where his mom was smiling beneath the sun hat.

He stayed for two days, sleeping in his old room which was exactly the way it was when he'd left it right down to the autographed glossies of Ernie Banks and Minnie Minoso pasted above the bed and the turtle bowl on the bedside table. There was even a little rubber turtle in the turtle bowl. In the downstairs den, displayed in vast gilded pyramids, were his trophies. He and his mom studied them: most valuable this, first place that. His all-state certificates were framed on the walls, sandwiched around photos of President Kennedy. They ate supper in the dining room surrounded by his baby pictures. She made him all his favorite dishes—baked ham and pineapple, sauerkraut and potatoes au gratin—fattened him on apple cobbler and lemon meringue pie. In the afternoon she watched from the window while he drove for the hoop. He gagged it up for her, bouncing them in off his head. For her he walked his funny walks, fell down, slammed doors on his nose. Before bed he serenaded her on the ukulele.

He stayed for two days and he would've liked to stay longer except he couldn't stand to be around his old man, even though the guy spent most of his time sitting on a camel-colored easy chair on the porch, which was equipped with special locks so he wouldn't hobble out and be at large in the neighborhood. His old man was nuts and had been for as long as Buddy could remember. He had gotten up every morning at five-thirty for thirty years and gone to the copper mill with a lunch box that looked like a small locomotive under his arm, and by the time he finally got his leg messed up by falling down in some heavy industrial machinery he had been no better off than when he'd started, the stupid shit. He had played short on the company team, swilled incalculable amounts of gin, and known everything. There was nothing you could tell him he didn't know first. He taught Buddy to play ball. He would pitch and Buddy would bat, and every so often he would clip the kid on the ankle or the shin to teach him not to fear the ball. Then Buddy would pitch to his old man who would crowd the plate, encouraging his son to move him back. When Buddy did so, plunking his father in the ribs, he would draw back his arm and whistle the bat at his son's head. "You got to fight," he would lecture, "for every fucking inch you can get."

There was nothing you could do about the guy. He just kept getting meaner and meaner; for the last couple of years all he did was snarl. It was a particularly repellent expression encompassing the entire left side of his face beginning with the eye, which was the size and color of a whiskey cork, running down his cheek in two long crevices, wrinkling his bright red blister of a nose, and falling into his twisted mouth. The right side of his face was a normal old guy's face, creased and pitted here and there with prehistoric-looking marks; it was the other side that got people. Some assumed he had had a stroke or gotten his face messed up by some heavy industrial machinery, not realizing it was just Willie Barnes's natural way of looking at things, the facial equivalent of a hard slide into second. Buddy couldn't stand to see it. Though his old man looked at everyone and everything the same way, Buddy always felt the snarl was directed especially at him. Not once, in his whole life, had he ever done anything that was good enough. Not one single time. They had not spoken for almost three years, not since the time Buddy got drunk and went out on the porch to get a few things off his chest and his old man had trained the snarl on him and then, without warning, lashed out with a right cross that caught Buddy on the jaw and knocked him down.

On the second day he was there, Buddy had been watching a ball game and eating a peanut butter and jelly sandwich in the den when he looked up and saw his old man snarling at him across two rooms, judging him. He had immediately put his sandwich down and reached for his keys.

"I got to be hitting the road," he said to his mom, who was standing in the kitchen furiously stirring up some chocolate cake frosting with those special stirring muscles women have. He couldn't handle his old man looking at him that way. Also, he knew that sooner or later his mom was going to start asking him about his life. He didn't want to talk about that just now. "I'll keep in touch."

"Eat the cake, at least."

"I can't, Mom. I got stuff to do."

"Well then give me a kiss, you big goof." Her eyes glistened. Before he left she slipped a ten in his pocket.

∞∞∞

When Buddy returned he found the Glicker sprawled across the sofa, his blue champ robe tightly sashed and a washcloth on his forehead. An unsheathed thermometer lay on the table amid the cellophane and torn wrappers from innumerable snacks. The air was ripe with the smell of the locker room. All the shades were drawn.

Buddy went over and woke Herman by prodding him with a sand wedge. Herman groaned. He had come down with something.

"Up and at 'em, Herm. We tee off at one."

"I'm sick."

"What ails you?"

"Everything. My joints ache. My throat's sore. I've got this pain."

"Where?"

Herman pointed to the vicinity of his heart.

"You just got a hangover."

Herman shook his head. "I feel like I'm dying." He licked his lips. "Where you been anyway, shacked up with that waitress again?"

"Home, like I told you." Buddy scuffed the carpet with a few practice swings. "C'mon, get your ass up off of there and let's get going. Some fresh air is what you need."

"I'm not playing any golf," Herman said. "I'm sick."

Buddy paused, studying him. "You really sick?"

"I'm dying, I told you. I feel like shit."

"I'll tell you what's making you sick." Buddy pointed to an empty container of Sara Lee banana cake on the table. It was sandwiched between a nearly empty jar of hot peppers and the chocolate-smeared cardboard from assorted Hostess treats. "It's all this crap you been eating that's doing you harm."

Herman rolled over, facing the wall. "Give me a break."

"I'm serious." Buddy picked up a box of caramel corn and examined the contents on the back. "This shit is terrible for you. It's totally lacking in essential nutrients." Herman covered his head with a piece of foam rubber. "What you need is a square meal. You ever have my deluxe spaghetti?"

Herman made a retching sound.

"Just leave it to me," Buddy said. "I'll have you on your feet in no time." He went out into the kitchen and stuck his head in the refrigerator, liberating an evil smell. "I'm going to pick up a few things at the store, Herm. You want anything in particular?"

"Yeah," Herman said. "Bring me a banana cake."

Since all Doc had in the refrigerator was a carton of cherry yogurt, a jar of olives, a melon with some type of fuzz growing on it, and a hunk of stinky tinfoil Buddy was afraid to open, he loaded up at the supermart. He eschewed the fruits and vegetables and went right for the necessities. He went for the pimiento loaf and the wieners. He picked up some jelly and a huge tub of peanut butter. He laid in a supply of Manhandler soup. He got his hands on some Eskimo pies. Even though it was against his principles, he bought Herman another banana cake. He picked up the spaghetti, of course, and chunk of ground round and about five dollars' worth of spices, and while he was over there he scored a jar of pickled herring.

"That be all?" the salesgirl asked.

"No," Buddy said. "Reach back there, honey, and get me one of those Pez, will you?"

Back at Doc's, Buddy boiled the noodles, fried the hamburger, then poured a jar of sauce over the hamburger and laced it heavily with the spices, leaving the whole works to simmer until it achieved that distinctive tangy quality. He also slid a torpedo-sized loaf of garlic bread into the oven. Then he went back into the living room and listened to an Ornette Coleman record on Doc's headphones while he waited for the tang to set in. Herman was still on the sofa, the washcloth still on his head, watching the *Beverly Hillbillies* on Doc's portable black and white set, the picture telescoped into a small square patch in the middle of the screen. Doc himself was not there. He was at the library. He'd been spending a lot of his time at the library lately. Rain beat tediously on the roof and blew in through an open window onto Doc's books.

Buddy picked up an illustrated *Star Trek* paperback and leafed through it while he listened to the record. He was the type of guy who just wasn't satisfied doing one thing at a time. The way he saw it, his mind was too sharp to be entirely occupied by one thing; it needed a couple of things to work on. After a while he reached behind the turntable for the small yellow roach he'd left there the other day, fired it up, and sat back enjoying himself. He was having a fine time. He took a poke on the jay, squinting his eyes, and began thinking about the game that night. He couldn't wait to get out there and put on a show for his fans. His hands itched to make solid contact, to feel the smack of the clincher boring in on a hard shot to left. He wanted to sprint from first to third and hook the bag with a fadeaway. He longed to score. He wished it would quit raining. Rain was a downer. He wondered what he would do if the game was washed away. He supposed he could go down to the Corner and see what was doing, or maybe check out that new bar on Irving—there was a chick who told him to meet her there the other night, she wasn't bad, good legs, nice handles, maybe she'd be there. Maybe if nothing else materialized he would drop in on Nan. It was something. Anyway you looked at it the night was shaping up.

It was Herman who smelled the smoke.

"What?" Buddy said, wrenching off the phones.

"I said, whatever you got going in there is on fire."

"Jesus H. Christ!" He jumped up and rushed into the kitchen. Opening the oven door, he discovered a huge black tongue therein; he picked it up with an undershirt and flung it into the sink. Then he went over and peered down at his deluxe sauce. It was black, all but a small portion having adhered to the sides and bottom of the skillet. Cursing monotonously, he shoveled the tongue onto a platter, heaped the noodles onto two chipped plates, spooned on as much of the black sauce as he could loosen from the skillet, and loaded everything onto a tray which he carried into the living room and shoved onto the table directly under Herman's nose. "Down the hatch," he said morosely.

Herman looked questioningly at the repast spread out before him. He was questioning the black sauce. He looked like a man who'd been invited to eat something growing on the bottom of a ditch. "What is this?"

"Spaghetti, what do you think it is?" Buddy was chewing. He felt like he had a mouthful of wet ash.

"What's this black stuff on top here?"

"Sauce."

"You got to be kidding. You expect me to eat this?"

"It's a little burned, that's all. It isn't going to kill you."

"No." Herman pushed his plate away. "I'm not eating anything with any black sauce on it."

"Look." Buddy put down his fork. "You don't have to eat it. Nobody's forcing you. If you don't want it, make your own eats, Chef Boyardee."

"Don't worry about it." Herman got up off his sickbed and went into the kitchen and rooted in the refrigerator. Moments later he returned with the banana cake and a knife. The cake came in a large tinfoil container, the sides of which Herman had to peel back before he could get at it. He hacked out about a fourth of it and stuffed it into his mouth. Buddy broke off a piece of the garlic bread, which disintegrated in his hand.

They chewed awhile.

The *Beverly Hillbillies* was no longer on. A cartoon show was on now, featuring Woody Woodpecker. Buddy stared at the bird, listened with annoyance to its woodpecker laugh. Presently he got up and went over to the set and turned the sound off, putting the other side of the Ornette Coleman record on instead. As soon as he sat down, Herman got up, turned off the record player, and switched the sound up on the television. Buddy watched, his fork poised, his mouth open. Herman sat down and hacked out another piece of cake. The woodpecker was laughing that laugh.

Buddy put down his fork. He got up, turned the sound off on the television, switched the record on again. Herman watched, chewing slowly.

Herman got up.

Buddy said, "Sit down."

"I can't stand this racket. It makes my head hurt. Anyway, I want to watch the cartoon."

"I hate that woodpecker," Buddy said. He was massaging his forehead. Herman was over by the set again, turning up the sound. For an instant, Ornette and the woodpecker clashed loudly.

"All right." Buddy got up and took the record off; then he switched the television off completely. "Are you satisfied?"

"No, I'm not satisfied. I want to watch the show." Herman was sticking out his lower lip. "I'm sick."

"Look," Buddy said, "there's no use arguing with each other. Let's just sit here and eat our supper in peace, can we?"

They chewed some more. Herman chewed deliberately. He was thinking. All his features were bunched together in the center of his face as if they were holding a meeting. Suddenly he stopped chewing and looked directly at Buddy and said, "What are we going to do?"

Buddy was sprinkling some cheese on the black spaghetti. "We got the eight o'clock tilt. I figure if it gets washed out we go down to the Corner and see what's doing."

"I'm not talking about tonight. I'm talking about what we're going to do."

"What are you talking about?" Buddy stuffed a burned crust into his mouth and clapped off the crumbs. "We're going to do just what we been doing. We're going to relax, play some ball, have a few beers. Take it nice and easy."

Herman made an impatient coughing sound in the back of his throat. Beads of sweat bloomed on his face.

"What's your problem, anyway," Buddy said. "We're in good shape." He was tapping his fork against the plate. The fork was black and had a formidable coil of noodles glued around it. "Haven't we been having some fine times?"

"We got to *do* something," Herman said, waving his arms. "We got to *go* somewhere. We can't stay here forever. I'm tired of sleeping on the goddamn floor every night." He gripped the back of his neck. "It's making me sick."

"Fine," Buddy said. "We can switch. It's all right with me."

"We got to get some money," Herman said. He was rooting around on the floor for his wallet. He found it under a pile of dirty clothes and withdrew some bills. He counted them twice. "I got forty-five dollars here, including my severance pay." He flung the money onto the table. "Forty-five lousy dollars! What do you got?"

Buddy swallowed. "About a hundred." This was a lie; he had less than fifty. "And don't forget what the meat guy owes us."

"The meat guy," Herman said. He jumped up and began to pace, a ridiculous thing to do in such a tiny, cluttered room. He was muttering to himself. Suddenly he stopped and looked at Buddy, his head hanging. "I'll be honest with you. I'm not doing so good. I miss her. I can't help it. I miss her a lot. I miss the kid. I even miss the dog." He wrung his hands. "I admit it, Bud. I been going off and calling her."

Buddy looked at the mess on his plate and said nothing.

Herman was cracking his knuckles. His face was red, sweaty. "I been sneaking off. I can't help it. I miss everything. I get down on this goddamn floor at night and shut my eyes and I can't stop thinking. I'm thinking all the time."

Buddy said, "Sit down."

Herman sank into a chair and looked at the wall. Buddy went over and squatted down in front of him.

"You say you been calling her?"

Herman snuffled. "Yes."

"What she been saying?"

"Hi, how ya doing. Like that. Nothing much."

"She say she was sorry?"

"No," Herman said. "Not exactly."

"She apologize for taking your dough?"

"No."

"She apologize for beating you in front of the kid?"

"No."

"She take back what she called you?"

Herman didn't speak.

"You remember what she called you, Herm?"

Herman looked at him blankly.

"A boar, Herm. A lousy stinking boar. You ever see one of those things?"

Herman shrugged. "I been called worse."

Buddy stood and went behind Herman and laid a hand on the big man's shoulder; he might have been an elder ordaining Herman in some strange sect. "Look, do what you feel is best. Hey, I mean, who am I—Buddy Barnes—to be telling the Glicker what to do? He's his own man. Me, I'm just a left fielder, an easygoing guy. Herm's the guy with the wife, the kid—"

"Don't forget the house."

"Sure, the house. Furniture, too. Who am I to be telling a guy with furniture how to make his moves? This is one responsible individual we're talking about. Who knows better than Herm the Germ that there's more important stuff than just playing ball, having some beers, hanging out, getting it on with certain well-built waitresses. He doesn't need me—"

Herman cocked his head. "What's this?"

"What's what?"

"What you just said. The part about the well-built waitress."

"Oh that. It's nothing. Forget it. I was just planning to set something up for this week, but now that I think about it I'm completely out of line. Who am I—Buddy Barnes—to be taking it on myself to set up the Glicker with strange waitresses? This is a married guy we're talking about. How long, Herm, eight years?"

Herman cleared his throat. "Ten."

"Dig it. Ten years. A decade. How's it go?" Buddy drew erect, folding his hands in reverence. "In good times and bad times, in sickness and in health. Dig *that*. Nobody said it was going to be easy. The Glicker knows it. He knows that sometimes there's going to be a certain amount of friction, misunderstanding, a little wear and tear around the edges. Where does it say there's no aggravation? What about the silences, the petty cruelties? Let's not forget the staleness—may I use the word nausea—that sets in after night after night of her coming to the sack looking like one of those Russian discus chicks. Don't mistake me—I'm not assessing blame here. What woman gets dolled up every night? Can you blame her for getting just the least little bit tired of Mister Meat? Can you blame her if she's more than a bit peeved when you spend five nights a week playing ball and not even giving her the time of day and then going down to the Corner to have a few after the game and coming in lit, and pretty soon you got the wazoo out again and poking it at her and we've already established she's more than a little weary of *that*. I mean, who can blame a person for being fed up to here with that noise night after night after night?"

Buddy paused. He reached for a half-empty can of Old Style that had been decorating the table for several days, took a couple of big swigs, and passed it down to Herman, who took it and drained it and passed it back without moving more than his hand. Light gleamed off the bald spot on the top of his head. His jaws were working.

"Of course," Buddy continued, "you'd think she'd be able to understand the other side of the coin. You'd think she'd be able to get it through her noggin that a guy works hard all day, day after day after day, he wants to enjoy himself once in a while. A guy spends forty a week on company time, he wants a few lousy hours to himself. We're talking about a breadwinner here, a provider, a hardworking dude. So he wants to play a little ball, have a few after the game with his pals, where's the crime? Plus, it's not any old team he's playing with. He's not playing with the Bozos or the Turds. He's no Boll Weevil. He's a Stick. You think she knows what it's like to play with the Sticks, to be the best, to have people applaud when you step up to the dish? Does she know what it feels like to hit the seats? Not a chance. No way. She thinks it's a small matter, this hitting of seats. You're a Stick, you want to look sharp out there, you'd think she could keep from ironing wrinkles in your suit. You don't want to get up there in front of everybody in some nasty suit. You don't want to be looking like you slept in it. You want to be looking good out there but—let's face it—she doesn't care how you look. She fucks with your hat. She doesn't think much of how the breadwinner chooses to spend the few precious hours he has to himself. If the truth be known, she isn't too hot about your fellow Sticks either."

"Dorks," Herman said.

"What's that?"

"She called the Sticks dorks. Right to my face."

"Well, there you have it. These are guys—let's not forget —you've known all your life. You take the field with these guys. Dorks? Wait a minute here. These are your best pals she's talking about. You know the Sticks—name me one dork among us. Think about it. You go back a long way with these guys. Of course"—Buddy examined his fingernails —"there are certain guys you go back with longer than anybody, who she has a particularly low opinion of."

Herman was leaning forward in the chair. He had begun smacking his fist into the center of his forehead. "You were right there," he said. "She was saying stuff and you were standing right in front of her. Name-calling. Using vulgar language." He shook his head. "She was way out of line with that toilet mouth. I says, 'Woman, hold your tongue.' "

"Hey, never mind me," Buddy said. "I'm not important here. Sure, she called me some lowdown stuff, but it's you I'm talking about. I was there when it happened. I saw the whole thing." Buddy looked away, making little clucking sounds. "Do you remember it, Herm?"

Herman was looking at his feet. He had on one brown sock and one blue. His big toe was sticking out of the blue one. "Yeah, I remember it."

"You remember how she looked at you, the stuff she said?"

"I remember."

"You remember how she sneaked out and took your dough, cleaned you out, and you're standing there like a dork in the middle of the bank?"

Herman nodded, remembering it.

"You remember how she hung up when you called her from the Corner that time? 'The Glicker,' you said, and she hangs up."

Herman remembered that too.

"Above all else, let's not forget that she took a stick to you, Herm. She drove you out of your house and home."

"The kid was there," Herman said. His face had turned liver-colored. "That's what gets me. He was standing there the whole time. He heard things he shouldn't of. He saw it all." He got up and began to pace again, stooped over, hurling himself from one end of the room to the other. He knocked stuff over.

"Look," Buddy said, standing clear of this muscular pacing, "I didn't want to get you worked up. I just thought that if you were going to make your move there were certain things I, Buddy Barnes, your best friend, ought to remind you of, that's all."

Herman said, "Let's do something."

"Like what?"

"I don't know. Anything." He was hunting through piles of dirty clothes for a pair of trousers, picking garments up and flinging them aside. "I got to get out of here. Goddamnit to hell, where's my fucking pants?" He began kicking at the piles of clothes. Suddenly he turned and rushed over to Buddy and gripped his arm. "Listen. I have to ask you. What are we going to do?"

"We can't turn back."

"No turning back," Herman said.

"We gotta forge ahead."

"Forge ahead."

"All right." Buddy sat down, clapping his hands. "We

gotta get something together here, I agree completely. We gotta figure out our game plan. So we don't know what to do. So here's what we do . . ." Buddy had his index finger at his temple, as if he were drilling for answers. "Okay, I got it. We sit down and get out a piece of paper and write down what we can do. Follow me? I'm talking about our qualifications, our strong points. Get it all down in black and white."

"Yeah," Herman said. "Then what?"

"Then we look at it and go from there."

Herman mulled this suggestion, stroking his savage beard. "You think it's a good idea?"

"Of course. Listen, guys like us, with as many strong points as we got, we can completely overlook certain things. You'd be amazed. Get it all down in black and white, that's what I say. Where's some paper?"

"There's some in the kitchen by the phone," Herman said. "I'll get it."

"While you're up, Herm, how about getting us a couple."

Herman went into the kitchen while Buddy cleared an ample space on the table, sleeving aside the plates and the silverware and the remains of the bread, which had disintegrated into a mound of black crumbs.

Buddy had a jumpy feeling in the pit of his stomach like the first time up in a new season. His hands were shaky. He held them up and looked at them, observing his naked fingers. While he'd been counseling Herman he'd neglected to mention that he, too, had sneaked away. One night when the game had been rained out and there was nothing doing, he'd gotten into the Olds and started driving, his arm out the window and his hand thumping on the roof, trying to figure out what to do. He thought maybe he'd check out that new bar on Irving. He thought maybe he'd stop by and see Nan. He drove around some more, debating the possibilities, and then before he knew it, without having planned on it, he found himself in a phone booth dialing his old number.

He waited, counting the rings. He counted five. He was about to hang up when somebody picked up the phone and said hello. It wasn't Jo. It wasn't Jo's voice. It was a man's voice. Buddy had hung up immediately. Then he got back into the Olds and drove very fast to the apartment and, pulling around back in the alley into which she had dumped his stuff, he discovered a small, foreign-made automobile parked in his old space, a sleek red job with fancy hubcaps parked there in his old spot. He remembered it very well. He remembered staring at it and feeling that panicky feeling he got when he lost an easy one in the sun.

Herman came back with beers, a big sheet of lined yellow paper, and a piece of purple crayon. Buddy looked questioningly at this implement. "What's this?"

Herman shrugged. "It's the only thing I could find."

"Never mind." Buddy drew a line down the center of the paper with the crayon. On one side he wrote "Herm," on the other "Buddy."

"All right," he said, clapping his hands again, "where do we start?"

They looked at each other.

"All right," Buddy said, "we'll start with me. What, in your opinion, are some of my strong points?"

Herman glanced at the ceiling. "Geez, Buddy. There's so many."

"I know, I know, but we got to start somewhere."

"Well"—Herman tweaked his nose—"you're a funny guy."

"How do you mean that, Herm?"

"You can make guys laugh, loosen them up and so forth. You're a lot of laughs."

Buddy considered this. "You're right. I am a pretty funny guy." He jotted with the crayon. "Funny guy . . . gets along with people. All right, there's one. How about some more?"

"You're one helluva athlete. Name the game and you can play the shit out of it. I still say if your arm—"

"Helluva . . . athlete," Buddy said, writing it. "Okay. Now we're getting somewhere."

They thought a minute.

"I can play the trumpet," Buddy said. "Guitar, too."

"Sure. Get it down there." Buddy got it down. "You're a handy guy with your hands," Herman added. "You can fix stuff. You're real good at that type of thing."

Buddy wrote "good hands."

They drank their beers and considered some more of Buddy's strong points. When they were finished Buddy held up the paper, flicked it with his fingertips, and examined his résumé. It added up to a funny, artistically inclined, trumpet-playing individual who had good hands, was a helluva athlete, got along with people, and knew a great deal about books and music. In addition, he was a real nice guy. Buddy nodded, impressed with himself.

"Okay," he said. "Now you."

Herman shrugged sheepishly.

"C'mon, don't be modest."

"I don't know," Herman said. "I guess I'm kinda strong."

"Strong? Are you kidding me? You're the strongest son-uvabitch I've ever seen." Buddy wrote down "strong" beneath Herman's name and put three exclamation marks behind it.

"I'm a good driver," Herman said. "I can handle all type of rigs."

Buddy wrote it down.

They drank their beers and considered Herman's strong points. The list, when Buddy examined it, was not so long and diverse as his own, but it contained a lot of real good strong points nonetheless. The Glicker, it was agreed, was dependable, hardworking, honest, loyal, and a guy you could count on when the going got tough. He was a superb driver and a pretty fair athlete in his own right. He was extremely strong. Like Buddy, he was a real nice guy.

"Here." Buddy handed him the paper. "Take a look for yourself."

Herman studied it. "Geez, I got a lot of strong points," he admitted. "I'm not a bad guy."

"I told you this was a good idea, didn't I? Sometimes it helps to sit down and think about these matters and get it all down in black and white. You get it all down in front of you and look at it and the picture becomes a lot clearer, you know what I'm saying?"

"Dig it."

"I'm hanging on to this baby." Buddy folded the paper and put it in his wallet. "It's a start, you know what I mean?"

"It's a good start," Herm agreed. "How'd you hear about this anyway?"

"Jo," Buddy said. "She used to make me do it about once a month."

7

One day, without warning, the Sticks began to slump. They lost their edge, began missing cut-off men and pulling jackass stuff on the bases. There was no life in their lumber. Stretch was slumping, and so was the Bull; Red was not getting a solid piece of the ball. Herman? Slumping badly. Doc was falling behind on the mound, getting tattooed, and Buddy was worn out from chasing deep drives. He was still playing some swell ball, especially in the garden where he bailed the team out of deep trouble with his one-hand stabs and over-the-shoulders, but even he suffered lapses of concentration out there, due primarily to the little red foreign-made automobile with the flashy hubcaps. He could not seem to get this vehicle out of his mind. One minute he'd be bent at the waist with his hands on his knees, concentrating on the pitch, in the game, ready to move in any direction, and then the little red sports car with the flashy hubcaps would start tooling around in his head and he'd find himself throwing to the wrong base, getting a late jump on the ball. One night he broke the wrong way on a piece of cake and it dropped in front of him for a three-run double.

For a while the Sticks were able to overcome their boners with late-inning rallies, edging the Shooters and Maulers and Hit Men. Whitey, however, was not fooled. "That's it," he said. "Keep it up. We'll pay." The Sticks kept it up and they paid, getting clipped by the Swatters and the Strokers and the Chi-Guys and, on a sweltering Thursday with everybody there, catching their lunch from the Amalgamonsters, Stretch and Herman taking the collar and the ordinarily sure-fingered Red stone-handing innumerable balls at second.

After the game Whitey held a meeting.

"Fellows," he began, "we have evidently hit a little slide here. We're not playing good ball. Quite the contrary: we stink. In my opinion this is because we've got some guys who are not one hundred and ten percent in the game. Some of you Sticks are snoozing out there. Your minds are elsewhere. I realize certain things crop up from time to time, but this does not excuse getting doubled off second on infield pops and some of this other farcical shit we're pulling out there. Let's get in the game, gents. Let's play baseball. If you take the field as a Stick be prepared to play like one. If you aren't, please stay home and take up a hobby."

The next day Buddy and Herman had lunch with Stretch. Buddy had run into the first-sacker at the unemployment office. Stretch had been on the dole ever since the layoff at the copper mill, but this was Buddy's first check. Herman had pressured him into it. He had not wanted to go. He felt it would be unseemly for a guy like him to be seen standing in a bread line with a bunch of jigs and beaners and old dudes.

"I'm not going," he had told Herman.

"You got to," Herman said. "We're broke."

"If you think it's such a good idea, why don't you go?" Buddy said.

"I can't," Herman said. "If I went they'd just kick me out of there." He was examining his big useless hands. "I quit my job, remember?"

Once Buddy had actually gone down there, though, it hadn't been so bad. All he'd had to do was fill out some forms and tell a few lies, and when he went to pick up his check a couple of weeks later he was surprised to see that it wasn't just jigs and beaners and old dudes standing in line. Some regular white guys were standing in line, too. He'd even seen Stretch. He was standing a couple of lines over, his head sticking up above the masses. He had his baseball cap pulled low over his eyes.

"Hey, Stretch," Buddy called out to him. He'd had to holler at him a couple of times before he finally got his attention. "Get a job, you bum," Buddy had hollered, and Stretch had frowned and looked away.

"That wasn't so bad, after all," Buddy said to him on the way out. He was looking at his check. "How often you come down here, Stretchman?"

"Every two weeks," Stretch said. He had stuffed his check into his toolbox without looking at it. "Every two weeks I'm in that line."

They had lunch with Herman at the delicatessen by the old park where, as kids, they had hung out with their cream sodas, pitching quarters at cracks in the sidewalk and spitting several different ways. First they got out their clinchers and sticks so Stretch could take some extra batting practice, Herm pitching and Buddy standing way off by the big tree and hoping Stretch, a notorious pull hitter, didn't club long fouls into the tennis courts, in the bushes surrounding which, no doubt, Ferd was hiding with his trash spear. He needn't have worried. Stretch hit a few dribblers, then threw his stick down and waved them in.

Herm went across the street for a couple of meatball sandwiches while Buddy pried mud off his spikes with a twig. Occasionally he glanced out at the big tree with its

low and inviting limb into which, one day, he had leaped
from the back of a moving lawn mower. It seemed like this
had happened a long time ago. The air was wet with a fine
mist that seemed to be falling upward into the sky from
the damp, unmowed grass. In the distance some kids were
jamming sticks into the mouth of a water fountain. Stretch
had pulled his lunch out of a paper bag and was sitting on a
low bench, a napkin across his gray work pants, his legs
nearly up to his chin. He had the big crude features of a re-
cent immigrant and the longest neck Buddy had ever seen
on a human being. The layoff at the copper mill, where
Stretch drove a fork, was supposed to have lasted a month,
but it had gone on and on and on.

"I'm fucking terrible," he was saying.

"Don't worry about it," Buddy said. "Everybody hits a
slump. I've had slumps. Herm, you've had slumps, haven't
you?"

Herm belched. "Certainly."

Stretch was bent forward chewing on a baloney sandwich.
He chewed tentatively, as though he wasn't sure what ex-
actly he was chewing. He left his thumb prints in the bread.
Buddy and Herman were slurping on their sandwiches.

"You know those guys in the towers," Stretch finally said.

"Which guys are those?" Buddy said.

"The guys in the towers," Stretch repeated, gesturing
broadly with his sandwich. Held together with pieces of ad-
hesive tape, his glasses were two panes of moisture; you
couldn't see his eyes. "The guys who climb way up there
with a box of ammo, a couple of hunting rifles, and a pistol
in their pants, and start blasting. The guys who hole up in
the attic. The guys who stand on roofs and open up on the
trafficopter. You know the guys I'm talking about?"

"Those burnouts," Buddy said. "What about them?"

"When they finally nab those guys it always comes out
what good guys they were. Family men. Hard workers. You
know what I mean? A guy'll come on and say, 'He was a

quiet guy. Good neighbor. Treated all the kids on the block to Hershey bars.' " Stretch wiped his mouth on his sleeve. "That kills me. Who did they expect, King Kong? Sure they were regular hardworking guys. That's why they climbed up there in the first place."

"Yeah," Buddy said. He had stopped chewing and was looking at Stretch with steepled eyebrows. "So?"

Stretch didn't answer right away. He had put down his sandwich and was rooting around in his toolbox for something. After a minute he found what he was looking for and brought it out into the mist: a huge black pistol. Buddy and Herm looked at it.

"I can't take it anymore," Stretch was saying. "I drive the fork but the mill's shut down. Another month, the guys say, maybe more. The dole's running out on me. I'm running out of time. My wife, let me tell you, has gone completely off the wall. She's missing screws. She's on this religion thing. Wears this long white dress and reads the Bible. Me? I'm a beast. All men are animals, she tells me. She tells me it's a sign from God that I'm out of work. Change your ways, she says. That isn't all. Get this. She says I got the mark on me. The mark of Satan. Satan! I mean, what do you say to something like that? But that isn't the half of it. Now she's got me looking. Where is it? I ask. I don't see it. If I got it, please tell me where it is. She hides her face from the sight of me, gives me a mouthful of Scripture. Repent, she says. She's my wife, I drive the fork, and she won't let me near her—how do you like that?" He was passing the pistol from hand to hand; his glasses had slid down his nose and his eyes were lit weirdly from within, like a jack-o-lantern's. "So I get a little out of line once in a while and whip out the trouser snake. So I eat her Bible. I'm not proud of it, but it's getting to me, you know. It's messing me up. I'm slumping, hurting the team. I'm not in the game."

"Easy, Stretch," Buddy said. He was looking at the pistol. It occurred to him that he had never been this close to one before. "Tell you what, why don't you hand me that thing and then we'll sit down and talk this thing out. We can work it out. Herm, don't you think we can work this out with Stretch?"

"Sure we can," Herman said. He was sitting absolutely still and was following the pistol out of the corner of his eye.

Stretch held the weapon away. "Yesterday, when Whitey was talking about guys pulling stupid stuff, he was talking about me. I know it. I forgot how many outs there were and got doubled up. Jesus." He lowered his head, sniffling on his sleeve.

"He was talking about all of us," Buddy said. "We're all playing like shit."

"Thanks, Bud, but it's no use." He paused, looking from the pistol to the half-eaten sandwich on his lap as though trying to decide which one to put in his mouth. Suddenly he sprang to his feet. "You guys excuse me a minute."

He disappeared behind a tree and, squatting, began firing point-blank into a mud puddle, the shots muffled, the bullets embedding, the muck flying up and splattering his hands and face and the front of his faded blue work shirt. Buddy and Herman were glued to the bench. After a minute Stretch came out from behind the tree, the slimed gun still smoking, the tension drained from his mud-covered face.

"For Christ sake, Stretch," Buddy said.

"I'm sorry, you guys," Stretch said. "I just felt so damn terrible."

∞∞∞∞

The Sticks continued to stink. They gave each other pep talks, wore talismans and fetishes, even shuffled the batting order, and they were still getting beat in three different leagues. They were plagued with errors, infected with pop-ups. They were fumbling around out there, coughing it up, heaving the pill into dugouts. They were hitting corn, swinging like a bunch of tired old Moose at the Fourth of July picnic. They were riddled by the Shooters, mauled by the Maulers. They were overrun by the Roaches, a bunch of young creeps with ponytails and bib overalls who shouldn't have lasted the slaughter rule. They were ambushed by the Assassins, rubbed out by the Hit Men. The Amalgamonsters destroyed them. Word was out they were getting old.

Whitey held a meeting.

"Fellows," he began, "all right already. It should be evident to each and every one of you that we're smelling up the city. We're making spectacles out of ourselves. In the last few weeks I've seen things I've never seen on a diamond before. I've never, for example, seen two base runners collide going in opposite directions. That isn't a double play, it's a disgrace. Are we Clowns or Misfits? Are we Porcupines? Let's cut out the bonehead stuff, shall we? There's no excuse for being in the toilet when you're due up. There's no excuse for batting out of order. Let's each and every one of us go to the toilet before the game."

The Bull hung his head. It was he who'd been in the can, a mental error which had caused Herman to bat out of order and cost the team runs. Nobody spoke. The only sound was the clacking of cleats in the gravel lot where the Sticks were assembled. Occasionally a player brought up some phlegm.

"Don't mistake what I'm saying here," Whitey continued. "What I'm saying goes for each and every one of us. I'm not saying one guy's doing this, another guy's doing that. I'm not naming names. What I'm saying is, we're all fucking up, and let me add that if we don't cut it out I just might have to make some changes and let some of these younger ballplayers show me what they can do. All right. That's it. Everybody get away from me."

The meeting broke up. Whitey turned to Buddy, who was thoughtfully chunking mud off his spikes, and said, "Where the hell was my second baseman tonight?"

"Beats me."

"Something's up," Whitey said. "It isn't like Red to miss a tilt."

The next game the happy-go-lucky infielder showed up in civilian clothes with his throwing arm in a sling.

"What happened to you?" Buddy asked.

"I was stabbed."

"Get out."

Red wasn't shitting him. It seemed that for some time he'd been seeing two women, frequently on the same night. Whitey told him to cut it out on the grounds that it was bound to affect his play. "It's always been my theory," he had said, "that excessive copulation takes a lot out of a ball-player." Red paid no heed. He kept seeing the two women, making them the same promises, feeding them the same lines. One grew suspicious and decided to follow him, a steak knife concealed in her purse. She followed him down broad boulevards and narrow one-way streets; she followed him through alleys. Red was fairly easy to follow inasmuch as he drove a bright red Edsel with a Cub banner waving from the antenna. She followed him to the apartment of her rival, waiting in the corridor for several moments, listening to squeals of horseplay and the music of Barry White. When it grew silent she barged in, steak knife drawn, and discovered Red and the other woman copulating in a La-Z-Boy recliner. She went for his heart but Red got his shoulder in the way. She stabbed him three times before he could get the weapon away from her. "For Christ sake," he said. "Can't we talk about this?"

"Sure, you miserable prick. Go ahead. Talk. Explain to me what's been going on."

The other woman, who had been dialing the police, put down the phone. She was a short busty blonde with a large nose; the other was pretty and slim. Red hadn't been able to make up his mind.

"Yeah," the busty one said. "I'd also like to know the story."

"Girls," Red said. He was holding his shirt against his badly bleeding shoulder.

"Isn't it obvious?" the slim one said.

"I guess it is. C'mon into the kitchen. I'll make some coffee and we'll talk."

"I'm Claire."

"Hi, I'm Shirley."

They went into the kitchen.

"Hey," Red said. "I'm stabbed."

He had finally had to put on his clothes, reel out to the Edsel, and drive himself to the nearest hospital, where he collapsed in the emergency room while filling out some forms.

"Are you kidding me?" Buddy said.

"It's a bitch, isn't it? What gets my goat is that now I'm out of the playoffs. She sliced me good."

Whitey told Red to get out of his sight, replacing him at second with Squirrel, a young wiry guy who, Buddy had to admit, could really cover the hole. Still, he was accustomed to firing his strikes to the veteran now resigned to watching the games from the last row of the bleachers, his perforated wing balanced gingerly across his knee.

Red wasn't the only Stick to go down. One night Harv rounded second and went down clutching the back of his leg, and they had to help him off. Sammy raced out for a pop, stepped in a hole, and went down with an ankle sprain, and they had to carry him off. Then it was the Bull going down from the momentum of one of his murderous cuts, losing his balance and doing the splits, and they had to get a stretcher to cart him away. "Sure," Whitey said. "This too."

One night Stretch failed to show. Whitey came up to Buddy after the game and said, "Where the hell was my first baseman?"

"Beats me, Whitey," Buddy said.

"Something's up," Whitey prophesied. "I've never known the man to miss a game."

They got the lowdown from Crawford, who now worked as a watchman at the copper mill, fingerprinting visitors and waving to his friends from a lookout tower. "It was fucking terrible," Crawford was saying. He was at the bar, shaking his head and wiping his eyes with a filthy bandana. His safety goggles lay on the counter. The team gathered round.

It had happened during the night shift when the mill was shut down. Crawford, who was supposed to be keeping an eye on the place, had been sitting up in the tower listening to a transistor radio and monkeying with his new hand when he heard what sounded like shots coming from the loading dock. After a minute he got down from the tower and eased around back to see what the story was and found that the entrance had been blasted open. "My momma didn't raise no fools," Crawford pointed out. "I called the cops." While he waited for the cops to show up, he climbed up on some trash and peeked in the window and saw Stretch mounted on his fork, impaling empty crates and stacking them up by the door, his hydraulic lift making an eerie whine in the dark silent factory. "He had about ten crates stacked up, working like a bitch," Crawford said. "I go up to him and says, 'Stretch, what's the story here? We're all shut down.' 'Keep away from me, Crawford,' he says, without even stopping. 'I'm unclean,' he says. His eyes had this crazy look like a bunch of snakes were after him. Then he went past me and I saw the pistol in his pants."

Meanwhile, squad cars were screeching into the parking lot along with news crews from all the major affiliates. As soon as he heard the sirens, Stretch leaped off his rig—which ran amok for a while, knocking over the water cooler and several garbage bins before fixing on a course of aimless circles in the middle of the plant—and barricaded himself in the locker room. The cops moved in, sharpshooters taking cover at strategic vantage points. The news crews set up their lights and cameras. Crawford was crying into a bullhorn. Every so often Stretch would open up with the pistol, the bullet ricocheting around the damp smelly room.

"Stretch!" Crawford would cry out. "You still there?"

"What do you want, Crawford?" Stretch would say. "Let me alone."

"Come on out, Stretch, there's a million cops out here. Just throw out the piece and come on out." The cop from whom Crawford was taking instructions leaned over and said something to him. "Oh yeah. When you come out, Stretch, make sure you got your dukes on top of your head."

"It's no use," Stretch said. "I got it on me, Crawford. I got it and I can't find it."

"What's that, Stretch?"

"The mark."

"Mark? What mark is that, Stretch?"

"The mark of the devil. I looked all over for it and I can't see it, but the sonuvabitch is there all right. I know it's there. It's driving me crazy."

Crawford paused. There was nothing in his brain that could produce a reply to this. He huddled with the cop. "A priest, Stretch. There's a priest out here. He'll help you."

"A priest?"

"Sure. He's right here. Not a bad guy, Stretch."

"Send him in."

"Uh-uh, Stretch. You got to come out."

A shot rang out.

"Stretch!"

"What?"

"Just a second. He's coming in."

They put a fake collar on one of the cops and sent him in, heavily armed. Moments later Stretch and the false priest emerged. Stretch's hands were cuffed behind his back, and the priest had a gun to his head. Stretch was not wearing any clothes.

"I couldn't talk to him," Crawford whined. "I couldn't

hardly get a look at him. They jumped all over him and took him away . . ." He broke off, snuffling.

"Jesus H. Christ," somebody said.

"You got to be shitting me."

Sticks grew quiet, fathoming this tale.

"You say he was naked?" Harv asked.

Crawford nodded.

Buddy shook his head. "We had a little batting practice. We talked. I thought he was okay." He was smoothing a piece of crumpled cellophane between his fingers.

"Wait a minute," Froggy said. "What's this mark he was talking about?"

"Who knows," Crawford said. "I caught a look at him and he didn't have no marks on him except on the side of his head where the cop hit him with something."

"Sure, he was a little uptight," Buddy said, remembering the crazy tower talk, the pistol, the shooting of mud. "But he seemed okay. Didn't he seem okay to you, Frog?"

"Sure. Stretch is Stretch."

"The guy was naked," Harv said. "That's what gets me."

◎◎◎◎

When Buddy got back to the apartment Herman was sitting on a small folding chair in the center of the living room, soaking his feet in a tub of hot water. He was surrounded by mounds of clutter—dirty dishes, books, stacks of unjacketed records, piles of beer cans, empty banana cake tins, tangled balls of clothing. He was still feeling poorly. Whatever he had he could not seem to get over. He coughed, took his temperature a lot. His skin had turned the color of banana cake, which was about the only food he could get down. He was going through about three cakes a day. Every so often he would sash his blue champ robe and get up and pace, clutching at his heart, moving back and forth through the clutter which had been spreading more every day until it had finally squeezed him into a narrow patch in the center of the room where he sat in his robe with a blanket around him and a thermometer in his mouth. A naked light bulb glowed faintly above him. All the windows were closed. Doc had moved in with his brother.

"We got edged in the seventh," Buddy said.

Herman grunted, not surprised. He had the thermometer clamped at the side of his mouth like a cigar. About every thirty seconds he would take it out and cough and then put it back again.

"Listen." Buddy gripped his arm. "I have to tell you about Stretch. You won't believe what happened."

"Your friend was here."

"Huh? What friend?"

"Pastrami. Salami. The dago with the hat."

"Noselli."

"Whatever. He was over here a little while ago."

"Here? He came here?"

"About an hour ago. Comes in in that slick jacket and that little wop hat all huffy and pushy and wants to know where you are. I told him you were playing ball, where did he think you were. Give him a message, he says. Tell him I'm getting tired of waiting on him. Tell him he's diddling. Tell him he better see me soon if he knows his ass from his elbow. Tell him yourself, I says. I threw him out."

Buddy had picked up one of the empty beer cans and was crushing it in his hand, no big feat considering the quality of aluminum they were making nowadays. "Let me get this straight. Noselli came here? He was here tonight? Right under my very roof?" He threw the can into the kitchen where it rattled across the floor and thudded into garbage bags stacked three deep in the corner. "I don't believe this. You say he was here, huh? Saying stuff. Wearing the hat." He flailed his arms. "Honest to shit, Herm, I just wish I was here to bust his ass in person."

"I was here," Herman said. "Sick as a dog and I got to get up off that couch and fuck with a greaseball. My nose is out of joint about it, let me tell you."

"He's pushing me, Herm. He's looking for grief." Buddy was now demolishing one of the cake tins. "Diddling, huh?"

They lapsed into an angry silence, watching the rain drip down from the cracked ceiling into a configuration of pans.

"Well," Herman finally said.

"Well what?"

"Well what are you going to do about it—you given any thought to that? You given any thought to the fact that you owe him? You given any thought to the fact that we are broke again?"

"The meat guy pays us Friday."

"The meat guy—what's that? Fifty bucks apiece. Big deal."

"Don't forget the government."

"The government," Herman said. "How long you think that lasts? You think they're going to keep paying you forever? No way." He lifted his toes out of the water, wiggled them a couple of times, and stuck them back in. "They're not that dumb."

"Well, what else do you want me to do, Herm? I'm doing what I can. I was the guy who went down there and signed up, remember? You didn't."

"I couldn't," Herman said. "I quit my job." He gripped his head.

"I just wish you'd quit worrying all the time. All you do is bitch anymore." Buddy turned himself into a sourpuss, his voice a nagging whine. "No money. What are we gonna do? Meat guy. Just like an old woman." He snapped his fingers. "Besides, if we need some extra money all I have to do is hunt up the nearest poker game. We need ready cash, all I have to do is bring my stick to the bar."

Herman took the thermometer out of his mouth. "Look

yourself. The last time you brought your stick to the bar you lost your ass and mine. What was it, eighty-five clams?"

"The guy was unconscious," Buddy said, remembering him, a little guy with hair like a rooster, wearing a flannel shirt with the tail sticking out. For three games he'd banged the balls around and then, with the money on the line, he cleaned the table in about ten minutes with a Chesterfield stuck in his mouth. Buddy might as well have been holding a divining rod. Herman had watched the guy scoop up the money, and then Herman disappeared into the toilet and stayed there a very long time. The noises he was making had kept everyone away. "He was making shots he never dreamed of," Buddy added. "You saw it."

"Certainly. That's how it goes when you're going bad. Slump a little, and bad news comes out of the woodwork."

Buddy threw up his hands. "Okay, Herm. Lighten up. I don't need it. We just dropped one in the seventh—which you wouldn't know about since you weren't out there."

"Well pardon me, I'm only sick as a dog." Herman glanced at his surroundings with counterfeit cheer. "I can't understand it, either. We got everything you could possibly want. Great digs. Modern conveniences at our fingertips. Wealth. Plenty of eats. We even got our own weather." Buddy was breathing heavily through his nose; irony was not Herman's strong suit. "Yes sir, we're doing just fine. Action? I can't believe all the action we're getting." Herman jammed the thermometer back into his mouth and spoke around it. "The closest I been to a woman in the last two months was that stroke place on Clark you stuck your nose up at."

"Action?" Buddy said. "You want action?" He fished out a scrap of paper from a back pocket of his baseball pants, then went over and picked up the phone.

"What are you doing?" Herman said, but Buddy was already talking in a low, sugar-coated voice. After a minute he hung up and came back, his cap cocked at a rakish angle. "You want action, you got action."

Herman was working his jaws. "What are you talking about?"

"I'm talking two babes come up to me after the game. Say they been following us, coming to all the games. One of them slips me her number." Buddy was picking up empties and shaking them until he found one that had something in it. "I figure you're not feeling so hot, I'll just sit on it for a day or two until you're feeling better. I didn't know you were raring to go. My mistake." He reached in back of the sofa and found a half-full Old Style. "They'll be over around ten."

Herman was squinting at him. "You serious?"

"No, I just made a date with the weather guy. Of course I'm serious. They're red hot, Herm. Legs? Let me tell you."

Herman jammed his hands into the pockets of his robe. "I'm not interested in any action tonight. I don't feel good."

"Fine. I'll take them both. Tits? Out to here, brother."

Herman took the thermometer out of his mouth and held it up to the light: his temperature was 98.7. The fact that it wasn't higher irritated him no end. "This goddamn thing must be broke." He shook it, stuffed it into his mouth again. "Well?"

"Well what?"

"Well what happened to Stretch?"

"Jesus Christ. Stretch. I almost forgot." Buddy pulled a chair close. "Listen to this, Herm. You won't believe it." He told Herman the story Crawford had related at the bar, emphasizing the pistol, the alleged mark of the devil, Stretch's nakedness. Herman listened impassively, hunkered over the tub and splashing his feet in the murky water.

"Stretch," Buddy would point out from time to time. "We're talking about a solid, hardworking guy here. Decent. Good moral character. Straight as an arrow. We're speaking of a man who wouldn't even do the twist at his own wedding, and there he is, running around naked in a factory with a goddamn pistol in his hand."

"Where'd they take him?"

"Jail? The nuthouse? Who knows. They just took him." Herman shrugged. "At least wherever they took him he'll be able to score a hot meal."

Buddy stared at Herman in astonishment; then he erased him with broad sweeps of his hands. "Listen to Mr. Heart here. We're only talking about a teammate, a guy we've known for twenty years."

"What do you want me to do? The guy went goofy. You heard him. You saw him shoot the mud puddle. You were there."

"Never mind. Forget it. I'm sorry I even brought it up." He was standing in the center of the room, assessing the mess. "C'mon, help me get this dump straightened up. Those babes'll be here in a minute."

"You go ahead." Herman coughed, baying like a coon hound. "I don't feel good."

Buddy did it himself, shoveling the empties into a plastic leaf bag, stacking the dirty dishes in a fantastic pyramid by the kitchen sink, and bulldozing the rest of the junk into one corner of the room and covering it with blankets. Then he went into the bathroom, removed the dirty magazines from the tub, tied the shower curtain back up with a piece of string, and took a scalding hot shower. After forty-five minutes he emerged, his hair slicked back, his skin shiny pink and anointed with various oils.

"You oughtta clean up your act before the chicks get here," he told Herman. "You'll feel like a new man."

Herman hadn't moved. He was still sitting in the middle of the room with his feet in the tub of water and looking at a Bowery Boys movie on the television. "You're wasting your time," he told Buddy. "It's already quarter after ten."

"Give them time. They'll be here."

He put on *Return to Forever,* jammed the headphones over his ears, scooped a Luke Short western off the floor, and settled back to wait for the babes. After a minute he reached behind the turntable and found a little tiny roach which he wedged into a bobby pin and fired up. Herman continued to cough and watch television, getting up every now and then to adjust the rabbit ears on top of the set. It made no appreciable difference in the reception. The rain continued to plop into the pans, splat on the carpet. The babes never showed.

∞∞

The Sticks were hurting. They were playing in physical and psychological pain, a fact that failed to inspire them. The team was down. They weren't hustling, weren't talking it up. Harv was down and Sammy was down. Doc was playing in a funk. He had grown extremely fussy about the mound, obsessed with cleaning away twigs and pebbles and tidying up between innings. Farber forsook baseball entirely, claiming he needed the time to work on his calves. Whitey replaced him with Goose, a rangy guy with a honking laugh and the longest arms Buddy had ever seen on a human being. Dog was in right, Harv having been switched to first, replacing Stretch who had been transferred to the psychiatric ward for observation. These young guys were swell players but Buddy, now the lone holdover, began to feel like a stranger in the garden.

One day he assumed a new role on the team: holler guy. He tried to pick guys up. He was a geyser of enthusiasm.

"Let's hear it," he gushed. "This is our inning. Here we go. We're rolling now." He clapped his hands raw, stuck his fingers in his mouth and whistled so piercingly that the Sticks nearest him bumped their heads on the dugout ceiling.

"C'mon, c'mon," he hollered. "Let's hear some noise. What's the matter with everybody? Are we Dummies? Are we Stiffs?"

Doc glared at him. "Why don't you put a lid on that shit?"

"We're dead," Buddy explained. "I'm just trying to pick us up, is all."

"Well go over there and do it." Doc pointed to the other side of the dugout. "By the way, you got any idea when you're moving out?"

They couldn't snap out of it. They went through the motions, and when the game was over they changed shoes and trudged to the parking lot, moving with the gingerly preoccupation of the arthritic.

"Hey," Buddy chirped, "who's going to the bar? Anybody going to the Corner for a quick one?" Nobody answered. Those whom Buddy owed money glared at him—practically everyone on the team. "I'll be down at the Corner anybody wants to join me there."

Buddy would throw his shoes in the Olds and drive to the Corner and have a few beers and play the machines and wait for his teammates to join him. Nobody showed.

ⓞⓞⓞⓞ

The Glicker was down, down. Between licks he sat in the dugout looking at his shoes, his lower lip curling downward. Every so often he coughed abjectly into his hat. He seemed to have completely lost his incredible strength. He would go up there and take his usual mighty lick but the ball wasn't going anyplace. After one puny blow he pounded his trusty black stick into the ground so hard it snapped in two, and he continued to rage on the sidelines, kicking bats and shoes and throwing forearm shivers into the chain-link fence as though he meant to bring it down.

Buddy went over to him. "Easy, big guy."

"Get off my back," Herman muttered. "Just leave my ass alone."

Buddy had never known Herman to behave like this. Even though they had neglected to put it down on the paper with the rest of his strong points, the Glicker had always been an easygoing guy. Lately, though, he'd become a cranky guy—touchy, moody, collared inside himself. Never a big yakker, he had practically quit talking altogether. He never wanted to do anything. He would get up off the floor where he slept each night on a pallet of cushions and the hairy tan blanket Buddy used as a seat cover in the Olds and switch on the television and sit in front of it all day, watching game shows and cartoons in his blue champ robe, shivering and coughing, the thermometer wedged in one corner of his mouth. When Buddy got up, the first thing he saw each morning was Herman hunched over in front of the set with his hands on his knees like an old man waiting for a bus. Occasionally he would spot Herman going through his wallet, counting the bills or staring at pictures of Sam and Mitchell, pressing the snapshots between his thick fingers. About the only time he really came alive was when they put on a food commercial and Herman would hunch way over and stare at the set, his eyes glazed and his jaws working, as though he meant to take a bite out of the picture tube.

Buddy didn't like to see the Glicker down like this. He didn't like to see him moped in front of the television all day with the thermometer in his mouth when they should be out at the ball game or catching some rays, having a fine time. He especially hated it when Herman got his wallet out and started looking at the pictures. When he caught Herman doing this, Buddy tended to think about the small foreign-made sports car with the flashy hubcaps he saw one night in the alley, parked in his old spot, and when he thought about that he knew he was in trouble. It got him to thinking about other things, such as what the automobile was doing there in the first place. When he thought about the sports car it was an easy step to begin to think about the owner of it, whom he pictured as this detestable Mediterranean guy with perfect teeth and a fancy shirt opened down to here and eight or nine medallions gleaming against a densely haired chest. And once he had the car and the guy it was real easy to imagine him and Jo together, doing things, and when he thought about *that* he was in big trouble. Although they had neglected to put it down on the paper with his innumerable other strong points, Buddy had a fertile imagination—he had, after all, been a writer—and the scenes he sometimes imagined starring Jo and this Latin creep made him want to jump out the window or get in the Olds and drive one hundred miles per hour or until it fell apart. One time, having dreamed particularly graphic scenes, he woke up in the middle of the night and threw on some shorts and went across the street with his basketball to the school-yard and went at it until dawn, shooting fallaways and jumpers off the dribble, driving to the hole, pushing himself until when the sun finally came up he was on his back on the asphalt, totally drenched, every muscle exhausted from the effort of driving the little red sports car out of his head.

From then on Buddy knew for certain that all this sitting around could lead to no good. It got you thinking, and Buddy didn't want to think. He wanted to act. He was a doer, a mover and a shaker. He jumped out of bed, windmilling his arms. He did situps, pushups, ran in place. He opened windows, took deep breaths. "Looks good," he would say, sizing up the day. He would clap his hands and suggest they go to the ball game or catch some rays, and Herman wouldn't do anything but turn slightly and glare out of the corner of his eye. Well, bite my head off, Buddy would think.

ⓞⓞⓞⓞ

One day Herman began to steal food. He started with small items—Hostess snowballs, a pack of peanut butter cups, a couple of bags of barbecued potato chips—which he ate covertly in Doc's room, where for some reason, although Doc was almost never there, neither one of them ever slept. Buddy didn't know what he was doing. He would be sitting by the stereo with the headphones jammed over his ears and sucking at one of the little tiny yellow roaches he had stashed back there when, without saying a word, Herman would get up and hunt through the clutter for some clothes and disappear out the door. Half an hour later he would return and immediately squirrel himself in Doc's room. What the hell, Buddy would think. One afternoon he got up and looked into Doc's room and discovered Herman sitting off in a corner gnawing on a brick of chocolate.

"What's going on in here?" Buddy said.

Startled, Herman hid the chocolate behind his back. "Nothing. Let me alone."

It went on like that for about a week. Buddy didn't get worried about it until the time Herman left one afternoon wearing Doc's overcoat. He was gone longer than usual, and when he returned, red and huffing, he went immediately into the kitchen and started banging cabinets. Buddy thought: now what? He got up and went into the kitchen to see what the story was and discovered Herman with his hands on a huge piece of red meat. Spread out on the counter beside it were four or five potatoes, as many cobs of corn, and a head of lettuce. Herman was still wearing the overcoat.

Buddy's mouth was open. "Look out for this feast, Herm. How'd you score all this stuff?"

"Never mind. I got it." He was hacking at the lettuce with a knife.

Buddy watched him. "You lifted it, didn't you?"

Herman continued to mutilate the lettuce. After a minute he looked up. "So what?"

"So nothing. Hey, I'd have to be nuts to bitch at these eats. The thing is . . ." He paused, searching for a delicate way to say it. Theft, like irony, was not one of Herman's strong points. "I'm just telling you to watch yourself, is all. If you're going to go into the rob and steal business, you got to be careful, is what I'm saying." He tapped his fingers on the counter. "That overcoat, for instance . . ."

"Look." Herman pointed at him with the knife. "Don't be telling me how to do stuff. I don't want to hear about it."

Buddy shrugged. "Sure. No problem. You did fine." He stared at the piece of meat, trying to remember when he'd seen anything like it. "You mind if I give you a hand here?"

"Suit yourself," Herman said.

They prepared the food and brought it out into the living room, clearing junk off the table with broad sweeps of their arms. Buddy stared rapturously at what lay before him. Lately he'd been subsisting on Cheerios, pot pies, and Almond Joys; the meat he'd eaten came in a plastic bag. His ribs had begun to show, sticking out like the skeleton of a sunken boat.

"I got to hand it to you, Herm," he said, nibbling on a piece of corn typewriter-style, "this really hits the spot. Nothing like a good meal to give you a lift is what I always say."

Herman said nothing. He was chewing some meat. He chewed slower and slower and slower.

"You know, I been thinking. In my opinion we're definitely over the hump. We were down for a while, sure, but I think the worst is over. Take last night. We could've pulled that game out if the guy doesn't make a lucky stab on the ball Goose hits." He mashed a potato up against his face, scooped it clean, and threw the empty skin on the table. "Sure we were slumping—who doesn't—but come play-offs, the Sticks'll be there. What do you think, Herm, are we going to start rolling again or am I nuts?"

Herm was still chewing. Finally he spat out what was in his mouth and turned and faced the wall.

"What's the matter?"

"I can't eat."

"Something wrong with the food?" He leaned over and inspected the slab of meat on Herman's plate. It looked okay to him. It looked just fine.

"I can't eat," Herman said. His voice was shaky. "I chew

and chew and I just can't swallow it." He got up and went into Doc's room and shut the door.

Buddy shrugged and continued eating. He cleaned his plate and then he looked at Herman's, which had been barely touched. "Hey, Herm," he shouted, "you sure you don't want any of this?" He waited a minute and when Herman didn't answer he picked up the plate and put it down on his side of the table.

Two days later they caught Herman at the supermart stealing a banana cake, and Buddy had to go down and talk the manager out of prosecuting. He paid for the cake and sweet-talked the guy, a short indignant man with a square mustache, wearing an apron, while women in babushkas gathered round. Herman sat over by the carts in Doc's overcoat, looking out the window.

As soon as they were out in the car Herman reached for the cake and started prying it open. "Just don't start on me," he said, gouging out a big hunk and stuffing it in his mouth. "I don't want to hear about it."

ⵔⵔⵔ

The employment agency no longer called him. The day after they had made out their list of strong points, Herman had gone to an agency on Fullerton and presented himself for opportunity. The agent, a young bird-faced woman in a Queen Victoria blouse, asked him for his qualifications. Herman whipped out the list and showed it to her. The woman glanced at it briefly and handed it back. She flipped her aviator glasses onto her head and rubbed her eyes.

"That list isn't complete," Herman said. "It was just off the top of my head."

"Mr. Glick, what work have you done?"

"I move goods."

"How did you move these goods?"

"By truck."

"I see. You're a truck driver. What kind of truck did you drive, Mr. Glick?"

"A beer truck."

"A beer truck. Good." She got up and went to a file cabinet. "Let me check and see what we have on that."

"Wait," Herman said. "I'm not interested in that line anymore. If I wanted to haul drinks I wouldn't have quit in the first place. I'm interested in something different."

"Like what?"

"I don't know." Herman thought a minute, working his jaws. This had become a lot more difficult than he had expected. "Something worthwhile, you know? Something useful." He paused, looking at his hands. "I'm a qualified guy."

The woman slammed shut the file cabinet. "All right, Mr. Glick. Just put your telephone number on that card there. If something worthwhile comes up we'll give you a call."

"I'd appreciate it."

A few days later the woman from the agency called to tell him they had something he might be interested in.

"Good deal," Herman said.

The woman told him it was in transportation, right up his alley: a large corporation needed a chauffeur to drive big shots to and from the airport and to high-level meetings around town.

Herman politely declined this opportunity.

A few days later she called with another opportunity: driving a bus for retarded children. "It's only part-time, but you might be able to work something out with the principal. I understand they also need custodial help."

"Retards!" Herman shouted, after he had hung up. "Who wants to drive a bunch of little nuts around?"

After that the employment agency didn't call him anymore. Herman studied the want ads, but after a few unsuccessful and humiliating inquiries, he quit doing that too. He quit doing everything. Every night he fell asleep on the pallet of cushions with the crumpled snapshot of Sam clutched to his bosom. Every day, while Buddy sat with the headphones—and the reefer—keeping an eye out for the landlord who'd come by twice already wondering where the hell was his rent, Herman sat in the center of the room amid plaster chips and the multiplying clutter, staring at the television in his blue champ robe, the thermometer stuck in a corner of his mouth. And every so often he would glance at Buddy with eyes like two angry bees ready to burst out of his head and sting him. Well excuse me for living, Buddy would think.

8

Slumping on innumerable fronts, the Sticks eventually resorted to violence. Here was the story: fourth inning of the playoff game against the hot dog dagos, down 9–2, elimination staring them in the face, Herman at the dish. He'd popped up twice already, and the dagos were razzing him, blowing kisses, waving hankies, you-hooing him, gesturing with sissy wrists. Herman dug in, his face the color of a pomegranate. The pitcher showed him the ball twice, then came in with a gift down the middle. Herman took a murderous cut, spinning himself around. He went down. The ball went straight up. The pitcher settled under it and slapped it with his hands to the catcher, who caught it and tagged Herman with it daintily on the bill of his cap.

"You're out, sweetie," the catcher said.

Herman looked up at him for a second, nodding thoughtfully. Then he lunged at the asshole, goring him in the belly. They grappled at the plate.

The fight lasted nearly fifteen minutes and took both umpires, the league supervisor, and a bunch of cops who were just hanging out in their squads killing time to break it up. Small skirmishes erupted here and there, but the fight centered on home plate, where Herman had the catcher by the neck. A great mass of guys was on top of them, and every so often Herman would rear up out of the pile and knock people off his back, an arm still locked around the catcher's head. The bozo's tongue was sticking straight out like a lizard's.

The cops had to get out the riot gear to break it up, thumping guys on the shoulders and shins and noggin. When they finally pried Herman off the catcher, the guy was purple and had a series of welts running across his forehead from Herman pounding it against the dish. Herman himself was not unscathed. His shirt was a shredded rag hanging from his neck, and the bill of his hat had been torn off, the crown sitting on the top of his head like a skullcap. His nose was bleeding and a big knot, the size of a golf ball, was swelling out of the center of his forehead like a third eye. Banished, he left the field spitting teeth.

Buddy watched the whole thing from the refreshment stand, where he'd been slurping on a Sno-Kone.

Here's the real story, though. When the game finally resumed the dagos suddenly found themselves up against a different ball club. The Sticks were pissed. They stood in a line on the top step of the dugout and rattled bats. They shouted. They spat. Doc led off with a shot up the middle that spun the pitcher's cap off. Taped from calf to thigh, Harv grabbed a stick, went up there, and hit line. One angry ballplayer after another stepped to the plate, and when the inning was over the Sticks were up by five.

Suddenly alive they kept pouring it on, vets as well as younger Sticks contributing. Doc caught a guy looking with razzle dazzle, Sammy and Squirrel turned two. Goose gooned one. Whitey cracked a small bemused smile, seen by no one. Inning by inning the score mounted, until Buddy finally ended it with a leaping juggle job at the fence, the whole team pouring out to mob him. It was fives and tens, Dutch rubs, and soul shakes all around. Somebody said, "The cheer," and they all gathered around Harv, who led a lusty post-game version, an all but unprecedented occurrence in Stick tradition culminating in a blizzard of caps.

"The Corner," somebody said.

"Wait a minute. Where's Herm?"

"The Glicker!"

"Who sees the man that turned this club around?"

Nobody could come up with him. Buddy, who had been chunking mud off his spikes, got up and walked over to the car to see if the unsung Stick was sulking in there, but when he peered in he found instead of Herman two girls stowed away in the front seat, flushed and laughing at the crazy gig they were into.

"Hi," one of the intruders said. She was scooched down in the seat holding her bare feet in her hands. Buddy started at her dirty soles and went up, checking out the slim brown legs, the blue cut-offs cushioned tightly against her crotch, the bare tummy, the salmon-pink halter, the full mouth, the wide green eyes. She had wheat-colored hair braided in pigtails. Her cut-offs were cut off so high on her thighs that Buddy could glimpse white quarter moons of cheek. Her halter clung tightly to her breasts, revealing two prominent buttons the size of Hershey kisses. Buddy put her at seventeen. Beside her was a nearly identical copy, only her halter was yellow. They might have been the Doublemint Twins.

"Hello." Buddy did not say this. He sang it.

"I hope you're not pissed," the pink one said. "We been watching your games and—" She lapsed into giggles. The yellow one pushed at her shoulder.

"Mind? Why should I mind?" He stuck out his hand. "I'm Buddy."

"I'm Bobbi," the pink one said.

"I'm Ronnie," the yellow one said.

"Pleased to meet you." Buddy shook their moist little hands and slid in.

"That was some game," Bobbi said. "You were super."

"Thanks, Ronnie."

"Bobbi."

"Of course."

"Were you in the fight?"

"Sure."

"You didn't get hurt, did you?"

"Nope. Lucky, I guess."

"I'm glad," Bobbi said. "It was really humungous."

Buddy agreed. "Listen, now that we're acquainted, what would you girls like to do?"

Bobbi and Ronnie started to laugh and push at each other.

"We could go for a drink," Buddy suggested. "You want to go down to the Corner and have a few?"

"We're too young," Ronnie said.

"Of course. How dumb of me. Well, we could go for a ride."

"Why don't we get high and ball," Bobbi said.

Ronnie squealed and pushed Bobbi hard into Buddy. "I don't believe you said that."

"Well," Bobbi said.

"I don't believe you."

Buddy was sitting very still with both hands on the wheel. A small surprised smile had appeared on his face, but his mind was grinning from ear to ear.

"She's so bad," Ronnie said.

"Bad?" Buddy said. "Bobbi, are you bad?"

"If you think I'm bad," Bobbi said, "you should see her."

"Are you bad?" Buddy asked Ronnie.

"Very," Ronnie said.

"We're both bad," Bobbi said.

"Is that so?" Buddy said. "You know what? I'm bad too."

"We're all bad," Bobbi said.

"So," Buddy said, "you know what I'm wondering? I'm

wondering where we should go to do these terrible things. You bad girls have any ideas?"

They shook their heads. "We both live at home," Ronnie said.

Buddy suspected so. "We'll just have to go to my place then, won't we."

"I guess we will," Bobbi said.

Ronnie said, "Let's go."

Buddy started the Olds and had nearly pulled out of the lot when he remembered Herman. He slammed on the brakes, grinding metal. "Don't go away. I'll be right back."

He found Herman sitting under the huge tree beyond the center field fence, where the old guys went to watch the games and drink their cheap wine out of paper bags. Herman was sitting alone, facing away from the field. From a distance he looked like a stump rooted in the ground. Buddy came up and shook him.

"For Christ sake, Herman. What are you doing here?"

"What do *you* want?" Herman said. His eyes were puffy and his nose was swollen; the rims of his nostrils were red. The lump in the middle of his head now looked like the beginning of a horn. His suit might have been exploded off him.

"Get up," Buddy said. "I got a pair waiting for us in the car."

"A pair of what?" He spoke out of one side of his mouth only; he kept the other shut to hide his missing teeth.

"Babes! Young tomatoes! I'm talking seventeen, eighteen, brazen as anything. They're red-hot, Herm, I'm not shitting you."

"Tell me," Herman said, "these wouldn't be the same ones that were over the other night, would they?"

Buddy squeezed his forehead. "There's no time for this, Herm. I got them, take my word for it. They're back at the car, raring to go."

Herman spat blood. "I'm not interested."

Buddy flung out his arms. "Not interested? What's the matter with you? Are you nuts? These are sweet things—wait'll you get a load of them. Legs? Let me tell you."

"Legs?" Herman said.

Buddy made a whistling sound. "And tits! These are young girls I'm talking about. They're unabashed. One of them says, 'Let's ball,' just like that."

"Ball? She said, 'Let's ball'?"

"What do you think I'm trying to tell you. C'mon." He began tugging on Herman's arm. "Make haste, you homo. They're not going to wait all night."

Buddy's windows had quit rolling down, so that, when Buddy and Herman returned, the car was filled with a thick, pungent smoke. Bobbi and Ronnie were laughing. Bobbi held the jay.

"Ladies," Buddy said, "I want you to meet Herman. Herman, this is Bobbi and this bad girl over here is Ronnie."

" 'Lo, Herman," the girls chirped. They laughed and laughed.

Herman made a gruff sound and looked at Buddy. Buddy pushed him into the back seat. "Ronnie, why don't you climb in back with my friend Herman here. The guy, as you can plainly see, was in the thick of that humungous fight out there tonight. I think he'd appreciate it if you treated him nice."

They drove away. Buddy asked Bobbi for a poke on the jay. Bobbi scooched over so close she was practically sitting on his lap and handed it to him. Buddy took several rapid tokes, his eyes squinting, and handed it back to her. He immediately felt the top of his head swell. He smiled idiotically.

"Colombian," Bobbi said.

In the back, Ronnie was giving succor to Herman, running her fingers lightly over his wounds. "Quit," Herman said, knocking her hands away.

"Oh oh," Ronnie said. "Herman is grouchy." She repeated this a couple of times, pausing momentarily to suck on the joint. "Old grouchy Herman. Here, this'll mellow you out." She offered him the reefer.

"I don't want any," Herman muttered out of the side of his mouth. He was sitting stiffly to one side, as though he were traveling on the edge of a cliff.

Up front, Bobbi was fooling with the dials on the radio, punching one station after another. She had seized Buddy's hand and put it high up on her leg. Buddy could feel the silky hairs. Her other hand perched on the bulge in his pants. Buddy stepped on it.

∞∞∞

The apartment was in its usual ransacked state when they got there—the empties, the tins and cellophane, the piles of dirty clothes, the plaster chips, the pans full of rusty water; the place smelled like a wrestling mat.

"Hip digs," Bobbi said.

Buddy's head felt like a balloon. He took out a bottle of Wild Turkey he had bought on the way back and poured himself a shot, then offered the bottle to Bobbi. She made a face at it. "How can you drink that shit?" She reached into her pocket and produced an assortment of pills. "Ludes? Acid?"

"Acid?" Buddy said. "You got to be kidding. Nobody takes that stuff anymore. It's laced with horse dope, for Christ sake. It'll make you nuts." Many years ago, in his college days, Buddy had taken acid once and eventually had to admit himself into the infirmary, certain his heart had not beaten for forty-five minutes.

Ronnie was stretching in the center of the room. She began casually undressing, reaching around and unsnapping her halter, an act that caused Herman to grip the arms of his chair as though he meant to pull them off.

"Uh, Ronnie," Buddy said. "Herman and I are pretty tired from the game. I don't think either of us are into any group stuff at the moment."

Ronnie made a face. "Maybe later?"

"Maybe. Why don't you and Herm go into the bedroom there."

"Well, okay." She reached down and grabbed Herman's hand. "C'mon, old grouchy Herman. We might as well get it on." She dragged him to his feet and led him around the corner to the bedroom, Herman walking stiffly, his eyes glazed. She might have been leading a beast of burden.

Buddy poured himself another shot of Turkey. When he turned around, Bobbi was wearing only a pair of lime-green underpants. They were shaped like home plate, about a third the size. She had put on a jazzy Latin album and was reading the liner notes, her rump bouncing to the rhythm. Buddy watched her a minute, his blood roaring. He felt dangerous, crazy. He put down his drink.

"Hey."

"Hey what?" She faced him and ceremoniously undid her hair. It fell to the tops of her small, conical breasts, which were deeply tanned and peaked in tips that were all nipple. Jo, he dimly recalled, had a pair almost exactly like them. The points of her hips tapered to trim thighs that left plenty of space between her legs.

"Hey, come over here a second."

"Hey, what for?"

Buddy could dig this sort of sex play. Smirking, his brows arched, he went over to her and, starting at her shoulders, began running his hands down her sides. Her skin was buttery. He kissed her small wet mouth, sticky with some kind of fruity lipstick. There were tongues; his head reeled. He slipped a finger down the back of her pants, probing the cleft. Suddenly she eeled away.

"That tickles."

She skipped over to the couch and jumped on it, bouncing up and down. Dust flew. Buddy was ripping off his uniform.

"Wait! Leave it on."

"Huh?"

She smiled, showing him her tongue. "I was hoping you'd leave it on. When I thought about this, I always pictured you with your uniform on."

"Tell you what," Buddy said, slipping out of his pants. "I'll leave my cap on."

He sauntered over to her, letting her get a full load of his physique, then eased himself onto the couch and began kissing her mouth, her throat. His hand, splayed across her concave tummy, inched to the bristly hair. He twirled some around a finger, tugging just enough to make it hurt. He was not without his tricks. Her legs opened and closed, her heels bounced together. She began to make soft fluting sounds. Buddy reached up and snapped off the light.

She reached up and snapped it back on. "Everyone knows it's no fun in the dark."

Buddy happened to prefer it in the dark, but he wasn't about to make a big issue over it. When it came to screwing he was a fairly reasonable guy. Flinging off his cap, he bent his head to her breasts and went to town, sucking, licking, stiffening the nipples between his teeth. He pushed them together so he could get at them both at the same time. She put her palms on the top of his head and began pushing him down. Buddy resisted. He did not regard eating pussy the greatest joy in life. It had been his experience that once you started, some chicks wouldn't let you quit, and you'd have to stay down there for twenty or thirty minutes until your entire face was chafed raw. It was his belief that if you got some chicks started on this you could get completely sidetracked, delaying unnecessarily or postponing entirely the real stuff. Nevertheless, if this child wanted it so bad he supposed he could give her a taste. He moved down slowly, his tongue describing various geometric figures while she arched against him, gritting her teeth. He tarried at the mound and then dove for home, burying his face in her swampy center.

He gave her all the moves he knew. He licked and chewed her, sucked on her button. He spread her apart and thrilled her with a fluttering tongue. She was making loud throaty moans, her hands clamped to the sides of his head. He used his nose on her. She scissored him with her thighs and, placing her heels against the arm rest, began thrusting against him, rubbing herself against his entire face. This was just the sort of action Buddy had been talking about. Soon he was drenched from chin to brow. His tongue ached. Her hair was working over the bridge of his nose like sandpaper. Buddy thought, that's about all of that and, putting his hands on the inside of her thighs, pried her legs apart and extricated himself.

The girl gave a sharp cry. "I'm almost there."

"Don't worry about it," Buddy reassured her. He was a large guy, everywhere. He had a big one and was fully confident it would meet with her complete satisfaction. Rearing up, he guided himself with a finger and eased all the way in. She was surprisingly loose and yet, he thought, who but a fool argues about his place in heaven? Grinning, he looked at her for a reaction but she was playing it cool behind hooded eyes.

Buddy liked it slow. He liked to take his time. He went for the deluxe accommodations with champagne and a bubble bath at the end. He and Jo could go on forever, fooling with angles and positions, throwing in some fancy stuff, building it all up to a cymbal-crashing finish. Jo had great moves, good hands, stamina. She could work him over like a whole team of experts. Her pussy had nuance. He had no sooner checked into this youngster, though, than she started bucking against him so rapidly he had to grip the back of the sofa to keep from falling off. He felt like he had mounted an amusement park ride.

"C'mon," the girl was saying. "Move it."

"Don't worry about it." He thrust into her so hard the opposite end of the couch flew up.

So it was going to be a sprint. So he could handle that. He quit fooling. Putting both hands under her buttocks, he lifted her up until she was practically bent double, her legs high in the air. This was his Attila position, the one he and Jo usually saved for the cymbal-crashing finish. She shook her head and wriggled back down, planting her heels firmly in the cushion and cutting him off at the pass. Reaching back, he grabbed her ankles and lifted her legs high again. She tried to draw them back down, failed, then tricked him by locking them around his back and heeling him hard in the kidneys. Buddy put his hand under her jaw and pushed her head into the arm rest.

"Okay," the girl said. "That's it. Off."

"What?"

"You heard me. Lemme up."

"Now? You're out of your mind."

"Get the fuck off of me!" She began thumping him on the head and ears. Buddy grabbed her wrists and, pinning her with his full weight, began a series of quick deep thrusts designed to end this farce as quickly as possible. The girl went absolutely still. She examined her fingernails. Buddy felt himself losing it. He squinted shut his eyes and imagined him and Jo in a cymbal-crashing finish, imagined Jo rolling her ass, working, talking to him dirty. It was no good. He was shriveling up. He went slower and slower. Finally, when he stopped altogether, he had nothing left at all, his crank as small and useless as a stub under the belly of a fat guy.

He pushed himself up and rolled away and sat for a minute, contemplating himself with dismay and astonishment. Never before had such a thing happened, not even when he was so loaded he could barely see. Hadn't he always been ever-ready Buddy, a hard-charging guy, present and eager for duty? He hung his head, groaned. Presently he heard voices buzzing around him like mosquitoes.

"I got a dud," Ronnie was saying. "He couldn't get it up."

"Head?"

"Are you kidding me?"

"Yeah, well at least he didn't try to pull a King Kong number on you."

"Fill me in."

"Right in the middle of it he gets weird and starts like pulling my legs off."

"No shit."

"Swear to God. Me? I just fished out. Kong here couldn't pull it off. Zilch. Wipeout city. Wasn't it, Kong?"

Buddy shut his eyes. At that moment he was attempting to render himself invisible.

"Hey, how I look? I got any marks on me?"

"I don't see any. Hey, you got the book?"

"In my bag."

Ronnie went over to the bag and pulled out a little black book. She thumbed to the middle of it until she found a blank page. "Hey, Mickey Mantle, you got a pencil?"

"By the phone," Buddy said, gesturing feebly.

Ronnie went into the kitchen and got the stub of purple crayon, the self-same tool Buddy had used to jot down his strong points. Ronnie and Bobbi held a naked conference directly above him.

"You got the names?" Bobbi said.

"I got mine. Glick. Herman Glick, Mister No Dick."

They laughed, pushing at each other. Ronnie wrote it down.

"Hey," Bobbi called out. "What's your last name?"

"Barnes."

"Spell it."

Buddy spelled it for her.

"Well," Ronnie said, "what do you think?"

"Can't be a D," Bobbi said.

"No way," Ronnie said. "Not even an F."

"The way I see it, can only be one thing."

Ronnie nodded. "Wipeout."

"Worse, even."

Buddy lifted his head. "Worse than a wipeout?"

" 'Fraid so, Johnny Bench," Bobbi said. " 'Fraid you're a T.W."

Buddy groaned. "A T.W.?"

"Uh-huh," they both said. "Total Wipeout."

ΟΟΟΟ

Buddy was lying naked on the couch with a pillow over his useless tool and staring at the gaps in the ceiling when, at the crack of dawn, Herman got up and began stalking through the apartment, hunting up his things and stuffing them into his duffel bag. He looked like hell. His swollen forehead protruded Cro-Magnon fashion over his puffy eyes. His upper lip curled away from his teeth; a purple knot distorted a cheekbone. His hair was gathered on the top of his head like a wheat stalk. Periodically he would turn and cough abjectly in Buddy's direction. He did not appear to have slept.

Buddy had been lying on the couch with the pillow over his tool ever since the girls had split in an extravaganza of giggling ridicule. He too hadn't slept. He just kept lying there, thinking. Every so often he would shut his eyes and groan. He did not feel at all well. He felt like he was coming down with something. He had this pain. The bottle of Turkey, now half empty, lay on the table beside his last five-dollar bill.

He kept trying to change the subject, forcing himself to think about good things and happier times. He thought of ball, replaying some particularly outstanding games he'd had in which he'd climbed walls, made one-hand stabs and over-the-shoulders. He counted his conquests, a bountiful bunch which he arranged like a museum curator into various categories. There were the girls of his awakening, the girls of his young bullhood, the girls of his mature, golden years. He toured the premises, inspecting the gallery of redheads, the hall of blondes. He visited the moaners and the shriekers and the ones who shook all over. He spent an agreeable time in the Big Knocker Room. Some he dallied at—pancake Nan, kinky Flo, naughty Judy, zealous Dominique who later firebombed the local VFW and had her picture displayed in the post office. He stopped, of course, at his first, Arlene Glee, whom he'd possessed in a Studebaker behind diamond number three and who, many years later at a chance encounter in the bleachers at Wrigley Field, accused him of being the real father of Jeremy Clyde, her nine-year-old son.

He was still lying there, thinking about what it would be like going through the rest of his life without a hard-on, when Herman came over and started rooting around the couch on his hands and knees. Buddy massaged his eyeballs.

"You mind telling me what the fuck you're doing, Herman?"

"Looking for my fucking shoe."

"You got to find it right now, huh, at the crack of dawn?"

"Yes." He stood there, looming over him, looking like the creature that had crawled out of somewhere. "Get up. You're on my shoe."

Buddy passed a hand over his face and sat up, enabling Herman to pry his shoe out from behind a cushion. "Going somewhere?"

"Home."

Buddy grunted. "That figures."

Herman pointed the shoe at him. "Just lay off. I never should've listened to you in the first place."

"Sure," Buddy said. "I'm the guy. It's all my fault."

Herman didn't say anything. He continued to scoop his belongings into the duffel bag while Buddy muttered about what a bad person he was. "Blame me," he was saying. "It was all my doing. I'm a really terrible guy . . ." He looked over and saw Herman scoop the five-dollar bill off the table in passing. "That's it. Now rob me of my last five bucks."

Herman wheeled. "What are you talking about? This fin is mine."

"Your head is up your ass, Herman. It's mine. I left it there last night."

"You're crazy."

"Is that right. If you weren't such a moron you'd know that's where I always leave my dough." He wiggled his fingers. "Fork it over."

"Get bent. This is my bill. You screwed me over but you're not screwing me out of this." He stuffed the bill down his pants.

Buddy sat up, a murderous enzyme racing through his blood. "See if you can get this through that block of cement on top of your shoulders: that fiver is mine. Now fish it out of your pants and put it back on the table."

Herman laughed in his face. "You and what army?"

Buddy stood. "Okay, Herman. I'm through fooling. I want that bill."

"Guess what," Herman said. "I don't care if it is your bill. I'm taking it. How do you like that, asswipe?"

"Asswipe? You calling me an asswipe, Herman?"

"Definitely." Herman pointed rearward. "Your face and my buns, buster."

Buddy waved his hands. "Okay, Herm. Let's not be juvenile about this. Just put it back on the table and I'll forget the whole thing ever happened."

"Kiss this."

Buddy looked away momentarily and then lashed out with a sneaky right that collided with the side of Herman's head. He immediately flung his hand in the air in pain. Unfazed, Herman put his palm under Buddy's chin and pushed him backwards over the table, which cracked in two, Buddy falling amid the splintered pieces. Herman turned to scoop up his blue champ robe and Buddy leaped on his back, the two of them staggering through the living room knocking over furniture. The stereo went over. Herman steadied himself by pulling down a bookshelf while Buddy socked him in the ear, on top of the head. They lurched into the kitchen where Herman dislodged his assailant by swinging him into the sink. The fantastic pyramid of dishes teetered, fell.

They looked at each other, red-faced, panting. Buddy flung a saucer off his head and said, "Now you're going to have to kill me, ape-man." He scrambled to his feet and mounted another attack, but Herman dug a fist into his solar plexus, purging him of air. He sank back down, gasping, bright colors flaring in his eyes. His face wore a thoughtful expression, as though he were trying to remember how to breathe. He had still not quite gotten the hang of it again when Herman gathered up the last of his things and left, slamming the door so viciously the vibrations started several new avalanches in the living room.

After a while Buddy got up and dragged himself through the shambles back to the couch. Shoving aside broken pieces of table, he picked up the bottle of Wild Turkey which, he was glad to note, still had the cap on. He unscrewed it and took a swig. His hands trembled. His mind was as blank as a stone. He sat there for a long time, a tiresomely bright sun shining in his eyes, and listened to the hum of rush-hour traffic. He heard the sounds of shops opening, the blare of transistor radios, the voices of young girls calling out to each other as they got off buses, texts clutched to their loosely bound bosoms. The delicatessen guy right below him was sweeping off his stoop, whistling a happy tune. Buddy went over and slammed shut the window. He went around slamming shut all the windows, drawing down all the shades.

Around noon he began hitting the Turkey in earnest, drinking it out of a yellow plastic cup he had fetched from the bathroom. The cup had a picture of an alligator on it and some type of green scum growing inside. The alligator's name was Albert. "How's it hanging, Albert?" Buddy honked from time to time.

Around two he became filled with a sudden restless energy. The apartment was oppressively still and seemed to be shrinking in on him. Since he had nothing else to do, he decided to straighten it up, crawling over to the records fanned across the floor and putting them in their jackets. He slid three or four in, stacked them neatly against the wall, then got up and went back to the couch and poured himself a drink.

Around four, when Doc returned, Buddy was out, naked, on the floor. Doc looked at him, then took in the whole apartment with a sweeping glance. The books, the stereo, the broken furniture, the flotsam and jetsam of hasty meals —if he had put up a tribe of gorillas for the past three months, the place couldn't have looked any worse. Thoughtfully twirling his mustache, he got a pan from the kitchen, filled it with water, and poured it on Buddy who rolled over, shielding himself with an arm. Doc held the pan high for an instant, as though he meant to smite Buddy with it. His arm trembled. Finally, he lowered it to his side.

"You don't have to tell me," Buddy was saying. "I can take a hint."

9

Jo was sitting under an asparagus plant reading a book about the energy crisis when the phone rang. She looked up, wondering who it could be this time. Gary the appliance salesman had already called, but it could be him calling again—he had been known to call her two or three times the same night, like a teenager. It could be Bob the swinging dentist, who usually called about this time to ask her to spend the weekend with him on his cabin cruiser, *Lucky Lady,* which he piloted in all weathers in his navy blue skipper's cap ornamented with phallic anchors. It could be her marketing prof, Dr. Ted. It could even be Buddy. Jo didn't answer. She didn't want to talk to any of those individuals.

She held the book on her lap and counted the rings. She counted eleven before they finally quit. Sometimes she counted twenty. Sometimes the phone rang so much that she would finally have to pick it up and carry it to the closet and stuff it under the towels.

Gary was the worst. He would not let her alone. It was impossible to get away from him because they worked in the same department store. He was in appliances. He would come up on his breaks and watch her ring up purchases, his pudgy face transfixed in a cowlike expression, his elbow balanced on the counter. He would invite himself to lunch with her, follow her through the mall to a cafeteria specializing in tuna noodle casserole, follow her through the line and then to a table where he would stare at her the whole time she ate, methodically following the movement of her fork to her mouth with his large watery blue eyes, his hands clapped to the sides of his head. He would suddenly appear on elevators with her or materialize behind her, and she would turn around and bump into him.

"Gary," she would say, exasperated.

"At your service."

She supposed she had only herself to blame. The one time she had broken down over what had happened between her and Buddy, she had made the mistake of doing it in the store, in front of a stack of cootie games. Almost immediately Gary had stepped out from behind a display of Wiffle bats and stood beside her, weaving his head in agitation. Before she realized what she was doing, she was crying on his shoulder and saying things that were none of his business. This uncharacteristic demonstration of vulnerability affected Gary like a religious experience. His soul was uplifted. His heart was a zeppelin of love.

From that moment he assumed the role of her confidant. If she needed a sympathetic ear he would provide a pair of large ones, prominently lobed. If she needed a helping hand he would be there, chubby fingers extended. She continued to make mistakes. She made the mistake of going to a movie after work with him in one of the eight theaters the mall contained (she watched the movie; he watched her), and then she made the mistake of inviting him over for a pizza. Predictably, he got some on his trousers, and while she was dabbing at the stain with a rag he bent his head and quickly fastened his lips to hers. This intimacy proved too much.

doubt. Well—poor thing. I am sorry for women, but
there is nothing to be done since Nature has decreed
they shall grow old.

I got up and shook out the folds of my mackintosh
—a most useful garment in those damp places—and
threw away the end of my cigar. "I am now going
to retire for the night," I explained, as she turned her
head at my rustling, "and if you take my advice you
will not sit here till you get rheumatism."

She looked at me as though she did not hear. In
that light her appearance was certainly quite passable :
quite as passable as that of any of the statues they
make so much fuss about ; and then of course with
proper eyes instead of blank spaces, and eyes garnished
with that speciality of hers, the ridiculously long eye-
lashes. But I knew what she was like in broad day,
I knew how thin she was, and I was not to be imposed
upon by tricks of light ; so I said in a matter of fact
manner, seizing the opportunity for gentle malice in
order to avenge myself a little for her repeated and
unjustified attacks on me, "You will not be wise to
sit there longer. It is damp, and you and I are hardly
as young as we were, you know."

Any normal woman, gentle as this was, would have
shrivelled. Instead she merely agreed in an absent
way that it was dewy, and turned up her face to the
stars again.

"Looking for the Great Bear, eh ? " I remarked,
following her gaze as I buttoned my wrap.

She continued to gaze, motionless. "No, but—
don't you see ? At Christ Whose glory fills the skies,"
she said,—both profanely and senselessly, her face in

that light exactly like the sort of thing one sees in
the windows of churches, and her voice as though she
were half asleep.

So I hied me (poetry being the fashion) to my bed,
and lay awake in it for some time being sorry for
Menzies-Legh, for really no man can possibly like
having a creepy wife.

But (luckily) *autres temps autres mœurs*, as our unbalanced but sometimes felicitous neighbours across
the Vosges say, and next morning the poetry of the
party was, thank heaven, clogged by porridge.

It always was at breakfast. They were strangely
hilarious then, but never poetic. Poetry developed
later in the day as the sun and their spirits sank
together, and flourished at its full growth when there
were stars or a moon. That morning, our first Sunday,
a fresh breeze blew up from the Weald below and a
cloudless sun dazzled us as it fell on the white cloth
of the table set out in the middle of the field by
somebody—I expect it was Mrs. Menzies-Legh—who
wanted to make the most of the sun, and we had to
hold on our hats with one hand and shade our eyes
with the other while we ate.

Uncomfortable ? Of course it was uncomfortable.
Let no one who loves to be comfortable ever caravan.
Neither let any one who loves order and decency do
so. They may take it from me that there is never any
order, and even less frequently is there any decency.
I can give you an example from that Sunday morning.
I was sitting at the table with the ladies, on a seat
(as usual) too low for me, and that (also as usual)
slanted on the uneven ground, with my feet slightly

too cold in the damp grass and my head slightly too hot in the bright sun, and the general feeling of subtle discomfort and ruffledness that is one of the principal characteristics of this form of pleasure-taking, when I saw (and so did the ladies) Jellaby emerge from his tent—in his shirt sleeves if you please—and fastening up a mirror on the roof of his canvas lair proceed then and there in the middle of the field to lather his face and then to shave it.

Edelgard, of course, true to her early training at once cast down her eyes and was careful to keep them averted during the remainder of the meal, but nobody else seemed to mind ; indeed, Mrs. Menzies-Legh got out her camera and focussing him with deliberate care snap-shotted him.

Were these people getting blunted as the days passed to the refinements and necessary precautions of social intercourse ? I had been stirred to much silent indignation by the habit of the gentlemen of walking in their shirt-sleeves, and had not yet got used to that, but to see Jellaby dressing in an open field was a little more than I could endure in silence. For if, I asked myself rapidly, Jellaby dresses (shaving being a part of dressing) out of doors in the morning, what is to prevent his doing the opposite in the evening ? Where is the line ? Where is the logical limit ? We had now been three days out, and we had already got to this. Where, I thought, should we have got to in another six ? Where should we be by, say, the following Sunday ?

I cannot think a promiscuous domesticity desirable, and am one of those who strongly disapprove of that

worst example of it, the mixed bathing or *Familienbad*
which blots with practically unclothed Jews of either
sex our otherwise decent coasts. Never have I allowed
Edelgard to indulge in it, nor have I done so myself.
It is a deplorable spectacle. We used to sit and
watch it for hours, in a condition of ever-increasing
horror and disgust,—it was quite difficult to find seats
sometimes, so many of our friends were there being
disgusted too.

But these denizens of the deep at the points where
the deep was a *Familienbad* were, as I have said,
chiefly Jews and their Jewesses, and what can you
expect ? Jellaby however, in spite of his other
infirmities, was not yet a Jew ; he was everything
else I think, but that crowning infamy had up to then
been denied him.

But not to be one and yet to behave with the
laxness of one within view of the rest of the party
was very inexcusable. "Are there no hedges to
this field ? " I cried in indignant sarcasm, looking
pointedly at each of its four hedges in turn and
raising my voice so that he could hear.

"Oh Baron dear, it's Sunday," said Mrs. Menzies-
Legh, no longer a rather nice-looking if irreverent
cameo in a velvet case, but full of morning militancy.
"Don't be cross till to-morrow. Save it up, or what
will you do on Monday ? "

"Be, I trust, just as capable of distinguishing
between the permitted and the non-permitted as I am
to-day," was my ready retort.

"Oh, oh," said Mrs. Menzies-Legh, shaking her
head and smiling as though she were talking to a child

or a feeble-minded; and turning her camera on to me
she took my photograph.

"Pray why," I inquired with justifiable heat,
"should I be photographed without my consent?"

"Because," she said, "you look so deliciously
cross. I want to have you in my scrap-book like that.
You looked then exactly like a baby I know."

"Which baby?" I asked, frowning and at a loss
how to meet this kind of thing conversationally. And
there was Edelgard, all ears; and if a wife sees her
husband being treated disrespectfully by other women
is it not very likely that she soon will begin to treat
him so herself? "Which baby?" I asked; but
knew myself inadequate.

"Oh a perfectly respectable baby," said Mrs.
Menzies-Legh carelessly, putting her camera down
and going on with her breakfast, "but irritable and
exacting about things like bottles."

"But I do not see what I have to do with bottles,"
I said nettled.

"Oh no—you haven't. Only it looks at its nurse
just like you did then if they're late, or not full
enough."

"But I did not look at its nurse," I said angrily,
becoming still more so as they all (including my wife)
laughed.

I rose abruptly. "I will go and smoke," I said.

Of course I saw what she meant about the nurse
the moment I had spoken, but it is inexcusable to
laugh at a man because he does not immediately
follow the sense (or rather the senselessness) of a
childishly skipping conversation. I am as ready as

any one to laugh at really amusing phrases or incidents, but being neither a phrase nor an incident myself I do not see why I should be laughed at. Surely it is unworthy of grown men and women to laugh at each other in the way silly children do? It is ruin to the graces of social intercourse, to the courtliness that should uninterruptedly distinguish the well-born. But there was a childish spirit pervading the whole party (with the exception of myself) that seemed to increase as the days went by, a spirit of unreasoning glee and mischievousness which I believe is character- istic of very young and very healthy children. Even Edelgard was daily becoming more calf-like as we say, daily descending nearer to the level occupied at first only by the two nondescripts, that level at which you begin to play idiotic and heating games like the one the English call Blind Man's Buff (an obviously foolish name, for what is buff?) and which we so much more sensibly call Blind Cow. Therefore I, having no intention at my age and in my position of joining in puerilities or even of seeming to countenance them by my presence, said abruptly " I will smoke "—and strode away to do it.

One of the ladies called after me to inquire if I were not going to church with them, but I pretended not to hear and strode on towards the shelter of the hedge, giving Jellaby as I passed him such a look as would have caused any one not overgrown with the leather substitute for skin peculiar to persons who set order, morals, and religion at defiance, to creep con- founded into his tent and stay there till his face was ready and his collar on. He, however, called out with the geniality born of brazenness that it was a jolly morning; of which, of course, I took no notice.

In the dry ditch beneath the hedge on the east side of the field sat Lord Sigismund beside his *batterie de cuisine* watching over, with unaccountable and certainly misplaced kindness, the porridge and the coffee that were presently to be Jellaby's. While he watched he smoked his pipe, stroked his dog, and hummed snatches of what I supposed were psalms with the pleasant humming of the good, the happy, and the well-born.

Near him lay Menzies-Legh, his dark and sinister face bent over a book. He nodded briefly in response to my lifted hat and morning salutation, while Lord Sigismund, full as ever of the graciousness of noble birth, asked me if I had had a good night.

"A good night, and an excellent breakfast thanks to you, Lord Sidge," I replied; the touch of playfulness contained in the shortened name lightening the courteous correctness of my bow as I arranged myself next to him in the ditch.

Menzies-Legh got up and went away. It was characteristic of him that he seemed always to be doing that. I hardly ever joined him but he was reminded by my approach of something he ought to be doing and went away to do it. I mentioned this to Edelgard during the calm that divided one difference of opinion from another, and she said he never did that when she joined him.

"Dear wife," I explained, "you have less power to remind him of unperformed duties than I possess."

"I suppose I have," said Edelgard.

"And it is very natural that it should be so. Power, of whatever sort it may be, is a masculine attribute. I do not wish to see my little wife with any."

"Neither do I," said she.

"Ah—there speaks my own good little wife."

"I mean, not if it is that sort."

"What sort, dear wife ? "

"The sort that reminds people whenever I come that it is time they went."

She looked at me with the odd look that I observed for the first time during our English holiday. Often have I seen it since, but I cannot recollect having seen it before. I, noticing that somehow we did not understand each other, patted her kindly on the shoulder, for of course she cannot always quite follow me, though I must say she manages very creditably as a rule.

"Well, well," I said, patting her, "we will not quibble. It is a good little wife, is it not." And I raised her chin by means of my forefinger, and kissed her.

This, however, is a digression. I suppose it is because I am unfolding my literary wings for the first time that I digress so frequently. At least I am aware of it, which is in itself I should say a sign of literary instinct. My Muse has been, so to speak, kept in bed without stopping till middle age, and is now suddenly called upon to get up and go for a walk. Such a muse must inevitably stagger a little at first. I will, however, endeavour to curb these staggerings, for I perceive that I have already written more than can be conveniently read aloud in one evening, and though I am willing the same friends should come on two, I do not know that I care to see them on as many as three. Besides, think of all the sandwiches.

(This last portion of the narrative, from " one evening " to " sandwiches " will of course be omitted in public.)

I will therefore not describe my conversation with Lord Sigismund in the ditch beyond saying that it was extremely interesting, and conducted on his side (and I hope on mine) with the social skill of a perfect gentleman.

It was brought to an end by the arrival of Jellaby and his dog, which was immediately pounced on by Lord Sigismund's dog who very properly resented his uninvited approach, and they remained inextricably mixed together for what seemed an eternity of yells, the yells rending the Sabbath calm and mingling with the distant church bells, and all proceeding from Jellaby's dog, while Lord Sigismund's, a true copy of his master, did that which he had to do with the silent self-possession of, if I may so express it, a dog of the world.

The entire company of caravaners including old James ran up with cries and whistling to try to separate them, and at last Jellaby, urged on I suppose to deeds of valour by knowing the eyes of the ladies upon him, made a mighty effort and tore them asunder, himself getting torn along his hand as the result.

Menzies-Legh helped Lord Sigismund to drag away the naturally infuriated bull-terrier, and Jellaby, looking round, asked me to hold his dog while he went and washed his hand. I thought this a fair instance of the brutal indifference to other people's tastes that characterises the British nation. Why did he not ask old James, who was standing there doing nothing ? Yet what was I to do ? There were the ladies looking on, among them Edelgard, motionless, leaving me to my fate, though if either of us knows anything about dogs it is she who does. Jellaby had got the beast by the collar, so I thought perhaps holding him by the tail would do. It was true it was the merest stump, but at least it was at the other end. I therefore grasped it, though with no little trouble, for for some unknown reason just as my hand approached it, it began to wag.

" No, no—catch hold of the collar. He's all right, he won't do anything to you," said Jellaby, grinning and keeping his wounded hand well away from him while the nondescripts ran to fetch water.

The brute was quiet for a moment, and under the circumstances I do think Edelgard might have helped. She knows I cannot bear dogs. If she had held his head I would not have minded going on holding his tail, and at home she would have made herself useful as a matter of course. Here, however, she did nothing of the sort, but stood tearing up a perfectly good clean handkerchief into strips in order, forsooth, to render that assistance to Jellaby which she denied her own husband. I did take the dog by the collar, there being no other course open to me, and was thankful to find that he was too tired and too much hurt to do anything to me. But I have never been a dog lover, carefully excluding them from my flat in Storchwerder and selling the one Edelgard had had as a girl and

wanted to saddle me with on her marriage. I
remember how long it took, she being then still
composed of very raw material, to make her understand I had married her and not her *Dachshund*.
Will it be believed that her only answer to my
arguments was a repeated parrot-like cry of " But
he is so sweet " ? A feeble plea indeed to set against
the logic of my reasons. She shed tears, I remember,
in quantities more suited to fourteen than twenty-
four (as I pointed out to her), but later on did acknow-
ledge, in answer to my repeated inquiries, that the
furniture and carpets were no doubt the better for it,
though for a long time she had a tendency which I
found some difficulty in repressing to make tiresomely plaintive allusions to the fact that the buyer
(I sold the dog by auction) had chanced to be a maker
of sausages and she had not happened to meet the
dog since in the streets. Also, until I spoke very
seriously to her about it, for months she would not
touch anything potted, after always having been
particularly fond of this type of food.

I soon found myself alone and unheeded with
Jellaby's dog, while Jellaby himself, the flattered
centre of the entire body of ladies, was having his
wound dressed. My wife washed it, Jumps held the
bucket, Mrs. Menzies-Legh bound it up, Frau von
Eckthum provided one of her own safety pins (I saw
her take it out of her blouse), and Jane lent her sash
for a sling. As for Lord Sigismund, after having seen
to his own dog's wounds (all made by Jellaby's dog)
he came back and with truly Christian goodness
offered to wash and doctor Jellaby's dog. His

attitude, indeed, during these dog-fights was only one possible to a person of the very highest breeding. Never a word of reproach, yet it was clear that if Jellaby's dog had not been there there would have been no fighting. And he exhibited a real distress over Jellaby's wound, while Jellaby, thoroughly thick-skinned, laughed and declared he did not feel it ; which no doubt was true, for that sort of person does not I am convinced feel anything like the same amount we others do.

The end of this pleasant Sabbath morning episode was that Jellaby took his dog to the nearest village containing a veterinary surgeon, and Menzies-Legh was found in the ditch almost as green as the surrounding leaves because—will it be believed ?—he could never stand the sight of blood !

My hearers will I am sure be amused at this. Of course many Britons must be the same, for it is unlikely that I should have chanced in those few days to meet the solitary instance, and I could hardly repress a hearty laugh at the spectacle of this specimen of England's manhood in a half fainting condition because he had seen a scratch that produced blood. What will he and his kind do on that battle-field of, no doubt, the near future, when the finest army in the world will face them ? It will not be scratches that poor Menzies-Legh will have to look at then, and I greatly fear for his complexion.

Everybody ran in different directions in search of brandy. Never have I seen a man so green. He was at least ashamed of himself, and finding I was a moment alone with him and he not in a condition to get up and go away, I spoke an earnest word or two about the inevitably effeminating effect on a man of so much poetry-reading and art-admiring and dabbling in the concerns of the poor. Not thus, I explained, did the Spartans spend their time. Not thus did the ancient Romans, during their greatest period, behave. " You feel the situation of the poor, for instance, far more than the poor feel it themselves," I said, " and allow yourself to be worried into alleviating a wretchedness that they are used to and do not notice. And what, after all, is art ? And what, after all, is poetry ? And what, if you come to that, is wretchedness ? Do not weaken the muscles of your mind by feeding it so constantly on the pap of either your own sentimentality or the sentimentality of others. Pull down these artificial screens. Be robust. Accustom yourself to look at facts without flinching. Imitate the conduct of the modern Japanese, who take their children as part of their training to gaze on executions, and on their return cause the rice for their dinner to be served mixed with the crimson juices of the cherry, so that they shall imagine—"

But Menzies-Legh turned yet greener, and fainted away.

XIII

I AM accustomed punctually to discharge my obligations in what may be called celestial directions, holding it to be every man's duty not to put a millstone round a weaker vessel's neck by omitting to set a good example. Also, in the best sense of the word, I am a religious man. Did not Bismarck say, and has not the saying become part and parcel of the marrow of the nation, " We Germans fear God and nothing else in the world " ? In exactly I should say the same way and degree as Bismarck was, am I religious. At Storchwerder, where I am known, I go to church every alternate Sunday and allow myself to be advised and cautioned by the pastor, willing to admit it is his turn to speak and recognising that he is paid to do so, but reserving to myself the right to put him and keep him in his proper place during the fourteen secular days that divide these pious oases. Before our daily dinner also I say grace, a rare thing in households where there are no children to look on ; and if I do not, as a few of the stricter households do, conduct family prayers every day, it is because I do not like them.

There is, after all, a limit at which duty must retire before a man's personal tastes. We are not solely machines for discharging obligations. I see perfectly clearly that it is most good and essential that one's cook and wife should pray together, and even one's orderly, but I do not see that they require the assistance and countenance of the gentleman of the house while they do it.

I am religious in the best and highest sense of the word, a sense that soars far above family prayers, a sense in no way to be explained, any more than other high things are explainable. The higher you get in the regions of thought the more dumb you become. Also the more quiescent. Doing, as all persons of intellect know, is a very inferior business to thinking, and much more likely to make one hot. But these cool excursions of the intellect are not to be talked about to women and the lower classes. What would happen if they too decided to prefer quiescence? For them creeds and churches are positive necessities, and the plainer and more definite they are the better. The devout poor, the devout mothers of families, how essential they are to the freedom and comfort of the rest. The less you have the more it is necessary that you should be contented, and nothing does this so thoroughly as the doctrine of resignation. It would indeed be an unthinkable calamity if all the uneducated and the feeble-minded, the lower classes and the women, should lose their piety enough to want things. Women it is true are fairly safe so long as they have a child once a year, which is Nature's way of keeping them quiet; but it fills me with nothing short of horror when I hear of any discontent among the male portion of the proletariat.

That these people should have a vote is the one mistake that great and peculiarly typical German, the ever-to-be-lamented Bismarck, made. To reflect that power is in the hands of such persons, any power, even the smallest shred of it, alarms me so seriously that if I think of it on a Sunday morning, when perhaps I had decided to omit going to church for once and rest at home while my wife went, I hastily seize my parade helmet and hurry off in a fever of anxiety to help uphold the pillars of society.

Indeed it is of paramount necessity that we should cling to the Church and its teaching; that we should see that our wives cling; that we should insist on the clinging of our servants; and these Sunday morning reflections occurring to me as I look back through the months to that first Sunday out of our Fatherland, I seem to feel as I write (though it is now December and sleeting) the summer breeze blowing over the grass on to my cheek, to hear the small birds (I do not know their names) twittering, and to see Frau von Eckthum coming across the field in the sun and standing before me with her pretty smile and telling me she is going to church and asking whether I will go too. Of course I went too. She really was (and is, in spite of Storch-werder) a most attractive lady.

We went, then, together, Jellaby safely away at the veterinary surgeon's, Edelgard following behind with the two fledglings, who had achieved an unusually clean appearance and had more of the budding maiden about them than I had yet observed, and Lord Sigismund and Mrs. Menzies-Legh remaining with our patient, who had recovered enough to sit in a low chair in the shade and be read aloud to. Let us hope the book was virile. But I greatly doubt it, for his wife's voice in the peculiar sing-song that seems to afflict the voice of him who reads verses, zigzagged behind us some way across the field.

After our vagrant life of the last few days it seemed odd to be walking respectably along with no horse to lead, presently joining other respectable persons bent on the same errand. They seemed to know we were the dusty caravaners who had trudged past the afternoon before, and we were well stared at. In the church, too, an imposing lady in the pew in front of us sat sideways in her corner and examined us with calm attention through her eye-glass both before the service began and during it whenever the sitting portions of the ritual were reached. She was, we afterwards discovered, the lady of the manor or chief lady in the place, and it was in one of her fields we were camping. We heard that afternoon from the farmer that she had privately visited our camp the evening before with her bailiff and his dogs and observed us, also with the aid of her eye-glass, over the hedge as we sat absorbed round our supper, doubtful whether we were not a circus and ought not instantly to be moved on. I fancy the result of her scrutiny in church was very satisfactory. She could not fail to see that here she had to do with a gentleman of noble birth, and the ladies of the party, in pews concealing their short skirts but displaying their earrings, were seen to every advantage. I caught her eye so repeatedly that at last, quite involuntarily, and yielding to a natural instinct, I bowed—a little, not deeply out of considerations of time and place. She did not return my bow, nor did she after that look again, but attended during the rest of the service to her somewhat neglected devotions.

My hearers will be as much surprised as I was, though not half so tired, when I tell them that during the greater part of the service I was expected to remain on my knees. We Germans are not accustomed to our knees. I had certainly never used mine for praying purposes before; and inquiry later on elicited the information that the singular nation kneels every night by its beds before getting into them, and says prayers there too.

But it was not only the kneeling that shocked me (for if you ache and stiffen how can you properly pray? As Satan no doubt very well knew when he first put it into their heads to do it)—it was the extraordinary speed at which the service was run through. We began at eleven, and by a quarter to twelve we were, so to speak, ejected shriven. No flock can fatten on such a diet. How differently are the flocks of the Fatherland fed! There they grow fat indeed on the ample extemporisations of their pastor, or have every opportunity of doing so if they want to. Does he not address them for the best part of an hour? Which is not a moment too long for a meal that is to last seven days.

The English pastor, arrayed in white with two meaningless red ribbons down his back, preached for seven minutes, providing as I rapidly calculated exactly one minute's edification for each day of the week until the following Sunday. Alas for the

sheep of England! That is to say, alas from the
mere generally humane point of view, but not otherwise alas, for their disadvantage must always be our
gain, and a British sheep starved into socialism and
civil war is almost more valuable to us than a German
sheep which shall be fat with faith.

The pastor, evidently a militant man, preached
against the sin of bigotry, which would have been
all very well as far as it went and listened to by me
with the tolerance I am accustomed to bring to bear
on pulpit utterances if he had not in the same breath
—there was hardly time for more than one—called
down heaven's wrath on all who attend the meetings
or services of forms of faith other than the Anglican.
These other forms include, as I need not point out,
the Lutheran. Really I found it difficult to suppress
a smile at the poor man's folly. I longed for Luther
(a thing I cannot remember ever to have done before)
to rise up and scatter the blinded gentleman out of
his pulpit. But hardly had I got as far as this in
my thoughts than a hurried benediction, a hasty
hymn, a rapid passing round of the English equivalent
for what we call God's box, ended the service.
Genuinely shocked at this breathlessness—and you,
my hearers, who know no other worship than that
leisurely one in Storchwerder and throughout our
beloved Prussian land (I do not allude to Roman
Catholics beyond saying, in a spirit of tolerant
humanity, Poor things), that worship which fills the
entire morning, that composed and comfortable
worship during which you sit almost the whole time
so that no fatigue of the feet or knees shall distract

your thoughts from the matter in hand, you who
join sitting in our chorales, slow and dignified settings
of ancient sentiments with ample spaces between
the verses for the thinking of appropriate thoughts
in which you are assisted by the meditative organ,
and stand, as men should who are not slaves, to
pray, you will, I am sure, be shocked too—I decided
that here no doubt was one of the keys to the manifest
decadence of the British character. Reverence and
speed can never go together. Irreverence in the
treatment of its creeds is an inevitable sign that a
nation is well on that downward plane which jerks
it at last into the jaws of (say) Germany. Well, so
be it. Though irreverence is undoubtedly an evil,
and I am the first to deplore it, I cannot deplore it as
much as I would if it were not going to be the cause
of that ultimate jerking. And what a green and
fruitful land it is! *Es wird gut schmecken*, as we
men of healthy appetite say.

We walked home—an expression that used to
strike me as strangely ironical when home was only
grass and hedges—discussing these things. That is,
I discussed and Frau von Eckthum said Oh? But
the sympathy of the voice, the implied agreement
with my views, the appreciation of the way I put
them, the perfect mutual understanding expressed,
all this I cannot describe even if I would to you
prejudiced critics.

Edelgard went on ahead with the two young girls.
She and I did not at this point see much of each other,
but quite enough. Being human I got tired sometimes of being patient, and yet it was impossible to

be anything else inside a caravan with walls so thin that the whole camp would have to hear. Nor can you be impatient in the middle of a field : to be so comfortably you must be on the other side of at least a hedge ; so that on the whole it was best we should seldom be together.

With Frau von Eckthum, on the other hand, I never had the least desire to be anything but the mildest of men, and we walked home as harmoniously as usual to find when we arrived that, though we had in no way lingered, the active pastor was there before us.

With what haste he must have stripped off his ribbons and by what short cuts across ditches he had reached the camp so quickly I cannot say, but there he was, ensconced in one of the low chairs talking to the Menzies-Leghs as though he had known them all his life.

This want of ceremony, this immediate familiarity prevailing in British circles, was a thing I never got used to. With us, first of all the pastor would not have come at all, and secondly, once come, he would still have been in the stage of ceremonious preface when we arrived, and only emerged from his preliminary apologies to enter into the series of prayers for forgiveness which would round off his visit. Thus there would be no time so much as to reach the ice, far less to break it, and I am conservative enough and aristocratic enough to like ice : it is such an excellent preservative.

Mrs. Menzies-Legh was feeding her invalid with biscuits and milk. " Have some ? " said she to the pastor, holding out a cup of this attractive beverage without the least preliminary grace of speech.

He took it, for his part, without the least preliminary ceremony of polite refusal which would call forth equally polite pressure on her side and end with a tactful final yielding on his ; he took it without even interrupting his talk to Menzies-Legh, and stretching out his hand helped himself to a biscuit, though nobody had offered him one.

Now what can be the possible future of a nation deliberately discarding all the barriers of good manners that keep the natural brute in us suppressed ? Ought a man to be allowed to let this animal loose on somebody else's biscuit-plate ? It seems to me the hedge of ceremony is very necessary if you would keep it out, and it dwells in us all alike whatever country we may belong to. In Germany, feeling how near the surface it really is, we are particular and careful down to the smallest detail. Experience having taught us that the only way to circumvent it is to make the wire-netting, so to speak, of etiquette very thick, we do make it thick. And how anxiously we safeguard our honour, keeping it first of all inside these high and thick nets of rules, and then holding ourselves ready on the least approach to it to rise up and shed either our own or (preferably) somebody else's blood in its defence. And apart from other animals, the rabbit of Socialism, with its two eldest children Division of Property and Free Love, is kept out most effectually by this netting. Jellabies and their like, tolerated so openly in Britain, find it difficult to burrow beneath the careful and far-reaching insistence on forms and ceremonies observed in other countries. Their horrid doctrines have little effect on such an armour. Not that I am not modern enough and large minded enough to be very willing to divide my property if I may choose the person to divide it with. All those Jewish bankers in Berlin and Hamburg, for instance,—when I think of a division with them I see little harm and some comfort; but to divide with my orderly Hermann, or with the man who hangs our breakfast rolls in a bag on the handle of our back door every morning, is another matter. As for Free Love, it is not to be denied that there are various things to be said for that too, but not in this place. Let me return. Let me return from a subject which, though legitimate enough for men to discuss, is yet of a somewhat slippery complexion, to the English pastor helping himself to our biscuits, and describe shortly how the same scene would have unrolled itself in a field in the vicinity of Storchwerder, supposing it possible that a party of well-born Germans should be camping in one, that the municipal authorities had not long ago turned them out after punishing them with fines, and that the pastor of the nearest church had dared to come, hot from his pulpit, and intrude on them.

Pastor, approaching Menzies-Legh and his wife (translated for the nonce into two aristocratic Germans) with deferential bows from the point at which he first caught their eyes, and hat in hand :

I entreat the *Herrschaften* to pardon me a thousand times for thus obtruding myself upon their notice. I beg them not to take it amiss.

It is in reality an unexampled shamelessness
on my part, but—may I be permitted to introduce myself ?   My name is Schultz.

He would here bow twice or thrice each to the
Menzies-Leghs, who after staring at him in some
natural surprise—for what excuse could the man possibly have ?—get up and greet him with solemn dignity,
both bowing, but neither offering to shake hands.

Pastor, bowing again profoundly, and still holding
his hat in his hand, repeats :

My name is Schultz.

Menzies-Legh (who it must be remembered is for
the moment a noble German) would probably here
say under his breath :

And mine, thank God, is not.

—but probably not quite loud enough (being extremely correct) for the pastor to hear, and would
then mention his own name, with its title, Fürst,
Graf, or Baron, explaining that the lady with him
was his wife.

More bows from the pastor, profounder if possible
than before.

Pastor : I beseech the *Herrschaften* to forgive my thus
appearing, and fervently hope they will not consider me obtrusive, or in any way take it amiss.

Mrs. Menzies-Legh (now a Gräfin at the least) :
Will not the Herr Pastor seat himself ?

Pastor, with every appearance of being overcome :
Oh a thousand thanks—the gracious lady is
too good—if I may really be permitted to sit—
an instant—after so shamelessly—

He is waved by Menzies-Legh, as he still hesitates,

with stately courtesy into the third chair, into which
he sinks, but not until he sees the *Herrschaften* are
in the act of sinking too.

Mrs. Menzies-Legh, gracefully explaining Menzies-
Legh's greenness and silence :

My husband is not very well to-day.

Pastor, with every sign of liveliest interest and
compassion :

Oh, that indeed makes me sorry. Has the
Herr Graf then perhaps been over-exerting
himself ? Has he perhaps contracted a chill ?
Is he suffering from a depressed stomach ?

Menzies-Legh, with a stately wave of the hand,
naturally unwilling to reveal the real reason why he
is so green :

No—no.

Mrs. Menzies-Legh : I was about to refresh him
a little with milk. May I be permitted to pour
out a droplet for the Herr Pastor ?

Pastor, again bowing profusely : The gracious one
is much too good. I could not think of permitting myself—

Mrs. Menzies-Legh : But I beg you, Herr Pastor
—will you not drink just a little ?

Pastor : The gracious one is really very amiable.
I would not, however, be the means of depriving
the *Herrschaften* of their—

Mrs. Menzies-Legh : But Herr Pastor, not at all.
Truly not at all. Will you not allow me to
pour you out even half a glassful ? After the
heat of your walk ? And the exertion of con-
ducting the church service ?

Pastor, struggling to get up from the low chair, bow, and take the proffered glass of milk at one and the same time :

Since the gracious one is so gracious—

He takes the glass with a deep bow, having now reached the stage when, the preliminaries demanded by perfect courtesy being on each side fulfilled, he is at liberty to do so, but before drinking its contents turns bowing to Menzies-Legh.

Pastor : But may I not be permitted to offer it to the Herr Graf ?

Menzies-Legh, with a stately wave of the hand : No—no.

Pastor, letting himself down again into the chair with another bow and the necessary caution, the glass being in his hand :

I do not care to think what the *Herrschaften's* opinion of me must be for intruding in this manner. I can only entreat them not to take it amiss. I am aware it is an unexampled example of shamelessness—

Mrs. Menzies-Legh, advancing with the plate of biscuits :

Will the Herr Pastor perhaps eat a biscuit ?

The pastor again shows every sign of being overcome with gratitude, and is about to embark on a speech of thanks and protest before permitting himself to take one when Baron von Ottringel and party appear on the scene, and we get to the point at which they really did appear.

Now what could be more proper and graceful than the whole of the above ? It will be observed that there has been no time whatever for anything but politeness, no time to embark on those seas of discussion, sometimes foolish, often unsuitable, and always sooner or later angry, on which an otherwise budding acquaintanceship so frequently comes to grief. We Germans of the upper classes do not consider it good form to talk on any subject that is likely to make us lose our tempers, so what can we talk about ? There is hardly anything really safe, except to offer each other chairs. But used as I am to these gilt limits, elegant frames within which it is a pleasure to behave like a picture (my friends will have noticed and pardoned my liking for metaphor), it will easily be imagined with what disapproval I stood leaning on my umbrella watching the scene before me. Frau von Eckthum had gone into her caravan. Edelgard and the girls had disappeared. I alone approached the party, not one of which thought it necessary to introduce me or take other notice of my arrival.

They were discussing with amusing absorption a subject they alluded to as the Licensing Bill, which was, I gathered, something heating to do with beer, and were weaving into it all sorts of judgments and opinions that would have inflamed a group of Germans at once. Menzies-Legh was too much interested, I suppose, to go on being green, anyhow his greenness was all gone ; and the pastor sawed up and down with his hand, in which he clasped the biscuit no one had suggested he should take. Mrs. Menzies-Legh, sitting on the grass (a thing no lady should ever do when a gentleman she sees for the first time is present

—" May she the second time ? " asked Mrs. Menzies-Legh when I laid this principle down in the course of a later conversation, to which I very properly replied that you cannot explain nuances but only feel them), joined in just as though she were a man herself—I mean, with her usual air of unchallenged equality of intelligence, an air that would have diverted me if it had not annoyed me too much. And they treated her, too, as though she were an equal, listening attentively to what she had to say, which of course inflates a poor woman and makes it difficult for her to arrive at a right estimate of herself.

This is how that absurd sexlessness the Suffragette has been able to come into existence. I heard a good deal about her the first day of the tour, but on discovering how strongly I felt on the subject they kept off it, not liking I suppose to have their views knocked out of recognition by what I said. I did not, be it understood, deign to argue on such a topic : I just said a few things which frightened them off it.

And indeed, who can take a female Suffragette seriously ? Encouraged, I maintain, to begin with by being treated too well, she is like the insolent and pampered menial of a rich and careless master, and the more she gets the more she demands. Storch-werder does not possess a single example of the species, and very few foreigners come that way to set a bad example to our decent and contented ladies. Once, I recollect, by some strange chance the makings of one did get there, an Englishwoman on some wedding journey expedition or other, a young creature next to whom I sat at a dinner given by our Colonel. I was contemplating her with unconcealed pleasure, for she was quite young and most agreeably rounded, and was turning over the collection of amusing trifles I kept stored in my mind for purposes of conversation with attractive ladies when, before I had either selected one or finished my soup, she began to talk to me in breathless German about an Education Bill our Reichstag was tearing itself to pieces over.

Her interest could not have been keener if she had been a deputy herself with the existence of her party depending on it. She had her own views about it, all cut and dried; she explained her husband's, which differed considerably; and she was anxious to hear mine. So anxious was she that she even forgot to smile when speaking to me—forgot, that is, that she was a woman and I a man able, if inclined, to admire her.

I remember staring at her a moment in unfeigned astonishment, and then, leaning back in my chair, giving myself up to uncontrollable mirth.

She watched me with surprise, which made me laugh still more. When I could speak she inquired whether anyone at the table had said anything amusing, and seemed quite struck on my assuring her that it was she herself who was amusing.

"I am?" said she; and a faint flush enhanced her prettiness.

"Yes—you and the Education Bill together," said I, again overcome with laughter. "It is indeed an amusing mixture. It is like," I added, with happy readiness of compliment, "a rose in an ink-pot."

"But is that amusing?" she asked, not in the least grateful for the flattery, and with a quite serious face.

She had had her little lesson, however, and she did not again talk politics. Indeed she did not again talk at all, but turned to the gentleman on her other side and left me nothing to look at but a sweet little curl behind a sweet little ear.

Now if she had been properly brought up to devote herself to the woman's function of pleasing, how agreeably we could have discoursed together about that curl and that ear and kindred topics, branching off into all sorts of flowery and seductive byeways of compliment and insinuation, such as the well-trained young woman thoroughly enjoys and understands. I can only trust the lesson I gave her did her good. It certainly cured her of talking politics to me.

Listening to the English pastor heating himself over the Licensing Bill which, with all politics, is surely as distinctly outside the pastoral province as it is outside the woman's, I remembered this earlier success, and not caring to stand there unnoticed any longer thought I would repeat it. I therefore began to laugh, gently at first, as though tickled by my thoughts, then more heartily.

They all stopped to look at me.

"What is the joke, Baron?" asked Menzies-Legh, scowling up.

"Forgive me, Pastor," said I, taking off my hat and bowing—he for his part only stared—"but we are accustomed in my country (which, thank God, is

Germany) never to connect clergymen with politics, the inevitable wranglings of which make them ill-suited as a study for men whose calling is purely that of peace. So firmly is this feeling rooted in our natures that it is as amusing to me to see a gentleman of your profession deeply interested in such questions as it would be to see—to see—"

I cast about for a simile, but nothing occurred to me at the moment (and they were all sitting waiting) than the rose and inkpot one, so I had to take that.

And Mrs. Menzies-Legh, just as obtusely as the little bride of years ago, asked, " But is that amusing ? "

Before I could reply Menzies-Legh got up and said he must write some letters ; the pastor got up too and said he must hurry off to a class ; and Lord Sigismund, as I approached the vacated chair next to him and was about to drop into it, said he felt sure Menzies-Legh had no stamps, and he must go and lend him some.

Looking up from the grass on which she still sat, Mrs. Menzies-Legh patted it and said, " Come and sit on this nice soft stuff, dear Baron. I think men are tiresome things, don't you ? Always rushing off somewhere. Tell me about the rose and the inkpot. I do see, I think, that they're—they're funny. Why did the vicar remind you of them ? Come and sit on the grass and tell me."

But I had no desire to sit on grass with Mrs. Menzies-Legh as though we were a row of turtle doves, so I merely said I did not like grass, and bowing slightly walked away.

XIV

THE next day one of those unfortunate incidents
happened which may, of course, happen to anybody,
but really need not have happened just to me.

We left our camp at twelve, after the usual feverish
endeavour to start much earlier, the caravans as
usual nearly capsizing getting out of the field, and
breaking, also as usual, in their plungings several
hitherto unbroken articles, and with the wind and
dust in our faces and grey lowering clouds over our
heads we resumed our daily race after pleasure.

The Sunday had been fine throughout, and there
had been dew and stars at the end of it which,
together with windlessness, made us expect a fine
Monday. But it was nothing of the sort. Monday
provided the conditions I always now associate with
caravaning—a high wind, a threatening sky, clouds
of dust, and a hard white road.

The day began badly and continued badly, so that
even writing about it at this distance I drop un-
consciously into a fretful tone. Perhaps our dinner
at the inn on the Sunday had been more than con-
stitutions used to starvation could suddenly endure,
or perhaps some of us may have eaten beyond the

210

fingers in people's mouths all day and you go out with him."

"You should see his bedroom."

"Don't worry about it. A dentist, huh." He couldn't get over it. "If I ever get my hands on him he better be a dentist. I'll smash his teeth down his fucking throat."

Jo threw up her hands. "That's right. Same old story. When you can't get your way, use force." She pointed at the bedroom where one of her suitcases lay on the floor with its handle broken off. "I suppose you thought you could keep me from leaving by breaking my luggage—something, incidentally, a full-grown ape couldn't do."

"That was just an accident. I only wanted to rest a minute." He pointed at his heart which, at the moment, was killing him. "If you want to know the truth, Jo, I happen to be a sick man."

"You're telling me?"

He couldn't get through. He had used all his moves on her, tried all his lines, and come up empty. Hadn't he said he was sorry? He had borne gifts, summoned every ounce of that certain something—she was cold, cold. Immune to his animal magnetism, she wouldn't let him touch her with a ten-foot pole. He had been gone for a few short weeks and already she had systematically purged the apartment of every trace of him, getting rid of his barber chair, ripping down his posters, dangling plants all around the closet where his hoop once hung. And to top it all, here he was on the threshold of his greatest moment, the big tilt, the championship game, the one for the whole ball of wax, and what was she doing but getting out of town?

He had been about ready to throw caution to the wind and hit her over the head with something and load her into the Olds and drive away somewhere very fast when he thought of the rings. He had thought of this when he noticed she wasn't wearing hers. She was wearing a hunk of some turquoise junk that looked like it came out of a cereal box instead of her matrimonial band. Indignant, he'd put his hand on his hip and said to himself: what's the story here? And then he had thought: who am I to talk? His own finger was naked, his own band having been extorted off him by a minor wop shark. And then his eyes had lit up and he had thought, that's it, and he had slammed his hand on the counter and rushed out of the store.

Noselli had been in the Pin Palace, sitting in his usual dark corner of the cocktail lounge cracking peanuts open with his teeth. He had specifically requested cashews but the waitress had brought him peanuts instead. He hated peanuts. He found it difficult to crack them open with his fingers, so that he had to get at them by biting them between his front teeth. In this way he always got pieces of shell in his mouth, which he was spitting onto the floor when Buddy came over and slid in across from him.

"Nose, baby," he said cheerfully. "Howzit going?"

Noselli looked at him without expression. "Who cut your hair, Bozo the clown?"

Buddy laughed with false uproar at this remark. His fingers twitched. He told himself: be cool. "So, what you been up to? That Indian you were waiting on ever show up?"

"No," Noselli said. He was clapping peanut dust off his fingers. "That makes two of you."

Buddy sat back. "Hey, what are we talking about? Am I sitting here talking to you or not?"

"Sure. After I been hunting all over the city for you. After I showed up in person at that dump you were in and your fat friend gives me the heave." He shook his head. "*Me*. I show up in person to see *you*, and I get the heave. Bad. Very bad."

"Hey, I'm sorry about that," Buddy said. "The guy was a little under the weather at the time. He's basically a reasonable guy. Like us." He was leaning forward looking at his hand. It had gone numb on him again. He began biting his fingertips, nibbling for signs of life. "The way I figure it we're both reasonable guys. I'm a reasonable guy. Tell me, Nose, don't you consider yourself a reasonable guy, or am I way off on this?"

Noselli took a long time to answer. "Usually."

"Sure. We're a lot alike that way. Mature, reasonable men. Guys of the world. I wouldn't have come over here to discuss this with you if you weren't."

"Discuss what?"

Buddy was beating his hand against the seat with karate chops. "I have a proposition for you, Nose. You remember that ring I put up a while ago?"

"Yeah." Noselli was turning a peanut around in his fingers, trying to figure out a way to get at it. His sixth sense told him to get ready for some diddling. "What about it?"

"I got something better for you." Buddy was digging through his pockets. "Wait'll you see this item. You know value, you're gonna love it. Here." He reached across the table and opened his hand and showed him what was inside it: the dragon earrings. In the dim light, the glass tails had a soft green sheen; Buddy had breathed on them and buffed them on his pants before he came in. "Huh? Tell me those aren't the sweetest things you've ever seen."

Noselli stared at them. His nose twitched, like a dog sniffing out suspect turf.

"That green stuff there? You know what that is?" Noselli looked at him. Buddy leaned close and whispered it. "Jade."

"Jade?" Noselli was now holding the earrings up to the light, squinting at them like he'd seen jewelers do in the movies. He shrugged. He didn't know beans about jade. "You sure this stuff is jade? It looks like glass to me."

"It's jade all right," Buddy said. "The real goods. This is rare shit, Nose, let me tell you. It's not every day you get your hands on some." He sat back watching Noselli closely. Behind them, bowling balls rumbled down alleys, pins crashed. Occasionally there were loud shouts from happy keglers. "Comes from China," Buddy added.

"Tell me," Noselli said, pushing his hat back off his eyebrows. "If this stuff is so rare how'd you get your hands on it?"

"What difference does it make, I got it, didn't I? I said to myself: okay, I got some jade, now what am I going to do with it? I said: I ought to put the Nose on to this, a guy like him appreciates value, he'd know what to do with it." He was thumping his hand against his leg. "It's worth four, maybe five times what the ring is worth. Easy."

Noselli studied the earrings a little longer, then slid them across the counter. "I'd rather have my cash."

"I'm working on that, Nose, believe me. I just need a little more time. Meanwhile, you got the jade." He slid the earrings back at him. "What do you say?"

Noselli thought a minute, the luster of the bauble bringing out the green in his face. He was sucking on a toothpick. "I don't know," he said finally. "We made a deal. You said you'd be around. I figure anyone who jumps into a tree is gotta be a jerkoff, but I'm a reasonable guy, I go along with it. Then what happens? You don't show up and I got to go hunting after you like I didn't want to, you mole up on me, your friend gives me the heave . . ." He attempted to crush a peanut between his fingers, failed, then bit it open with his teeth. "If you ask me, I'd say you were diddling."

"Diddling?" Buddy said. "Okay. If that's the way you feel, fine, I got two, three other guys would give their right arm for an item like this." He scooped up the earrings and got to his feet. "Sorry we couldn't make a deal." He turned to go.

"Sit down," Noselli said. "Don't be a turkey. Be cool. I'm still thinking it over." He jammed a fresh toothpick in his mouth. "From China, you say." Noselli didn't know any Chinamen but he did know a Jap. He figured that was close enough.

"Look," Buddy said. "If you're still hung up on this I'll even throw in my uke. But that's my final offer."

Noselli said, "What about my dough?"

"You'll have it by the end of the month," Buddy lied.

The transaction took place between two big green trash bins in the alley around back. First Buddy handed over the dragon earrings and the ukulele; then Noselli slid Buddy a half-empty bag of peanuts, salted in the shell. Buddy shook the bag until he glimpsed the ring buried at the bottom. He plucked it out and slipped it on. It went on easy.

"You know my terms," Noselli said. "And be around."

"You know me, Nose."

He hadn't even had time to laugh about it. He had rushed back to the Olds and driven very fast to the apartment and hunted through it until he found the mate. She had stuffed it in the back of a drawer filled with cheap jewelry, roach clips, and assorted gewgaws he had lifted at one time or another from bargain counters and surprised her with. Then he had rushed back and gotten in the Olds and driven very fast to the mall and hurtled through it, his lean figure slicing through the masses, and taken the escalator to her department and waited with his head sandwiched by rubber apes, the rings in his sweaty pockets. He remembered when they had gotten them, just a couple of crazy kids, and the jeweler, a jolly mottled guy wearing a white apron like a butcher, had led them down to the end of a counter and said, "For kids like you I can give a deal on these," pointing a mottled finger at a pair of plain gold bands. And Buddy and Jo had looked at each other, and Buddy had said, "Wrap them to go." Jo had put up the cash, and the next day they had gotten up at sunrise and gone out into the woods, Buddy in his hairy brown sport coat and Jo in her pioneer dress, a rose in her hair, and a guy had whipped a collar out of his pocket and stuck it on and pronounced them man and wife. Two days later they were riding the coasters. Remembering it, Buddy could feel his stomach turning inside out. He felt dazed, feverish. The blood pounded through his pulverized heart.

The purple-haired woman bought a Three Little Pigs coloring book and the deluxe box of crayons and finally went away. She scowled at Buddy, who was approaching the register wearing a plastic nose he had selected from a bin of such items.

"You got some nice schnozzes here," he said to Jo. "I think I'll get this one." He tweaked it once or twice. "You can never have enough schnozzes, Jo."

Jo spoke distinctly. "Listen to me, Buddy. If you don't leave me alone I'm going to have authorities throw you in jail."

"Marry me," Buddy said.

Jo stared at him. "What's the matter with you? We're already married."

"So what. We can do it again. There's no law against it. I got it all planned out. We can get ahold of that guy again —the guy with the collar—and meet him in the woods and then—" He paused, fumbling through his pockets. "Look. I got the rings."

He held them out to her. Jo looked at them. They were the saddest things she had ever seen.

"I already married you once, Buddy," she said. "The last thing I want to do is marry you again."

"All right." He abruptly fell to his knees in front of her. He could feel his whole life, past and future, rushing away from him, going down the toilet. "Look. I'm on my knees, Jo. What do you say?"

"For God sakes, Buddy," Jo said. People were looking.

After a while Buddy got up and put the rings back in his pocket. "Okay. It was an idea. Just think about it, that's all I'm saying." He had picked up the March of Dimes cup and had turned it over, trying to shake some coins out. "At least you're coming to the game tonight, aren't you? It's for all the marbles, Jo. Us and the Monsters for the whole ball of wax. Dig the excitement." He fashioned grand vistas with his hands. "Everyone'll be out there."

Jo said, "Not me. Tonight I pack. Tomorrow I'm off to the Coast."

Buddy made a face. "Aw c'mon, Jo. You know you'll love it. The color, the pageantry—the mayor's going to chuck out the first ball. Besides, you know I always play better when you're by my side."

Jo didn't say anything. She had opened the register and was sorting through receipts.

Buddy removed his cap and placed it over his heart. "We've worked hard, Jo. It hasn't been easy. We've had to overcome a whole bunch of adversity. We're aging—let's face it—we might never get another shot." He reached over and shut the register drawer. "It'd mean a lot to me if you were out there."

"Listen," Jo said, "there's no power on earth that could get me to that game tonight. I've had all the baseball I'm going to take. I've had baseball up to here."

"I'm asking you for the last time: inspire me."

"If you want inspiration, stick this on." She handed him his schnozz. "They'll die laughing."

She went out from behind the counter to attend to a short block-shaped man waiting with his block-shaped son. They were both wearing gray T-shirts that ended just above their trousers, leaving a space where their bellies showed. The boy had on a cap cocked to one side. The man was chewing a piece of cigar.

"You got something he can't break?" the man said.

"What did you have in mind?"

"Anything, just so he can't break it. He breaks every god-damn thing he gets his hands on."

"How about a game?"

"Hey, you. You want a game?"

The boy screwed up his face.

"You don't, huh? What you want, a *doll?*" The man chuckled. "Listen, he don't want a game. Just show me something sturdy."

Buddy watched as they disappeared around a corner. He slammed both fists on the counter and then, making loud strangling noises, went over and sulked by the Big Wheelers. He inched one out and started pedaling awkwardly through the department, his knees coming up to his chin. He began going faster and faster in a kind of tantrum, churning past masks and games, battery-powered race cars, bins of false noses and barrels of sponge balls. Jo was showing the block-shaped man and his block-shaped kid an inflatable clown you could punch with your fists as Buddy whizzed by and they exchanged glances, his pleading, hers one of unplumbed weariness. He was still looking back when he came to the end of the aisle. He saw the kid grin slyly, someone shouted, "Look out!" and the next thing he knew he was traveling down the up escalator on Big Wheels, bouncing out of control, the toy cutting a swath through the crowded stairwell, people shrieking, Buddy hanging on, going faster and faster, eventually flying off into the foundation department and thudding into a stocking counter so that all the thighs fell down.

He lay on the floor a moment, his legs still sandwiched around the trike. A crowd had gathered, mostly large, parrot-like women who were watching him curiously. After a while he threw the thighs off of him and got up, glancing to the top of the escalator where Jo stood, hands on hips, looking down at him. Buddy waved.

"I'm fine. Not hurt at all. See?" He shook his arms and legs, danced a reassuring jig. "Don't forget tonight. Game starts at eight. I'll save you a seat." She hesitated a moment, then jerked her head out of view.

A man with a plastic I.D. card on the lapel of his suit was striding over. "What's going on here?"

"Get away from me," Buddy said, pushing past him. "You're lucky I don't sue."

◦◦◦◦

They started coming early, the knowledgeable guys, the turks, the old gents with their seat cushions and paper bags and a pack of White Owls in the shirt pocket, the guys with transistor radios wired into their heads. By seven-thirty the bleachers had completely filled and the crowd had spilled down both lines, mashed up against the fence and jockeying for position. Finger men worked this crowd, pinching wallets. A high school band was tuning up in the parking lot, and a bunch of army guys hung out in center field, waiting to haul out the colors. The press box was filled with so many real and bogus officials they finally had to station a cop there to turn phonies away. Cops were everywhere; it seemed like half the force had pulled championship duty. The mayor wasn't there but his lackeys were, hamming it up in the choice seats behind home plate, gabbing with cronies, dispensing cigars and ballpoint pens with their names on them, posing with the lucky handicapped kid designated to throw out the first ball.

Betting men were in this crowd. A couple of skinny guys were working the Sticks' side, taking all wagers. Del worked the enemy, wearing his white sponge hat. Frog worked the fences and Crawford worked the hill beyond center field, where a big clump of fans were huddled close together beneath the tree. There were fans in the tree. Fans stood on the roofs of adjacent apartment buildings, leaned out of windows. The sky was like a muddy pool but this had not stopped Del from getting his dough's worth from the airplane pilot he had hired who, even at that moment, unbeknownst to anyone, was flying back and forth above the field trailing a banner that said: "Sticks Kick Ass."

The Monsters were on the field, looking huge in their coalblack suits. They loosened up by swinging sledgehammers and throwing balls to each other as hard as they could, laughing at the pain. They had a couple of ex-Bears on the team, but these were not the largest Monsters. They had three or four even larger guys. Their catcher was the largest man Buddy had ever seen, about the size of a deluxe refrigerator. Even their batboy was big.

Having already worked out, the Sticks fidgeted in the dugout, pacing, mumbling, doing odd things with their bats. The vets were solemn, the rooks edgy as cats. Sammy was rewrapping his swollen ankles; beside him Harv kneaded his tender thigh. Red and Doc lobbed a ball back and forth, Red throwing gingerly with his damaged wing, wincing with every toss. He was going against his physician's explicit orders, but he didn't give a shit: he had penciled himself into the lineup. The Bull lurched back and forth down the line, still favoring his groin. He too had penciled himself in. His attitude was: if I walk, I play. At the far end of the dugout Whitey sat like an Indian chief, his arms folded across his windbreaker, his face impassive. He had nothing more to say.

At quarter to eight somebody looked around and said, "Where the hell is Buddy?"

Everybody looked for him. They checked out the can, thinking he might have gone there to comply with Whitey's directive that everyone go to the toilet before the game. They glanced up into the bleachers where the Stick fans sat in a blue and gold mass, scoped out the row of chicks down the left field line with the idea that he might be hot-dogging it over there. But Buddy was scarce in all these places. Nobody thought to look behind the refreshment stand where, at that moment, Buddy was leaning against some trash bins with his head in his hands. He'd been sitting there for some time. He was not up for the game. He was down, down. He felt terrible. His legs were rubbery, his arms were filled with cement. Every time he breathed he felt like he was being stabbed in the heart with a pitchfork. His hands were shaky. In practice he had dropped two balls.

He was certain now she wasn't going to come. All during practice while he was out there shagging flies and taking his cuts and feeling worse and worse, he kept scanning the bleachers, triggering noisy reactions from his fans. They yelled to him, "Hey Buddy!" "Buddy, over here." Young chicks waved, blew him kisses. He didn't see them. He was studying the big clump of Stick kith and kin sitting in the middle of the stands. They were all there, even Stretch, who stared uncomprehendingly at the color and pageantry all around him, heavily sedated and guarded closely by two white-smocked orderlies who had a hand on each of his shoulders. Herm, of course, was there, wearing his gold Stick jacket with the blue all-star patch and wishing to Christ he was out there. Every time he saw Buddy whom, for the past few days, he'd been secretly harboring in his garage, he would nod and flash the power sign. Buddy didn't see it. He was looking at the empty seat right next to the Glicker he had saved especially for Jo.

She wasn't coming and he was feeling real bad. His legs seemed impossibly heavy, as though they were glued to a stand, like a toy soldier's. He had the chills. Nausea gripped him. After the warmup he wandered off to the can in compliance with Whitey's directive, and he remained there a while, waiting to see if he would throw up or not. The noise, the smoke, the color and pageantry—it was making his head hurt. He wondered why he couldn't just stay in the toilet until everything was over. This seemed like a good idea, but after a few moments the Bull came by and pounded on the door and Buddy got up and left and went to hide behind the hot dog stand.

He sat there hunkered between the trash bins with his head in his hands while the army guys hauled out the colors to the accompaniment of the high school band, which played a lame and tinny rendition of the anthem. He sat there while one of the mayor's lackeys said a few appropriate words and the afflicted kid threw out the first ball, a feeble toss that landed five feet short of the Bull's waiting hands. He was still sitting there when Whitey found him and came over and spiked him on the ankle.

"For Christ sake," Buddy said.

"Have you lost your noodle? We're ready to take the field. Get your ass out there."

Buddy made a shooing motion with his hand. "I'm not playing tonight. Put Mole out in left."

"Don't trifle with me."

"I'm not trifling. I'm serious. Scratch my name."

Whitey wrenched off his cap. His brush cut bristled like silver quills; he looked like a porcupine. "This is no time for jokes. We're playing for the whole shebang." He thrust out his arm, pointing commandingly. "Take your position."

"I don't want to," Buddy said. He clutched at his chest. "I don't feel good. I'm sick."

"You don't feel good?" Whitey leaned over him, sneering. "What's the matter, you got a tummyache?"

Buddy refused to dignify this with an answer.

"Look," Whitey said, "don't give me this tummyache shit when all the chips are on the table. Half my squad is hurting. I've got guys with hamstrings, sprains, charley horses —one of my guys is playing with a severe knife wound, I've got a guy who's favoring his groin. And not one of them is sitting down."

"Look yourself," Buddy said. "I told you I was sick so get off my case. Besides, I carried this team all year. I'm the reason we're in here. I started hot and stayed hot. When we were slumping, hitting mush, pulling Bozo stuff on the bases, Buddy Barnes was playing swell ball. When we were down I was up. You're looking at the holler guy. If it wasn't for me we wouldn't even be here; you know it and I know it, so back off."

"True," Whitey said, "but it doesn't cut any mustard with me if you go chickenshit in the big one."

"Chickenshit?" Buddy said. "It's got nothing to do with chickenshit. I just can't play tonight." He brushed a speck of grime off his shoe. "I've got my reasons."

Whitey waved his fists. "But this is for all the marbles!"

"Big deal. Being the manager of the Sticks you may have lost sight of this, Whitey, but there are more important things than playing ball. Don't forget there's about fifty billion people behind the Iron Curtain who couldn't give a shit who wins tonight. Ditto for Africa. Show me the spear-chucker who's into this game. And don't forget those guys less fortunate than yourself, don't forget your crippled guys, the downtrodden and hungry."

Whitey was gouging his eyes. He was thinking, it's never easy. You play this crazy game for thirty years, you think you've seen it all, you get hot sometimes, you have your slumps, your guys get stabbed, go nuts, fall asleep in the toilet, finally you put it all together, you're playing for the big banana, and your left fielder develops a tummyache and a social conscience. He jerked his hat back on his head and spat a big tobacco clam about an inch from Buddy's shoe. "So you're sitting it out, huh?"

"Yes," Buddy said. "I am."

"Okay. Fine. We're only in the main event tonight, that's all. It's only something we worked thirty years for and may never get another shot at. But never mind. You don't want to play, I'll just put someone else out there who does. I'll be fucked before I beg." Whitey pointed a finger at him. "Just let it be known that Buddy Barnes spent the biggest game of his life sitting on his ass behind the hot dog stand." He spat and walked away.

Buddy remained where he was, crouched over like a big crab between the trash bins. Presently he heard the Stick-man cheer—hubba hubba hubba HO!—heard the crowd go wild as they took the field. He heard the P.A. guy announce the change in the Stickman lineup—Mole Molarski in left for Buddy Barnes—heard the groan that followed, the buzzing commotion, and still he didn't move, just crouched in a little tighter between the trash to shield himself from the noise that was splitting his head open. He wondered if he might be dying. It was possible. What he would've really liked to do was to get up and go over to his car and lie down in it and die there instead of behind the hot dog stand, but he understood he lacked the strength to do this. He supposed he would just have to die behind the hot dog stand, then. On the other side of the stand people were buying refreshments. "A dog and two chips," he heard one guy say. Buddy laughed. For some reason he found this very ironic.

He was still sitting there, idly feeling his pulse disappear, when a couple of kids sprinted past. One—a little tousle-haired yard-ape with a bottle of grape stuck in his mouth—stopped and edged back and peered in at him.

"Ain't you Buddy Barnes?"

Buddy hid his face in shadows and ignored him.

"Sure you are. I seen you before." The kid squinted up his face. "How come you're hiding back here instead of playing?"

Buddy lifted his head. "I'm not hiding. I'm just sitting here. Besides, you got the wrong guy. I'm not Barnes."

"You are too."

Buddy made a move as if to charge them, and they ran away. He crouched back in the shadows, holding his head. They just wouldn't leave you alone. They just weren't satisfied unless they had their pound of flesh. Not this time. Not tonight. They want a show, fine, let them go out there and play left field in a coma. Buddy Barnes was sitting it out.

The game was well under way and there was a lot of noise coming from the Monsters' side of the field. Evidently they were kicking Stick ass. It sounded bad. He shrugged. There was nothing he could do about it. He had gotten them here, carried the whole goddamn team on his back, and if they took the lump in the big one it wasn't his fault. All year he'd been out there knocking his head against the fence while the rest of them were pulling up lame, losing screws, running off to join the freak show. They had dropped like flies and nobody had said word one. But let him miss one game and all of a sudden the term *chickenshit* is being tossed around fast and loose. Buddy found this highly ironic. At that moment he thought he knew what Jesus felt like when the Guy sweated it out in the garden while his pals were passed out on the ground, drunk, not one of them remotely hip to the situation. He too had been betrayed. Hadn't he had to sleep in his car in the ballpark when, having been attacked by large, aggressive rats and had a junkie pull a heater on him, he called his teammates one by one and not one of them would give him shelter?

A whole lot of shrieking and clamor was still coming from the Monsters' half of the stands; the Sticks' side was absolutely still. Buddy removed his cap, scratched his head. It seemed like the Sticks had been out there forever. He jammed his cap down over his forehead and began creeping out from behind the hot dog stand, meaning to get a peek at the score. He creeped out to the edge of the parking lot and, hiding behind the bus the band had come in, peeked out at the big board in center where a yellow "7" was posted in the Monsters' half of the first. The Sticks had not even gotten a lick in yet and already they were out of it. Their body language said they were done for. Harv had his face in his hands, Red cradled his wing, Sammy was on his knees, the Bull lurched from side to side favoring his groin. On the mound Doc was holding the clincher closely to his face and staring at it as though he had never seen one before. Out in left Mole had the paralyzed look of a man being sniped at in an open field. Buddy watched as he minced toward the line for an easy one, tripped over his own feet, and fell flat on his face, the ball coming down foul a foot from his head like a mortar round. There was loud braying from the Monsters and their fans. Buddy looked away.

Suddenly, a strange mournful sound began coming from the stands. It started slowly, a low rumble issuing from the Sticks' half of the field. Buddy cocked his head to listen. More plea than cheer, it began building in volume and tempo until it became a locomotive chant, accompanied by stomping feet: "We want Buddy! We want Buddy!" He shrank back behind the bus with his hands clapped to his ears while it went on and on and on. It spread from the stands to the trees, to the roofs of apartment buildings. The noise swelled all around him. He paced, clenching and unclenching his dukes. What could he do? What choice did he have? The whole town wanted him. They'd called for the Gipper, hadn't they? And demanded Houdini jump in the lake. In every generation there were certain individuals, guys like him, who didn't have the luxury of sitting one out. Even the Big Guy had had to go out there. He waited for the cry to build to stentorian proportions, then began moving resolutely toward the field.

∞∞∞∞

When it was over, after they had revived him and peeled him off the plate and carried him around on their shoulders and gone to the Corner to celebrate, they wouldn't even know where to begin.

They would talk of course how the Monsters came out gooning, putting a seven spot up in the first and making it look easy, yukking it up in the dugout while the Sticks keystoned it on the field, falling down and running into each other, zombied out and demoralized with their main man scratched from the lineup. They would talk how, suddenly, out of nowhere, number one sprinted out on the field to the standing O, holding up the game for a good five minutes, and how, sick as a dog, he still managed to put an end to the Monsters' fun with a one-duke grab at the fence. They would talk then how the Sticks came back, peppering shots to all fields and jackrabbiting it on the base paths. They would remind guys that these were not the Sticks of yore. These were a bunch of kids and a few vets who were playing with pain, all taped up, not even fifty percent out there. They would talk Sammy's ankle, Harv's thigh, Red's punctured wing. They would talk how the Bull squatted behind the plate all night favoring his groin. They would talk how these bandaged guys, these walking wounded, somehow put it to the Monsters with line-drive sticking and wall-to-wall D. They would talk how this emergency room squad Whitey had patched together took a five-run lead into the final inning only to have the Monsters demolish it with a series of goon shots that had everyone blinking and pointing to ridiculous distances beyond the fence and which, when it was finally over, had put them up by a pair.

But when they got together to talk this game, the guy they would talk about was Mr. Left Field. They would talk, of course, about his garden work, how, sick as a dog, he still came in on low shots and took them off his ankles, tumbling over and coming up showing ball. They would talk about the way he cut off the gaps, smothered the line. They would talk his wing. Was it three or four guys he burned going for the extra base, including that one guy at the plate who was so freaked at seeing the ball there ahead of him he just stopped right in his tracks and let Bull put it on him. They would certainly talk how he climbed the fence. Was it three or four guys he sent back to the pines with over-the-shoulders and leaping stabs, including the one he took going full blast into the barrier, knocking himself stupid and suffering a series of nasty gashes on his knee and arm and skull—but rolling over with the clincher held high in his bleeding duke!

They would talk all this and his stickwork too. His first two times he'd hit chalk and taken third standing. The third one spun the shortstop around and he'd Jungle-Jimmed it into second. The fourth one was a goon shot to dead center that scattered guys in the tree and had even the biggest Monsters gawking. The last time he'd come up it was the final frame, one dead and two alive and the crowd going ape-shit, and he'd gapped the Monster outfield with a shot to right center and Frog, coaching third, practically had to jump out and tackle him to keep him from trying for home. Harv, hitting next, poked a soft one to center, raging his stick against the fence. The guy drifted in, ready to unload. Buddy tagged, ready to go for it. Later they claimed he took off early but the ump said no way. He and the ball and the Monster catcher—a guy the size of a meat locker—came together at the plate. The ball went one way, the meat locker went the other; Buddy went straight down, out cold on top of the dish with the goddamn ever-loving son-of-a-bitching can-you-dig-it winning run.

ᴏᴏᴏᴏ

They'd had to get the salts out to revive him. Buddy opened his eyes and saw a circle of faces pressing in on him; everyone had a twin. After a minute the fake faces merged with the real ones—Harv, Red, Herman, the Bull . . .

"He's coming to."

"He took a vicious blow."

"Back off. Give him some fucking air."

They edged away while Buddy lay on top of home plate, testing things. He wiggled his toes, flexed his fingers. He rolled his neck gently to see if his head was still screwed on right. Suddenly he sprang to his feet.

"I'm fine."

They immediately mobbed his ass. Sticks climbed all over him, thumping him on the back and shoulders, giving him Dutch jobs, his hands smarted from so many fives and tens. They hoisted him up and bore him around like a rajah.

"You put him down, man."

"Wham. Right on his ass."

"He was a big fucker."

"He took a vicious blow and still he scored."

Nobody could actually believe what had happened, and every few seconds Sticks would blank out, trying to fathom it. Then it would dawn on them again that they were the kings of the whole town and they would have to do something—jump up and down, screech, give someone a monkey burn. Sammy and Doc hugged like lovers, Harv prayed to God on his knees. The Bull was completely out of control. He kept going around thumping people. He was a thumping machine. He thumped Red on his punctured wing and Red didn't even feel it, that's how high the keystone man was flying. Frog had his glasses off and was wiping his dewy eyes. Alone in the dugout Whitey kept going over the score sheet like he'd done after every game for thirty years. Not too bad, he was saying, but we could've played better, we gave them too many outs, that first inning was a carnival act . . . He more than anyone could not get it through his schoolhouse that after thirty years they had finally won the whole shebang.

On the other side of the field morose Monsters were rowed along the dugout aimlessly fooling with equipment, zombied out, while Stick fans surged against the fence, shouting and waving.

"Hey, Buddy!"

"Buddy, over here."

Buddy smiled wanly, curiously remote. His senses were beginning to send messages again; the message said he was in pain. Chunks of flesh from his legs and shoulders had been flayed off by the fence, the base paths. His arms were bruised, his shins barked. He felt as though he'd been dragged across the field from the back of a tractor. A series of gashes ran up his forearm. Blood dripped from his chin. His temples throbbed, and reaching up he felt a thick, dome-like swelling growing on the top of his head. He took a step toward the dugout and his legs bent funny like a rubber guy's.

"Easy." Herman braced him. "You okay?"

"Sure."

"Tell me we didn't do it. Tell me we're not the champs." He was banging his fists together, a kite-sized grin on his meaty face. Abruptly he grabbed Buddy by the shoulders and held him up like a newspaper. "I saw it, I was sitting there, and I still don't believe it. I've seen guys play their asses off but I never saw anything like tonight. Hit, run, throw—"

Buddy said, "Jo didn't happen to show up, did she?"

"To tell you the truth, Bud, I didn't see her."

A brace of Sticks swooped past bearing a huge trophy that looked like the Parthenon. "We're hitting the Corner," Frog said. He stopped and reached into the equipment bag and handed Buddy the game ball. "It was unanimous."

Buddy looked at it, curiously unmoved. It might have been something from the moon. "It was a team effort, Frog."

"Don't be ridiculous," Frog said. "Without you we get our lunch out there." He hurried off to catch up with the others, who were piling into vehicles and splitting for the Corner in clouds of dust, horns blaring. Buddy watched them leave.

"C'mon, c'mon, let's get going." Herman was tugging his arm. "I shouldn't but what the hay. It's not every day you take the town."

Buddy said, "I think I'll pass it up."

Herman stared at him. His hands were red and swollen from being wrung through championship pressure. He spoke in hoarse croaks. "Are you nuts? Everyone'll be there. We took the town, remember?"

"I know it. I just don't feel like going, that's all." He was bouncing the game ball on the sidewalk. Over by the fence a group of his fans were still hanging around, hoping to get a word from him, a nod, a hand on his body. Buddy didn't see them. "Listen, Herm, do me a favor, will you?"

"Name it."

"Drive me to Jo's."

The Glicker raved all the way there. He couldn't stop talking the show his partner had put on. He talked his snags, his sticking, his strikes to all bases. He talked the collision at the plate. "You should've seen it. The guy's waiting there, see, blocking the dish. A big fucker. What would you say he went, Bud?"

"Huh? I don't know." He was looking out the window, stroking the top of his head as though it were a magic lamp. "Three?"

"Oh, yeah. Easy. I'd say at least three and a half. So there he is, this fucking tank just standing there waiting for you, he can't wait to put it on you, and here you come down the line—whooosh—a blur and here comes the ball and the next minute the ball's over here and this outhouse is way over there and you're on top of the dish and we're the kings of the whole goddamn town." He whistled through the gaps in his teeth. "I'm telling you, you should've seen it."

Buddy was silent. An idea had been swelling in his mind corresponding to the dome on the top of his head. He turned it over, poked at it from various angles. The idea surprised him and disappointed him at the same time. More than anything, though, it struck him as being right. He'd miss it, sure, but there was a time to play and a time to quit playing, a time to run and throw and field and hit for both average and power, and a time to hang them up on the wall. Hadn't he always wanted to go out like a champ?

"They won't forget tonight," Herman was saying. "No way. I want to see the guy who can top that act."

"I've played better."

"Listen to him," Herman said. "He wins the city all by himself and he acts like it was a waltz." He reached out and pummeled Buddy's leg. "What a guy."

Buddy took a deep breath. "There was a reason for my inspired play, Herm."

"Sure there was. You were playing for the whole ball of wax. Each and every marble was on the line."

"It was more than that."

"Huh?"

"I'll let you in on a little secret, Herm." He paused, placing his fingertips together. He wondered how best to put it. "Buddy Barnes will play no more."

Herman grinned over at him. "Sure."

"I'm serious."

"C'mon. This is the Glicker you're talking to, remember."

"I've thought it over and I've made up my mind: Buddy Barnes has played his last game."

Herman's smile slid off his face and he lapsed into silence, confounded by this news.

When they got to the apartment Buddy told Herman to pull around into the alley. "We'll go up the back. Give me a hand, will you, Herm? I'm still woozy."

Herman got out, and as he was coming around to the other side of the car, Buddy grabbed hold of the frayed neck of his jersey and tore it down the front, baring one of his tits. Then, cradling the game ball in the crook of his arm, he draped himself on Herman's shoulders and together they lurched up the stairs.

oooo

Jo was studying the small print on her airplane ticket when she heard a stampede around back. She put the ticket down and went into the kitchen just as Buddy and Herman barged through the door.

"Make way," Herman said. "We got an injured man here."

Jo stared at Buddy. He looked as though he'd been shot out of a cannon. "My God. What happened?"

Buddy lifted his head, struggling to speak.

Herman said, "He played his goddamn heart out, that's what happened."

They lurched through the kitchen into the hallway, Herman cracking his head on basketed plants. "He's all beat up, Jo. He gave his all. Where should I put him?"

Before she could answer, Buddy pointed to the bedroom. Herman dragged him in there and, sweeping suitcases aside, dumped him onto the bed.

"I don't understand," Jo was saying. "He hurt himself like this just playing ball?"

Herman's face was creased with emotion; his heart overflowed. "You should've seen him, Jo. You should've been out there. He didn't care about the fence. He didn't care that the fucking guy—pardon my French—was as big as a fucking bus. He went in there anyway." He reached down and put a hand on Buddy's shoulder. Buddy winced. "Didn't ya, kid?"

Jo frowned. "He did this to himself just for a baseball game?"

"You don't understand," Herman said. "This was the big one. The town was at stake. This man here won it. This guy right in front of you took it all by himself. Ran and threw, fielded his ass off. Hit for the cycle. You should've seen the size of that guy. He had the plate blocked, see." Herman crouched over, blocking an imaginary dish. "Buddy tags and starts tearing down the line. The throw comes in, the ball's right there, and Buddy hits this guy at full speed and knocks him on his ass." Herman jolted himself with a powerful blow, roughing himself up. "He's in there. He scores. Numero uno. Right now they're raising the roof on account of him. I shouldn't go but, what the hay, how often do you take the town." He reached down and pressed Buddy's hand, the one still holding the clincher. "Take it easy, Bud. Get your rest. You deserve it."

He left the room, then stuck his head back in, motioning Jo close. "Another thing. I almost forgot to tell you. Listen to this: Buddy Barnes has played his last game." He paused, letting the full weight of this announcement sink in.

Jo said, "I should hope so."

Herman went away. Jo came over and sat down on the edge of the bed and looked at Buddy, the ends of her mouth drawn down. "You're crazy, Buddy. You really ought to have your head examined." Buddy didn't speak. He was lying on his back with his eyes half closed, a suffering angel. "You play too hard," Jo said. "You really ought to quit, but I know you won't."

Buddy moistened his lips. "I'm finished, Jo. I'm hanging them up." He struggled to rise, succeeding halfway, and handed her the ball. "I dedicated my last game to you," he whispered thickly, falling back.

Jo held the ball, studied it, began plucking at a seam. She bounced it gingerly in her palm as though it were a big yellow egg. Abruptly she pitched it into a corner. She got up and began pacing rapidly at the foot of the bed, rubbing at her temples, muttering to herself. Every so often she would pause and point at Buddy, like a lawyer pointing at the accused. Buddy watched her beneath hooded eyes. Every so often he coughed abjectly.

She came back to the bed, examined his wounds. "Look at you. You're a mess." She probed a bruise on his cheekbone that resembled a ticktacktoe diagram. Buddy sucked in his breath. "All right. Just a minute." She went into the bathroom, returning momentarily with a washcloth, a big hunk of cotton, and a bottle of antiseptic. Buddy made a feeble protest but she knocked his hands away. "You want to turn green?"

She helped him remove his tattered jersey and began ministering to him, washing the cuts and dabbing antiseptic on them with pieces of cotton. Buddy endured it without a whimper. She washed his arms and shoulders and back. "All right," she said, "take off your pants." She helped him struggle out of them. She washed his legs and feet, gently stroking the bruised shins and battered knees. Buddy reached out his hand and began to gently smooth her hair. He ran his fingers down the nape of her neck, across her shoulder, passed them fleetingly over a breast. She washed his discolored thighs.

She adjusted herself and, looming directly over him, began dabbing at his face. She brushed the cotton across his speckled cheekbone, patted his nose. She began dabbing where there wasn't any need to dab. They were looking at each other, reading each other like crystal balls. She reached out and touched his lips. He put his hands behind her neck and drew her down.

In a minute she was peeled open, languorous, while Buddy knelt above her, sucking her in with hungry eyes. He was better. He had never felt better in his whole life. He reached up and snapped off the light, then threw himself on her like a sailor washed up on a friendly shore.

12

The woman sitting next to Jo on the plane was talking about one of her husbands—her third or fourth, Jo wasn't sure—who used to keep a loaded gun in every room so that he wouldn't be caught unarmed when the jungle bunnies finally stormed his property. She was about forty, with severe black hair that fit snugly over her head like a shower cap. She wore a fur stole with the claws still in it and smoked long brown cigarettes.

"I travel," the woman was saying. "I'm always in the air. I fly to the Coast often—this is my seventh or eighth time, I can't remember. The first time was with Arnie, my second. He complained about everything, the hills, the weather, the food—imagine complaining about the food in San Francisco. He kept talking about queers all the time, making these jokes. His feet hurt. I dumped him like a bad habit." She lit another cigarette. Her breath smelled of Listerine and gin. "Now I come by myself. I take off whenever I feel like it. I'm not like a tourist either. I mix right in. I know the shops, the restaurants." She reached out and patted Jo's leg. "Listen, if you want to see Frisco, stick with me."

Jo nodded and looked out the window. She was wishing the woman would be quiet so she could concentrate on the trip. She was enjoying it thoroughly. She had liked the take-off best—the noise and speed and power had knocked her out—but the feeling of gliding through the clouds at five hundred miles per hour wasn't bad either. She wished the pilot would throw in a few tricks—some steep turns, a dive, maybe even a loop-the-loop—and show her what this baby could really do. She felt buoyant, restless; she could hardly keep herself in the seat. She wanted to get up and walk around, check out everything, inspect the cockpit, talk to the passengers. Most of them were young, smartly dressed people like herself and like herself they were on the go. Some had open briefcases on their laps and were sorting through important papers. Jo wished she had a briefcase too and made a mental note to bring one on her next trip. She kept glancing at the people, studying their faces, their style. She hoped she fit in, hoped that the stewardesses who kept walking by would think she was one of them. The only ones who didn't fit in were a couple of cards with big square sideburns and peach leisure suits sitting way up front, and an extremely thin man with the wrinkled, leathery face of an old cowboy in the row ahead of her. He was wearing a toupee several shades darker than his real hair, the rug sitting crookedly on his head like a hastily replaced divot. Beside him his wife, a queen-sized woman with a face that looked like it belonged on a jar of preserves, was telling him there was nothing wrong with the wing.

The plane banked steeply, giving her a view of the countryside. Looking down, she saw empty land divided into big rectangles by patches of woods, strips of highway. Towns clustered here and there, the buildings tiny and uniform as Monopoly houses. Minute cars traveled. Jo was impressed.

Everything was neat, tidy, like an illustration in one of the picture books she sold. She realized, however, that this was a trick. She wasn't fooled. The world was messy, life changed. Some people could handle that, some couldn't. If somebody couldn't, it wasn't her fault.

He was still sleeping when she left, his head burrowed under a pillow and a leg hanging over the edge of the bed. She could have set off a cherry bomb in the room and it wouldn't have disturbed him, which was all right with her; she didn't need to have him wake up on her while she was leaving and start on her all over again. She wanted to leave easy. When she was finally ready she had called a cab and gone into the bedroom for her luggage. He had turned over on his back uncovering himself, the sheet twisted around his ankles. Bruises had bloomed on his body like odd flowers; his chest rose and fell. He slept like a boy, his lips parted, his hair down over his eyes. She watched him until she heard the cab honk, then turned and closed the door.

She hadn't left him a note. There was nothing to explain. It had been sensational, like the good old days, but it had meant little, changed less. She supposed she had used him but she didn't feel bad about it. Things happen, people get hurt—who said life was fair? Maybe now when he woke up and found the place empty he would finally get the message.

The woman sitting next to Jo nudged her leg and muttered, "Idiots." She gestured toward the front of the plane where the two cards were giving the stewardess a hard time.

Jo nodded.

"Business or pleasure?" the woman said.

"Pardon me?"

"The trip?"

"Oh." Jo hesitated. "Business. Of course, I've got some friends out there too that I'd like to see—if I can fit it in. My brother lives on the Coast. He flies big jets for the air force." For some reason Jo wished she hadn't mentioned that.

"Really? George, my third, flew in Korea. Never got over it. Every chance he got he'd get together with his old squad and they'd get drunk and talk about how MacArthur was right. Saturdays he'd go out to a park and fly one of those model planes you fly on the end of a stick. In my opinion he should've stayed in. Boring?" She lit another cigarette. "I dropped him like a hot potato."

Jo wasn't listening. She was thinking about Buddy. The more she thought about it, the more she felt that he wouldn't get the picture. He would probably spend the whole time she was gone hanging around, getting drunk and wrecking stuff, knocking over plants. He'd set things on fire. After last night she wouldn't be able to get him out of there with a crowbar. She supposed she would have to move. The idea still appealed to her. She needed a bigger place anyway, maybe in one of those fashionable buildings on the Near North Side. The women she had seen coming out of those buildings were smartly dressed, self-assured. They were on the go. There was some danger, certainly, but she wasn't worried, she could take care of herself. She pictured herself coming out of one of those buildings, smartly dressed in one of her new ensembles, hailing a cab; she liked what she saw. It was a fine idea and she made a mental note to look into it as soon as she got back. She wanted to move as quickly as possible. She supposed she would have to trick him somehow, wait until one night when he was really stewed and move out from under him. And yet, on the other hand, she wondered what good moving would really do. He would just find her, show up again with some hideous bauble he had lifted from the dime store and barge right in and put his feet up on her furniture and pop open a beer and switch on the ball game. Or one night, just when she would be thinking she was finally rid of him, he would show up under her window with the ukulele. No, the more she thought about it the more she felt that to be rid of him once and for all she would probably have to get out of town. It wasn't a bad idea. Not at all. She made a mental note to discuss this possibility with Sara Lee when she got to the Coast. Sara Lee would be able to offer some good advice on the matter. She could help her clear up all sorts of things.

The woman reached down and adjusted her hose. "You married?"

Jo shook her head.

The woman thrust a handful of fingers in Jo's face. "Five times, do you believe it? I ought to have my head examined. The last one I had, all he did was sleep. I woke him up and told him to beat it." She was blowing smoke through her nose. Her face was as small and hard as a dead sparrow's. "Now I'm on my own. Got a small place right on the lake, maid service, the works. I don't even make my bed. Most nights I eat out. I used to think the town was dead until I woke up. Now I entertain twice a week." She nudged Jo's leg. "I've taken up painting."

Jo stifled a yawn. "Really?"

"Absolutely. This man I know, an artist, says I have a natural gift. Imagine having this natural gift all these years and not even knowing. Listen, when you get back you'll have to come by and see my oils."

Jo made a noncommittal gesture.

The woman stuck out her hand. "I'm Susu."

"Jo."

"Listen, Jo, let's have a drink." She raised a jewelry-laden arm and snapped her fingers as though she were in a cocktail lounge.

Jo closed her eyes and smiled.

ΟΟΟΟ

Buddy was sitting in the living room with his feet up on the coffee table, watching a cowboy movie and taking slugs of some sickeningly sweet liqueur that came in a fancy bottle he had found under the kitchen sink. He was feeling better.

He felt he had pretty good control of the situation, but for a while there it had been touch and go. He had to admit for a while there he'd been pretty shaken up. He had paced, shouted, smashed some pretty good shots into the walls. His fists still smarted from these shots. He had taken down a chair with a nifty kung fu kick; the thing lay in three big pieces in the corner. Had he snuffled by the window? He might have, he really wasn't sure.

He had awakened at noon, rolled over with a smile on his face, and fallen off the bed. He had blinked and said, "Jo?" Then he had observed that the luggage was gone and he sprang up and began going through rooms, calling her name uncertainly, as though she were hiding somewhere, playing a joke on him. He remembered checking the closets and behind the sofa; he had gotten down and looked under the bed. He distinctly remembered going out on the back porch and shouting her name into the alley, his voice ringing all across the neighborhood, rousing dogs. He remembered shouting out there a good long while.

He wasn't sure but he believed he had made an ass of himself at the airport. He could not recollect all he had done after he had hot-wired her car and speedballed out there— he had been out of his mind—but he did recall an ugly confrontation with a ticket guy at the United terminal who could not seem to grasp the seriousness of the situation— it was his wife, he kept explaining, had he seen her, she was on an airplane, she had to be stopped. But the guy just kept shaking his head and looking away. He had a thin black mustache that looked like he had Flaired it on that morning; it looked like a disguise. The man would just not look Buddy in the eye so that, finally, to impress upon him the fact that he was not fooling around, Buddy had had to reach out and grab the guy in a double nerve hold and bring him to his knees. After that he seemed to remember running a good deal, plowing around and through and over aghast travelers

—were there men in pursuit? The people would just not get out of his way, the noise was splitting his head open, he knocked down a gathering of Arabs near the Pan Am wing. At one point he managed briefly to seize control of the public address system and make several direct overtures to Jo: this is Buddy, he kept saying, his voice echoing down the concourses, if she was out there somewhere, if she could hear him, he was begging her, forget about the sports car, forget about the Dells, he was begging her to please stay home with her husband where she belonged. While he was on the air he also announced the temporary suspension of all departures until his wife was located. He doubted he had the power to do this, but he said it anyway just in case. Then he remembered running again, plowing through the same knots of people; the Arabs saw him coming this time and took cover. Uniformed guys were coming at him now, leaping out at him from all directions, which made him angry; it was tough enough trying to run up and down the whole goddamn airport looking for your wife without having guys leap out at you besides.

It all finally ended with him outside, on a runway, trying to flag down a 747. Had he left in the custody of armed men? He supposed he had.

It was nearly dusk when he got back and another hour after that before he finally calmed down. She had messed him up good. He never suspected she would leave him, not after last night. He guessed he had panicked there for a while and paced and shouted and damaged his dukes. He had made an ass of himself at the airport, he was certain of it, and it was only because the main airport cop was a softball fan that he had avoided a serious rap. Had he torn down the shower curtain? He supposed he had. Now, though, he felt he had a pretty good grip on the situation. He felt like a general who'd been temporarily outmaneuvered but who still held the ultimate weapon—which he yanked on from time to time in his agitation. The way he saw it, she could go off half cocked, run around with coastal fruits, maybe even have a fling—if she could find a joyboy out there who could get it up. Let her play these childish games. He wasn't going anywhere. Sooner or later she would come back and he'd be right here, waiting for her.

After a while he had gone into the bathroom and tied the shower curtain back up with some twine and taken his leisurely hour-long toilette, steaming the soreness out of his muscles. His body looked like it had spent a crazy night with the tattoo man. He gently patted dry his hair, feeling the egg-sized lump Humpty-Dumptying his noggin. He had really beaten the crap out of himself but—he grinned into the foggy mirror—every wound had been worth it. It had been sensational, like the good old days. They had done it this way and that way and every kind of way—he had never been better, she hadn't been able to get enough—and when they had finally finished she had curled up against his chest, completely uncled, and fallen asleep in his arms.

He had come out of the bathroom, leaving his footprints in the tub and several soggy towels balled on the floor, and gone into the bedroom and put his bloody uniform on. The rest of his clothes were in his car which was still parked by the ballfield. He figured he would get Herman to take him over later, then maybe he would spin over to the Corner and catch some of the action he had missed last night. It must have been humungous, a really wild-ass time, and he was sorry to have missed out on it. More than anyone he had belonged in the thick of it after the show he had put on. He would've liked to hear what people said about his stick and garden and wing work, not to mention his hell-for-leather dash for the plate. They would have goosed and toasted him all night, young chicks would've been there itching to get their hands on him, but—he grinned into the bedroom mirror, meticulously combing his hair into place—he had had more important business to take care of. It had gone on and on and on, she'd cried out, wept, clawed his ass, he couldn't even remember how many times he'd done it, and when she'd finally collapsed beside him he still had plenty left, it was still right up there ready for more, and where else, he wanted to know, was she going to find powerhouse loving like that?

A hungry guy, he had made himself an enormous breakfast—five eggs and half a pound of bacon—sucked it down standing, and fired the dirty dishes into the sink. Then he went out and bought both the *Trib* and the *Times*, sprinting back with the papers tucked under his arm like a kid with dirty magazines. He opened them simultaneously to the sports sections and scanned rapidly until he came to the game. At least this time they had given it a headline, but the writeups were ridiculously brief, conveying nothing of the flavor of the game, the color and pageantry, the spine-tingling drama, the thrilling climax when he bowled over the pachyderm with the winning run. "The Stickmen were led by Buddy Barnes who had five hits and made several fine defensive plays." Fine? He would've come up with a different adjective.

Disgusted, he thumbed through the *Trib* until he came to the want ads. It would behoove him, he knew, to have at least a few irons in the fire when Jo came back. He wasn't planning to rush out and take the first thing he saw; he still had his standards. He wasn't settling for small potatoes here. He would not be pressured. Still, it would be wise to have at least an interview or two lined up to keep Jo off his back when she returned. He ran his finger down the page, encountering the usual items—they wanted punch press operators, assembly line guys, hawkers and deliverers and pencil-pushing men. They had nothing that remotely resembled a true calling. Nothing there for a qualified guy.

He shoveled the papers into the garbage, went into the living room, and switched on the set. He wrenched the dial back and forth until he found a cowboy movie. It starred

John Wayne. He eased back onto the sofa and put his feet up on the table, nudging over a big prickly plant, and watched the Duke beat the crap out of a bunch of Indians. He had seen this particular flick several times already and it was getting stale. He made up joke lines for the actors awhile, but then he got bored with that. He picked up a book that was on the table and began leafing through it. It was all about endangered species. There was a big picture of an eagle on the cover. He looked at the pictures for a while, then pitched the book onto the floor. He thumped his hands on the sofa and wondered if she had any science fiction lying around, but then he thought she probably wouldn't, she had always hated science fiction, she lacked the imagination for it. He wondered if she had any reefer around. He got up and began checking out all the old places where he used to hide his stash, but he didn't find anything, not even a roach. More than a little irritated, he flounced back down on the sofa and watched the movie some more, fidgeting his feet, drumming his fingers on a cushion. He wondered what he could do. He wished his hoop were still up. More than anything, though, he wished he had a game tonight. The season was over and here he was, still raring to climb a fence, dive for a low one and tumble over and come up showing ball. He was still ready to drift back on one and take it over the shoulder. He wanted to get up there and go with the pitch. His wing felt great. Suddenly he sprang up, hustled into the bedroom, and found the game ball stuffed in the back of a closet. He picked it up, smoothed it, tossed it from hand to hand. He juggled it into the living room, throwing it higher and higher. He threw one over his head and, turning, made a leaping one-hand stab, jarring over several plants tabled by the window. He threw one back the other way.

Abruptly he stopped, a voice whispering in his head: *Buddy Barnes has played his last game.* Who said that? Had he said that? No way. How could he have said that, it wasn't possible. Not him. Not the kid. Not the best goddamn ball-player in the whole town—maybe the world. Had he really said that? Well, if he had he must've been hurt, badly dazed, talking out of his head.

◌◌◌◌

Noselli was sitting in the cocktail lounge of the Pin Palace mopping grease off a hamburger with a handful of napkins and talking with Threefeathers and a guy named Angel. He was pissed off about the burger. He hated greasy burgers. He had specifically told the waitress to watch the grease. Observing him with his flat button eyes, Angel seemed to be getting a kick out of it. He had a broad nose and a deeply pitted jaw. A wispy goat's beard sprouted from his chin. When he was sixteen he had cut the letters "FU" into his forehead with a pocketknife for the fun of it.

"Where's the dude live?" Threefeathers was saying.

"Over on Irving." Unzipping one of his innumerable leather pockets, Noselli palmed a piece of paper with an address on it and handed it to Threefeathers. Threefeathers studied it, then handed it to Angel. Angel studied it, then slipped it into the pocket of his army coat. Out front, balls rolled incessantly down the alleys, pins crashed.

Threefeathers lit a Lucky. "What I'm wondering is, do you want us to touch him, mess him up, or what?"

"I don't give a shit what you do to him," Noselli said. "Use your discretion." He stuck his head into the aisle and yelled at the big waitress who was going by. "What about my fries?" She gave him a sour look and kept right on going. Angel smiled, his gold tooth flashing.

Threefeathers was poking holes in a piece of cellophane with his cigarette. "What's your beef with this guy anyway?"

"None of your business. He diddled—just like you with those headphones."

"Hey, man, like I told you—"

"Forget it. I don't want to hear about it. Just be grateful I'm giving you this chance." He took a bite out of the burger and, chewing slowly, held it up to his face. It was nearly raw.

"How big is the dude?" Threefeathers said. He was still not real comfortable with the situation. He didn't want to be breaking in on some great big dude. "I mean, should we bring something with us or what?"

"You?" Noselli said. "You better bring everything you got. The guy's a ballplayer, right? Bring something that can break legs. Mess up his arm. Use your imagination."

Threefeathers nodded, considering this. "Can we cut him?"

"Look, I don't care what you do. Just do it."

Angel began beating his palms rapidly on the table, making it rock. Then he reached down and began beating it from underneath. He clapped his hands loudly, then brought them to his mouth and hooted at the ceiling. Noselli was staring at him. Angel turned to Threefeathers and said, "Let's split."

"Right now?"

"Sure. What are you waiting for, man?"

They got up, Angel doing a little rooster dance around the table, strutting, flapping his elbows at his sides. Threefeathers stubbed out his cigarette. "I want you to know I appreciate this, Nose."

Noselli said nothing.

He watched them leave, his dark eyes glittering, his mouth turned down in disgust. A pair of burnouts. Real losers. They would probably just fuck it up and he would have to take care of the matter personally. Either way, it had to be done. The Jap had laughed in his face. He had showed him the earrings and the Jap had laughed and laughed. A Jap, laughing at a guy like him! Bad news. The matter had to be dealt with. You let one guy get away with this, another guy get away with that, pretty soon you got the fucking Japs laughing at you. You had your reputation to protect. You had to draw the line.

"Hey," he yelled at the waitress. "I got some fries coming here."

The waitress turned and said, "I only got two hands."

He pushed his hat off his forehead and watched her disappear into the kitchen, walking right past his fries which were sitting on the counter getting cold. He hated cold french fries. He liked his fries hot, a little crispy, and watch out for the grease. He felt that a cold soggy fry was a fry not worth eating. He thought it over a minute, staring at the fries, then, making a loud hacking sound in the back of his throat to let her know how he felt about it, he pushed himself up from the table and went over and got them himself.

The waitress finally came by with the check. Noselli picked it up and looked at it.

"Got a problem?"

Noselli was still going over the tab, adding it in his head. "No," he said. "You got it right this time."

"Goody for me." She was reaching back to untie her apron. "I'm through for today," she told him. "Pay up."

Noselli glared at her, then reached into one of his pockets for his wad. As he brought it out, a small scrap of paper fell out of his pocket onto the floor. Noselli paused, staring at it without expression, afraid to pick it up.

"You dropped something," the waitress said. She picked it up and handed it to him, and Noselli opened it and looked at it and saw Buddy's address written on it in his small, tidy hand. He had given the burnouts the wrong goddamn piece of paper. He had put them onto the wrong guy. They were now on their way to break in on an auto man with the Cicero boys who had promised to put him onto some first-class tape decks and a load of CBs.

Noselli paid the waitress and sank back in his seat, his arms folded across his leather jacket. He thought about tearing after them, but he knew it was no use. He'd never catch them now. He let his hat slide down over his eyes. Some days it just didn't pay to get out of bed.

FOR THE BEST IN PAPERBACKS, LOOK FOR THE

In every corner of the world, on every subject under the sun, Penguin represents quality and variety—the very best in publishing today.

For complete information about books available from Penguin—including Pelicans, Puffins, Peregrines, and Penguin Classics—and how to order them, write to us at the appropriate address below. Please note that for copyright reasons the selection of books varies from country to country.

In the United Kingdom: For a complete list of books available from Penguin in the U.K., please write to *Dept E.P., Penguin Books Ltd, Harmondsworth, Middlesex, UB7 0DA.*

In the United States: For a complete list of books available from Penguin in the U.S., please write to *Dept BA, Penguin*, Box 120, Bergenfield, New Jersey 07621-0120.

In Canada: For a complete list of books available from Penguin in Canada, please write to *Penguin Books Ltd, 2801 John Street, Markham, Ontario L3R 1B4.*

In Australia: For a complete list of books available from Penguin in Australia, please write to the *Marketing Department, Penguin Books Ltd, P.O. Box 257, Ringwood, Victoria 3134.*

In New Zealand: For a complete list of books available from Penguin in New Zealand, please write to the *Marketing Department, Penguin Books (NZ) Ltd, Private Bag, Takapuna, Auckland 9.*

In India: For a complete list of books available from Penguin, please write to *Penguin Overseas Ltd, 706 Eros Apartments, 56 Nehru Place, New Delhi, 110019.*

In Holland: For a complete list of books available from Penguin in Holland, please write to *Penguin Books Nederland B.V., Postbus 195, NL-1380AD Weesp, Netherlands.*

In Germany: For a complete list of books available from Penguin, please write to *Penguin Books Ltd, Friedrichstrasse 10-12, D-6000 Frankfurt Main I, Federal Republic of Germany.*

In Spain: For a complete list of books available from Penguin in Spain, please write to *Longman, Penguin España, Calle San Nicolas 15, E-28013 Madrid, Spain.*

In Japan: For a complete list of books available from Penguin in Japan, please write to *Longman Penguin Japan Co Ltd, Yamaguchi Building, 2-12-9 Kanda Jimbocho, Chiyoda-Ku, Tokyo 101, Japan.*

☐ **IT WAS A DARK AND STORMY NIGHT**
The Best(?) from the Bulwer-Lytton Contest
Compiled by Scott Rice

Named in honor of Victorian literary has-been Edward Bulwer-Lytton, this annual competition hunts for the most atrocious opening sentence to a hypothetical lousy novel. Hilarious and perversely instructive, this collection of skilled ineptitude abounds in prize-winningly shameless sentences.
144 pages   ISBN: 0-14-007556-9   **$5.95**

☐ **WITH ALL DISRESPECT**
Calvin Trillin

In this wonderful collection of wry insights from his "Uncivil Liberties" column in *The Nation,* Calvin Trillin tackles issues large (the danger of having a President who thinks Polaris is a denture cleanser) and small (living with a scale-tampering wife) with equal parts wit and grump.
240 pages   ISBN: 0-14-008819-9   **$6.95**

☐ **MORE RUMOR!**
Hal Morgan and Kerry Tucker

Rumor has it that New York City's birthrate rose dramatically nine months after the 1965 blackout, that the country's sewers flooded during halftime of the Super Bowl, and that the grips on M-16s used in Vietnam were made by Mattel. Morgan and Tucker do the research others don't to discover the truth behind the rumors.
208 pages   ISBN: 0-14-009720-1   **$3.50**

☐ **NOBODY BETTER, BETTER THAN NOBODY**
Ian Frazier

First published in *The New Yorker* between 1978 and 1986, these five essays shed light on some very peculiar subjects. For example, Frazier discusses Heloise, the syndicated household-hints columnist, and reports on the centennial celebration of a Kansas Indian raid to which the Indians' descendants were invited and promised free bowling.   *182 pages   ISBN: 0-14-010603-0*   **$6.95**

☐ **HOW TO EAT LIKE A CHILD**
And Other Lessons in Not Being a Grown-up
Delia Ephron
With drawings by Edward Koren

This bestselling guide to thinking, acting, eating, and sleeping like a normal eight-year-old instructs in such behavior as eating animal crackers (legs first) and talking on the phone (never hang up first), inspiring joyous recognition of childhoods long past.   *112 pages   ISBN: 0-451-82181-5*   **$3.95**

FOR THE BEST LITERATURE, LOOK FOR THE

☐ **THE BOOK AND THE BROTHERHOOD**
Iris Murdoch

Many years ago Gerard Hernshaw and his friends banded together to finance a political and philosophical book by a monomaniacal Marxist genius. Now opinions have changed, and support for the book comes at the price of moral indignation; the resulting disagreements lead to passion, hatred, a duel, murder, and a suicide pact.　　　　　*602 pages　　ISBN: 0-14-010470-4*　　**$8.95**

☐ **GRAVITY'S RAINBOW**
Thomas Pynchon

Thomas Pynchon's classic antihero is Tyrone Slothrop, an American lieutenant in London whose body anticipates German rocket launchings. Surely one of the most important works of fiction produced in the twentieth century, *Gravity's Rainbow* is a complex and awesome novel in the great tradition of James Joyce's *Ulysses.*　　　　　*768 pages　　ISBN: 0-14-010661-8*　　**$10.95**

☐ **FIFTH BUSINESS**
Robertson Davies

The first novel in the celebrated "Deptford Trilogy," which also includes *The Manticore* and *World of Wonders*, *Fifth Business* stands alone as the story of a rational man who discovers that the marvelous is only another aspect of the real.　　　　　*266 pages　　ISBN: 0-14-004387-X*　　**$4.95**

☐ **WHITE NOISE**
Don DeLillo

Jack Gladney, a professor of Hitler Studies in Middle America, and his fourth wife, Babette, navigate the usual rocky passages of family life in the television age. Then, their lives are threatened by an "airborne toxic event"—a more urgent and menacing version of the "white noise" of transmissions that typically engulfs them.　　　　　*326 pages　　ISBN: 0-14-007702-2*　　**$7.95**

You can find all these books at your local bookstore, or use this handy coupon for ordering:
　　　　　　Penguin Books By Mail
　　　　　　Dept. BA　Box 999
　　　　　Bergenfield, NJ 07621-0999

Please send me the above title(s). I am enclosing _____
(please add sales tax if appropriate and $1.50 to cover postage and handling). Send check or money order—no CODs. Please allow four weeks for shipping. We cannot ship to post office boxes or addresses outside the USA. *Prices subject to change without notice.*

Ms./Mrs./Mr. _____

Address _____

City/State _____ Zip _____

Sales tax:　CA: 6.5%　NY: 8.25%　NJ: 6%　PA: 6%　TN: 5.5%

FOR THE BEST LITERATURE, LOOK FOR THE

☐ **A SPORT OF NATURE**
Nadine Gordimer

Hillela, Nadine Gordimer's "sport of nature," is seductive and intuitively gifted at life. Casting herself adrift from her family at seventeen, she lives among political exiles on an East African beach, marries a black revolutionary, and ultimately plays a heroic role in the overthrow of apartheid.

354 pages   ISBN: 0-14-008470-3   **$7.95**

☐ **THE COUNTERLIFE**
Philip Roth

By far Philip Roth's most radical work of fiction, *The Counterlife* is a book of conflicting perspectives and points of view about people living out dreams of renewal and escape. Illuminating these lives is the skeptical, enveloping intelligence of the novelist Nathan Zuckerman, who calculates the price and examines the results of his characters' struggles for a change of personal fortune.

372 pages   ISBN: 0-14-009769-4   **$4.95**

☐ **THE MONKEY'S WRENCH**
Primo Levi

Through the mesmerizing tales told by two characters—one, a construction worker/philosopher who has built towers and bridges in India and Alaska; the other, a writer/chemist, rigger of words and molecules—Primo Levi celebrates the joys of work and the art of storytelling.

174 pages   ISBN: 0-14-010357-0   **$6.95**

☐ **IRONWEED**
William Kennedy

"Riding up the winding road of Saint Agnes Cemetery in the back of the rattling old truck, Francis Phelan became aware that the dead, even more than the living, settled down in neighborhoods." So begins William Kennedy's Pulitzer-Prize winning novel about an ex-ballplayer, part-time gravedigger, and full-time drunk, whose return to the haunts of his youth arouses the ghosts of his past and present.

228 pages   ISBN: 0-14-007020-6   **$6.95**

☐ **THE COMEDIANS**
Graham Greene

Set in Haiti under Duvalier's dictatorship, *The Comedians* is a story about the committed and the uncommitted. Actors with no control over their destiny, they play their parts in the foreground; experience love affairs rather than love; have enthusiasms but not faith; and if they die, they die like Mr. Jones, by accident.

288 pages   ISBN: 0-14-002766-1   **$4.95**

FOR THE BEST LITERATURE, LOOK FOR THE

☐ **HERZOG**
Saul Bellow

Winner of the National Book Award, *Herzog* is the imaginative and critically acclaimed story of Moses Herzog: joker, moaner, cuckhold, charmer, and truly an Everyman for our time.

342 pages *ISBN: 0-14-007270-5* **$6.95**

☐ **FOOLS OF FORTUNE**
William Trevor

The deeply affecting story of two cousins—one English, one Irish—brought together and then torn apart by the tide of Anglo-Irish hatred, *Fools of Fortune* presents a profound symbol of the tragic entanglements of England and Ireland in this century. 240 pages *ISBN: 0-14-006982-8* **$6.95**

☐ **THE SONGLINES**
Bruce Chatwin

Venturing into the desolate land of Outback Australia—along timeless paths, and among fortune hunters, redneck Australians, racist policemen, and mysterious Aboriginal holy men—Bruce Chatwin discovers a wondrous vision of man's place in the world. 296 pages *ISBN: 0-14-009429-6* **$7.95**

☐ **THE GUIDE: A NOVEL**
R. K. Narayan

Raju was once India's most corrupt tourist guide; now, after a peasant mistakes him for a holy man, he gradually begins to play the part. His succeeds so well that God himself intervenes to put Raju's new holiness to the test.

220 pages *ISBN: 0-14-009657-4* **$5.95**

FOR THE BEST LITERATURE, LOOK FOR THE

☐ **THE LAST SONG OF MANUEL SENDERO**
Ariel Dorfman

In an unnamed country, in a time that might be now, the son of Manuel Sendero refuses to be born, beginning a revolution where generations of the future wait for a world without victims or oppressors.

     464 pages   *ISBN: 0-14-008896-2* **$7.95**

☐ **THE BOOK OF LAUGHTER AND FORGETTING**
Milan Kundera

In this collection of stories and sketches, Kundera addresses themes including sex and love, poetry and music, sadness and the power of laughter. "*The Book of Laughter and Forgetting* calls itself a novel," writes John Leonard of *The New York Times*, "although it is part fairly tale, part literary criticism, part political tract, part musicology, part autobiography. It can call itself whatever it wants to, because the whole is genius."

     240 pages   *ISBN: 0-14-009693-0* **$6.95**

☐ **TIRRA LIRRA BY THE RIVER**
Jessica Anderson

Winner of the Miles Franklin Award, Australia's most prestigious literary prize, *Tirra Lirra by the River* is the story of a woman's seventy-year search for the place where she truly belongs. Nora Porteous's series of escapes takes her from a small Australia town to the suburbs of Sydney to London, where she seems finally to become the woman she always wanted to be.

     142 pages   *ISBN: 0-14-006945-3* **$4.95**

☐ **LOVE UNKNOWN**
A. N. Wilson

In their sweetly wild youth, Monica, Belinda, and Richeldis shared a bachelor-girl flat and became friends for life. Now, twenty years later, A. N. Wilson charts the intersecting lives of the three women through the perilous waters of love, marriage, and adultery in this wry and moving modern comedy of manners.

     202 pages   *ISBN: 0-14-010190-X* **$6.95**

☐ **THE WELL**
Elizabeth Jolley

Against the stark beauty of the Australian farmlands, Elizabeth Jolley portrays an eccentric, affectionate relationship between the two women—Hester, a lonely spinster, and Katherine, a young orphan. Their pleasant, satisfyingly simple life is nearly perfect until a dark stranger invades their world in a most horrifying way.

     176 pages   *ISBN: 0-14-008901-2* **$6.95**

FOR THE BEST IN PAPERBACKS, LOOK FOR THE

☐ **CAN'T ANYBODY HERE PLAY THIS GAME?**
   Jimmy Breslin

Breslin's celebrated account of the New York Mets' first year of life—a year that produced a record number of losses and an unforgettable collection of oddballs—is a jubilant toast to the tenacity of the human spirit.

"Jimmy Breslin has written a history of the Mets, preserving for all time a remarkable tale of ineptitude, mediocrity, and abject failure."—Bill Veeck
                    124 pages   ISBN: 0-14-006217-3   **$5.95**

☐ **THE GAME**
   Ken Dryden

The veteran of eight years as goalie for the Montreal Canadiens, Ken Dryden reveals the texture of hockey—from the fundamentals to the rivalries and camaraderie—as only an athlete can.

"Extraordinarily insightful"—*Philadelphia Inquirer*
                          248 pages   ISBN: 0-14-007412-0   **$6.95**

☐ **THE LONG SEASON**
   Jim Brosnan

An inside account of the 1959 baseball season by a veteran National League pitcher, *The Long Season* presents an honest look at the game and many of its greatest stars, including Stan Musial, Hank Aaron, and Willie Mays.

"Probably the best factual book in the literature of baseball"—*The New Yorker*
                          278 pages   ISBN: 0-14-006754-X   **$6.95**

☐ **THE SHORT SEASON**
   The Hard Work and High Times of Baseball in the Spring
   David Faulkner

In a collection of anecdotes, stories, and interviews, David Faulkner captures the sunny, all-things-are-possible atmosphere, the conditioning and carousing, of the "Grapefruit League."

"A vivid, exciting account . . . David Faulkner is the most engaging baseball writer since Roger Angell."—*Philadelphia Inquirer*
                          276 pages   ISBN: 0-14-009850-X   **$6.95**

☐ **CHAMPION**
   Joe Louis: Black Hero in White America
   Chris Mead

This is a masterful biography of Joe Louis the man—more than the Heavyweight Champion of the World, Louis was the most recognized black American of his time and a dignified symbol of hope and achievement.

"A valuable addition to American social history"—Robert Creamer, *Washington Post Book World*   *330 pages   ISBN: 0-14-009285-4*   **$6.95**

☐ **WHY TIME BEGINS ON OPENING DAY**
   Thomas Boswell

From an affectionate and analytical perspective, veteran sports writer Thomas Boswell offers a penetrating look at the traditions, teams, ballparks, and games that make up the national pastime and inevitably the American grain as well.

"The writing is fresh, enthusiastic, and joyous."—*New York Times Book Review*   *298 pages   ISBN: 0-14-007661-1*   **$6.95**